Saving
Dr. Savannah

By

Connie Maynard Clark

i

Dedication

I dedicate this book to my daughter Tessy Marie Douglass. She is my number one fan!

Table of Contents

Prologue: A New Chapter

Saving Dr. Savannah is the sequel to my book, *Savannah*.

In the first book, Savannah was twenty-eight, working as an RN aboard a private yacht called The Lady Jane in the Bahamas. She met Mark Jenkins and Robert Malone, who helped her flee from the police and the wealthy Mason family after she was accused of murder.

Fast forward ten years, and Savannah is now a doctor. She has been asked to help save the Mason's child.

Flying from Florida to Virginia, she finds herself in hot water again!

The sequel brings back Robert Malone, Mark Jenkins, Cathi and Michael Mason, Dr. Kyle Clark, and his now wife, Lily Mason-Clark. Adam Jordan is also mentioned.

Warning: If you haven't read the first book, the sequel gives essential information about Savannah's past and may spoil the first book's plot.

Saving Dr. Savannah...

Chapter 1

Savannah Hayes entered her condo at 2 a.m. She removed her shoes and her white, knee-length medical coat. A pink stethoscope peeked out of her right pocket. She carefully hung the coat over a chair in her kitchen. She admired the black lettering on the left of the lapel on the upper jacket. She ran her hand softly over the embroidery: Savannah Hayes, MD.

She turned off the lights and walked into her bedroom. She could see the moon glistening on the Atlantic Ocean from her penthouse through the open draperies. She closed the drapes with blackout lining so the sun wouldn't wake her when it became daylight. She then headed to the shower to relieve the tension in her muscles.

She had a busy Sunday night working in the emergency room. She cared for two teenage boys with gunshot wounds. She had stabilized them enough before sending them to surgery. There had been an older gentleman who had a mild myocardial infarction. There had been children with colds and fevers. She worked nonstop during her twelve-hour shift. And she was exhausted. Her thirty-eight-year-old body felt more like eighty. Ten years ago, when she worked as an RN, she could stand on her feet and work tirelessly all day. Now her feet and back ached. She rubbed her feet and thought about soaking them in a foot tub with Epsom salt, but she was too tired to take the time.

Exhaustion clung to her body as she fell into bed. The soft mattress offered some brief comfort, but she tossed and turned, thinking about Robert. She tried to remember when she last saw him. It had been at least four years now. Nevertheless, he had always been the last thing on her mind every night when she crawled into bed for the previous ten years. She wondered if he had found someone else to love or was married.

She quietly kicked herself for losing touch with him. He probably didn't know she had finished her residency two years ago in Miami, Florida, and was now living in Palm Beach.

The fatigue took over, allowing her body to rest as she finally fell into a deep sleep.

She awoke at 10 a.m. on Sunday and wasn't surprised that she had dreamed about Robert Malone again. She stretched, stumbled out of bed, and walked to her dresser, where she kept a wooden box with the Rod of Asclepius on top. Her hand stroked the caduceus, a staff with two snakes that Robert had gifted her when she was twenty-eight. She remembered the sweet gesture and the warm kiss they shared before she exited the car to walk to her first day of medical school in Charlottesville, Virginia. She opened the box and smiled as she tenderly removed the shiny plastic tiara, a reminder that she was a strong individual who could handle life with courage and dignity. He and his best friend Mark Jenkins would call her My Lady, and she would curtsy and say, "Thank you, kind sir," as she pretended to straighten her invisible crown. A salty tear ran down her beautiful face, and she carefully placed the tiara back into its container.

A feeling of dread suddenly came over her. She felt a heaviness in her stomach, a sense of intense, overwhelming fear, almost like a threat that overpowered her. Her heart started racing, and she couldn't control the feeling of unease. She wondered if something was wrong with Robert and if he needed her.

She walked into her kitchen, pulled out cereal from the pantry, peeled a banana, and reached inside the refrigerator for the milk.

The milk slipped out of her hands and spilled on the floor. She stood looking at the white liquid, which gave her pause. She imagined it to be blood and remembered her dream several nights prior. In the dream, Robert had been shot and almost killed by a man he had been chasing. She knew he had taken a bullet when he had been a detective in West Palm Beach years before she met him. She reminded herself that the bad dream was why she was so apprehensive. Yet, the overwhelming sense of foreboding would not leave her. Her sense of loyalty and love of the medical profession and Robert Malone was too embedded in her not to take a premonition seriously.

Savannah's mantra was, "There is always a 'but' when life seems to be going well."

Luckily, she had the next two days off from work. A tear ran down her cheek as she cleaned up the mess on the floor, hoping her anxiety was just her regret over something she couldn't fix. So why was she crying over spilled milk?

She lost her appetite from feeling queasy.

She entered her bedroom and threw open the draperies, allowing the warm sunshine to flood the room. She made her bed and put on shorts and a white T-shirt. She placed her long, brown hair into a ponytail and thought about taking her daily stroll on the beach. While she was putting on her tennis shoes, her phone dinged.

She picked it up to see who was texting her. When she saw the name, Mark Jenkins, she dropped the phone and knelt to pray.

She knew Mark was Robert's best friend and would know everything about him, good or bad. She feared the worst. Why was he trying to reach her after all these years?

She sat on the edge of the bed and twirled her ponytail, a habit she had when she was anxious. She knew she couldn't ignore the text.

She took a deep breath to calm her nerves and gathered enough courage to call the number instead of texting back.

Mark answered immediately, "Hello, beautiful."

She didn't have patience for pleasantries.

"Please tell me Robert is alive and well."

Mark was silent, and her heart skipped a beat.

"My lady, Robert is fine. It's Danielle Mason. She's very sick, Savannah. She needs a bone marrow transplant because she has lymphoma. The Masons ask you to be tested to see if you qualify as a stem cell donor. You are her birth mother after all. They have run out of options."

Savannah felt faint; she felt lightheaded, her heart began to race again, and she was nauseous. Her memory of choosing to let her little girl be adopted by Michael and Cathi Mason ten years ago was all she could bear. Her heart literally ached. It was an immense emotional weight. She experienced a mixture of grief, loss, and love.

She looked at the wooden box on her dresser and pretended to put the tiara back on her head. She straightened her shoulders and her 5'9" physique.

"Yes, yes, of course. When, where, how?" She asked.

"I still have my condo in Fort Lauderdale. I can fly my plane to get you, wherever you are. We should get to Virginia as soon as possible," Mark answered.

"Mark, I'm in Palm Beach. I can meet you at the West Palm Beach airport later this afternoon. I'll need to take myself off the schedule at the hospital and take care of a few items first."

"Great, how about 3 p.m.? Does that work for you?" Mark asked.

Mark didn't want to sound alarmed or hurt by Savannah being so close and never reaching out to him. Although he realized they had lost contact because of Robert, it still hurt. He thought they were friends.

"Yes, I can be ready by then. Oh, and Mark?"

"Yes, I already know what you're going to ask. Robert will pick us up at the Norfolk airport. See you later, my lady."

Savannah packed clothing for a week and tucked her pink stethoscope in the suitcase. She never went anywhere without it. The stethoscope was 15 years old. She could afford a new one, but the old one was like a childhood friend, and she couldn't bear to retire it from service. It was the first stethoscope she had purchased after she had graduated from nursing school. A lot of memories were attached to it.

She gave the items she had packed one last glance, feeling she had forgotten something.

She named all the essential items that she should take as she dressed. She realized she had forgotten her phone charger, but she also questioned her choice of clothing.

She laughed when she saw three pairs of white jeans, white blouses, and two pairs of white tennis shoes in the luggage. Old habits die hard. She loved wearing white; what could she say? She was dressed in all white, so she changed her blouse to light pink. She threw a couple of blue and pink blouses in the suitcase for good measure. She didn't want Robert to think she wore the same clothing daily.

Savannah was a practical woman who never cared much about fashion. She cared about comfort.

Butterflies tickled her stomach. She was anxious yet excited to see Robert again. The butterflies quickly vanished when she thought about the task at hand. Her poor daughter had cancer.

She closed the suitcase and placed it near the front door. She would be back to get the luggage. First, she had to go to the hospital and explain why she had to have time off without telling them she had a daughter who needed help.

Luckily, it was Monday morning, and her boss was in his office when she arrived at the hospital. She knocked on the door, which read "Director of Emergency Medicine."

"Come in."

Savannah entered the office. "Good morning, Dr. May."

"Good morning, Dr. Savannah."

Dr. Jason May was not only her boss but also had become a good friend. She hated lying to him, but couldn't tell him the entire truth either. She felt her private life was nobody's business.

She explained that friends needed her in Virginia to help their sick child. She owed them a great favor.

"It's so important that if you can't give me the time I need, then I'm afraid I will need to resign, starting immediately."

Dr. May looked at her curiously and puzzledly. Savannah noticed the vertical wrinkle between his eyebrows and squinted eyes, knowing he was curious, but thankfully, he didn't ask any questions.

"If it's of utmost importance, Savannah, then I don't have a choice in the matter. You're a credit to the staff and the patients. You'll be missed around here."

Dr. May said he understood and graciously gave her the time off, but made her promise to keep him informed.

She promised.

Before returning home, she stopped and bought a gift for Danielle.

She had no inkling what lay ahead for her.

Chapter 2

Savannah took an Uber to the airport. When she exited the car, she saw Mark running toward her enthusiastically, waving his arms. He caught up to her, lifted her off the ground, and swung her around.

"Oh, my God, is it really you? And you are just as beautiful as I saw you ten years ago. And now you're no longer a nurse but a hotshot doctor."

He bowed and kissed her hand. "It's so good to see you again, my lady."

She laughed and curtsied, "Come here, funny man. You could always make me laugh."

She hugged him and kissed his cheek. He placed the top of his hand on his forehead and pretended to swoon, making her laugh again.

How long had it been since she laughed? She couldn't remember.

"The plane is ready. Shall we leave now?"

"Mark, I'm so nervous. I haven't met Danielle, and I hate to meet her this way. Yet, at the same time, that girl has been on my mind for ten years. I suppose we had to meet someday. She doesn't know about me, does she?"

"I'm not sure, Savannah. You're doing something wonderful for her. Robert says she's a beautiful little girl and sweet as pie, unlike her birth father."

"Oh, thank God, I was worried she'd get Noah's nastiness and flawed personality."

"She only looks partially like Noah, with curly blond hair. She has your green eyes and olive complexion, and your compassion for people and animals. Robert says she wants to be a veterinarian when she grows up."

"Speaking of Robert, I hope he doesn't hate me. It's been four years since we saw each other. He visited me when I was a Resident in Boston. I was so busy, and we only spent a few hours together. He was on board Daniel Mason's yacht, The Lady Jane, as the captain. I'm glad he continued working for the Masons."

"It's not up to me to tell you about Robert, but I guess he won't mind me telling you that he's a partner with DM Yachts now."

"Oh, my God. No wonder he stayed in Virginia. I thought he'd eventually move back to Fort Lauderdale."

Mark nodded, "He has moved up in the world, as have you."

He looked at his watch. "We'd better get moving. It's 3:15, and Robert is expecting us."

He picked up her luggage, and Savannah followed him to the Cessna Citation. She noticed Mark had also moved up in the world. The jet was much bigger than the plane she had flown in years ago.

The skies were cloudless, and only a soft wind blew as they effortlessly flew north to Norfolk, Virginia, her hometown. She was grateful for the smooth ride because she hated to fly.

She became lost in thought as she sat beside Mark in the co-pilot's seat, as they floated through the air. It seemed like a million years ago when she worked as an oncology nurse for Dr. Kyle Clark in Norfolk. So much had happened since then, and it seemed like the years had flown by, just like the diaphanous clouds they were flying through. Being with Mark also made her think of all the times they had spent together with Robert.

Although Mark wasn't handsome, his beauty lay in his generosity. He shared his wealth with those who needed help. He was easygoing and loved to laugh. He was 5'7" with soft, ample, curved lips and small teeth. His large brown eyes and big

13

personality could light up a room. He should have been a comedian. He was an entrepreneur and a mathematical genius who made a fortune in the stock market when he was young.

If you had to explain him, you'd say,

"He's one of the good guys."

Because he was.

*****

They landed at the Norfolk International Airport at 4:30 p.m. Mark taxied to the private hangar and helped Savannah with her luggage.

Robert Malone, now 52 years old, still looked like a Greek God to her. He was 6'1", strikingly handsome, with a muscular build. When he smiled, his white teeth were perfect, and she noticed he still had a nice tan. His skin seemed to glow. He had always worn his long, sandy blond hair in a ponytail or bun, but today, he wore it much shorter, which flattered his facial features. His thick hair was slicked back and cut conservatively, graying at his temples. He was stylishly dressed like he was Mr. GQ. He was very distinguished-looking, and she swelled with pride. He had become even more handsome with age. She took a deep breath as he walked up to her. Her hands were cold yet sweaty.

He, too, held his breath from seeing her. She was more beautiful than he remembered, and he wanted to take her in his arms and kiss her. Instead, he hugged her slightly as any gentleman would.

"Hello, Dr. Hayes," he teased.

"Hey, you."

She hugged him back and didn't want to let go. She always felt secure in his arms.

Mark interrupted, "Let's go eat. I'm starving."

Robert led the way to his parked Mercedes. "Come on, you two. I have steaks marinating at my place. I live fifteen minutes away in Willowby Spit. I purchased an older home on the ocean side that I renovated. It's comfortable. I also have two guest rooms, and I assume you'll both be staying with me while you're in town."

From the back seat, Savannah spoke, "But don't you just want to go to a restaurant? I don't want to be a bother."

"I don't think my girl will like that. It's no problem. You know I enjoy cooking."

"Oh, you live with someone?"

Savannah's heart sank in her chest.

"Just take me to a hotel. I'm tired, and it's been a long day."

15

"I insist. Ana is going to love you both."

Knowing Robert was sleeping with another woman, Savannah didn't think she could handle sleeping in the same house. She was determined not to show her jealousy. She quietly seethed in the backseat, trying not to show any emotion outwardly.

Mark continued, "How is Ana doing? I haven't met her yet, but you talk incessantly about her."

"She has arthritis pretty bad now. She can barely get into our bed."

"Sorry to hear that, Robert," Mark said.

"Yeah, she's an old fart like me."

Savannah wanted to cover her ears. She couldn't listen to the conversation any longer. She was going to demand that Robert take her to a hotel when he pulled into the driveway of a two-story wooden cottage painted aqua blue, sitting majestically upon stilts.

Ana came bouncing down the stairs when she heard Robert's car. The golden retriever's tail was wagging a hundred miles an hour. Robert exited the vehicle and opened his arms for Ana to fill them with her love.

"Savannah, meet my girl, Ana."

Savannah almost cried with joy when she saw that Ana was a dog. She didn't even know he loved dogs.

They entered a large living room decorated in a coastal style that was so inviting that Savannah instantly felt comfortable. Beyond was a larger room with tall ceilings and beautiful old wooden beams. Robert explained the beams had been honed from an old wooden boat. He called it his TV room. The kitchen was also part of the room. The cabinets were painted blue-gray. There was a kitchen island that could seat four people with a white quartzite countertop. Double sliding glass doors led to an inviting deck overlooking sand dunes and the ocean.

After unpacking her suitcase in the upstairs guest room, she entered the kitchen, where both men were catching up with their lives. Mark sat on a rattan barstool at the center island. Robert was placing three baking potatoes into the oven and making a salad. He removed three porterhouse steaks wrapped in Saran Wrap from the refrigerator and put them on the counter. The men were enjoying a cold beer. Robert opened a bottle of Chardonnay and poured a glass for her. Ana was sniffing Savannah's ankles.

She thought, "No need for jealousy here, girl, I'm only temporary."

Small talk was spoken throughout the delicious dinner. They laughed at the memories they shared, one of which was about the 43 Tiara LE yacht that belonged to Mark, which had run out of fuel when she and Robert were running from the police in the Bahamas.

"Did you ever get your boat back from impoundment, Mark?" Robert asked.

"Yes, most of the interior had been stripped down, but the main thing was, the guns hidden behind the custom wall in the master stateroom were never found. The insurance company took care of the damage. Otherwise, I would have been after your ass."

They clinked their beers and laughed. They continued talking about boats while Savannah sat, sipping her wine and reminiscing.

That had been a scary time in their lives, but it was when Savannah had learned to trust Robert and leaned on him for support. She would probably be rotting in a jail cell in the Bahamas or possibly dead from being hanged by a rope in the streets because she had been accused of Daniel Mason's murder. He believed in her innocence and helped her get away. He also stood by her while she proved her innocence. They had been in love once, and he stood by her when she found out she was pregnant with her rapist's baby. Sadly, they grew apart when she went to medical school.

Mark interrupted her chain of thoughts as Robert served them dinner.

The steaks were grilled to perfection. The rich, savory aroma of the meat reached her nostrils, and she realized she was hungry.

"Robert, do you have A1 sauce?"

Robert winced and answered, "I see you continue to destroy a perfect steak with that stuff."

She laughed. "Hey, some things never change. As I remember correctly, you always put ketchup on your eggs."

"Okay, you got me there." He had purchased the item in advance, knowing she liked her steaks smothered with the tangy sauce, but he still teased her about it.

Mark sat quietly listening to their banter.

After eating the delicious meal, Savannah picked up their plates and took them to the sink.

Robert said, "You're my guest, so I don't expect you to clean up, Savannah. We're going to the deck to have an after-dinner cigar. You want to join us?"

Offended that Robert was making her feel uneasy, she decided to join the men. It was his house, not hers. She didn't belong there.

"Yes, but no cigar for me, thanks."

They sat on the deck, sharing more memories. Savannah was relaxed, listening to the sound of the ocean and enjoying herself. The warm aroma of burning tobacco soon replaced the fresh, open-air smell.

When the men finished their cigars, it was dusk. Savannah finally convinced Robert to let her help clean the kitchen.

As they stood cleaning up the dishes, Savannah asked, "Robert, how bad is Danielle?"

Robert put his dish towel over the oven door. "It doesn't look good, Vanna." Robert was the only person, besides her late father, who called her Vanna.

"Will you take me to the hospital in the morning to meet her? I need your support again, even though it's unfair to ask that of you."

"Of course, Vanna, Mark is leaving early in the morning. We can take him to the airport, then we'll go to the Children's Hospital. I'll text Michael and let him know so he can meet us there. Cathi hardly ever leaves Danielle's side."

"It's good to see you again, Robert, but I need some rest. I have a feeling tomorrow is going to be a long day."

"Goodnight, Savannah. You'll find fresh towels in the bathroom and an extra pillow in the closet. We'll see you in the morning."

She hugged both men before heading up the stairs.

When Robert and Savannah lingered in their embrace, their chemistry was undeniable. It was so intense that Mark could almost feel the spark between them.

Ana followed Savannah up the stairs and into the guest room. With big brown eyes and a wagging tail, she lay on the floor next to the bed.

"Okay, sister, you can stay. But no snoring, got it?"

Ana immediately fell asleep and started snoring.

Savannah sat up in bed and thought, "Ana? He named the dog after me?"

She smiled and fell asleep, and for the first time in a long time, she slept like a baby, feeling secure, wrapped in one of Robert's soft blankets.

Chapter 3

Savannah woke at 7 a.m. She took a quick shower in the ensuite bathroom, donned a short-sleeved chambray blouse, and tucked it neatly inside her white jeans. Usually, she wore her long hair in a ponytail, but leaving it down today was more appropriate and would look more professional. She had women friends who wore hair extensions, but with her Mediterranean background, she was lucky enough to have a head of thick, rich brown hair. It flowed like an Andalusian's mane running in the wind. It reached down to her small waist because she never had the time to have it cut. It seemed she lived in the emergency room at the hospital in Florida and always wore it in a ponytail. She had offers to model her beautiful, shiny locks, but she thought that was ridiculous.

Mark howled like a wolf when she entered the kitchen. Ana followed her downstairs and wagged her tail at Mark, then went out the doggie door Robert had installed on the side of the house, where she could relieve herself in a fenced-in area outside.

Robert was busy making scrambled eggs, bacon, and English muffins when he offered her a cup of coffee with Truvia and French Vanilla creamer. She was flattered that he remembered how she liked her coffee.

His knees became weak at the sight of her. He thought she was the most beautiful creature he had ever seen, especially with her hair flowing past her shoulders.

"Do you need to leave us so soon, Mark?" She asked.

"Yeah, I'm picking Sara up in Fort Lauderdale, and we're going to the condo in Nassau. We haven't been there in six months or so."

Savannah asked if Sam Rolles was still the American Ambassador there. He nodded, and she said, "Tell him hello, and I send all my love."

"I see you're still with Sara. It's been over ten years. When are you going to make an honest woman out of her?" Robert asked.

"I've asked, but she feels marriage is only necessary when you have children. It works for us. She has her own place, and I have mine."

Savannah was uncomfortable with small talk about marriage. Robert had asked her to marry him, but she never answered. Instead, she had moved two and a half hours away to attend medical school. Sometimes, she wished she had said yes ten years ago, but her life was complicated back then. But she noticed that he had settled into his life nicely without her.

After breakfast, Mark walked upstairs to pack his small bag. Savannah helped clean the kitchen. She bumped into Robert when she leaned over to place the plates into the dishwasher.

"Excuse me."

"No problem," he said, rubbing his hands together while looking around the kitchen, making sure no food was left that Ana would find. He set out a bowl of food for her.

Ten years ago would have been a different story. Robert would have picked her up and twirled her around like Mark did at the airport. She noticed he had not called her "My Lady" like he used to.

Robert seemed cold and distant today. She hoped she had not offended him, but then she got angry with herself. Why should she care if he was in a bad mood? It wasn't her problem, whatever it was that caused him to be in such a mood. She had to concentrate on meeting the Mason family and the doctor at the hospital.

After dropping Mark off at the airport, Robert drove to the Children's Hospital. He called Michael Mason and told him they were on their way. Savannah tried not to twirl her hair with her fingers because, once again, she was anxious. Instead, she took deep breaths and slowly exhaled. Robert was quiet, but she knew him well enough to know he was probably worried about Danielle. He had graciously accepted the Mason's invitation to be Danielle's Godfather, even though he kept it a secret from Savannah. Danielle called him Uncle Robert.

Once inside the hospital, Robert led them to the elevator, which took them to the fifth floor.

Savannah noticed the brightly colored floor tiles in the hallway. The child-friendly environment could help distract and entertain the children during their hospitalization. She saw a bulletin board with pictures of the young patients who had been discharged. Yet, instead of fun-filled, the fifth floor was quiet. A large sign, "Sssh, Quiet" with a finger pressed against closed lips, was placed on the wall at the nurses' station. She could faintly hear the familiar dinging of an IV pump from one of the rooms, meaning the IV bag was empty and needed changing.

Savannah turned her attention to Michael and Cathi, who met them at the nurses' station. They hugged Savannah and thanked her profusely for coming.

Cathi and Michael had tried to have children for eight years before Savannah offered them to adopt her precious baby. Life had been happy until their child became sick. Cathi was so relieved and grateful that Savannah could once again give them the healthy child they loved so much.

They introduced her to Danielle's doctor, Kent Stone, who had not taken his eyes off Savannah since she exited the elevator. He wondered if she was married to the good-looking man walking with her. He couldn't wait to meet her, but standing before her, he was speechless. He marveled at her flawless skin and natural beauty. He noticed she wore no makeup except a hint of pink lipstick. Her short nails were manicured with clear polish. She was tall, even in her white tennis shoes.

He shook her hand, but had to excuse himself when his cell phone dinged. He walked to the other end of the nurses' station to return a text. He needed to see another patient, but realizing he had to be professional and caring to the Mason family and their friends, he rejoined them.

Savannah was whispering to Cathi,

"Who does Danielle think I am?"

"Dani thinks you're a friend of Robert…A doctor who flew in to help her."

"Dani, aww, that's so cute. Daniel would be proud that you named her after her grandpa."

Dr. Stone interrupted their conversation, trying not to sound blunt, but he had to go. He turned to Savannah and said, "I'm sorry to interrupt, but I have a full day planned. Danielle is a beautiful child; you'll see shortly, but she has been very sick. She's in isolation, so not everyone can be in the room at once. Her body is immunocompromised, so everyone must wear masks and gloves."

Savannah turned her attention to him, feeling he was rude to interrupt, but as a doctor herself, she knew how busy doctors are, so she would say what was on her mind.

Savannah started the conversation with the doctor as the others listened.

"I understand I need to provide a blood sample for HLA testing to see if I'm a match for a bone marrow transplant."

"Why, yes, but how would you know that term?"

"Let me formally introduce myself; I'm Dr. Savannah Hayes from Palm Beach, Florida."

Dr. Stone was more interested in her now.

"But why do you think you're a match when her father, mother, or uncle's DNA tests weren't good?"

Evidently, the doctor wasn't aware that Danielle was adopted or that Robert wasn't really her uncle. Dani just called him that.

"You can say it's a woman's intuition, Doctor, and that's all you need to know."

Dr. Stone knew not to argue. "I'll order the test now."

Michael Mason interrupted, "You need to expedite this as a priority, doctor. You know DM yachts donate millions to the hospital."

"Yes, I'm aware of that. Thank you. Your donations have helped save the lives of so many children. I'll have Nancy, the head nurse, draw the blood ASAP. I know you're anxious to get the samples to the lab, so I will wait and take them myself," Dr. Stone said.

He quickly walked to Nancy. They watched him as he leaned over to speak with her, sitting in her chair, typing on her computer. He pointed to Savannah.

Nancy stood and motioned for Savannah to follow her into her private office.

Once Savannah was in the office, Nancy excused herself. "I'll be right back. I need to go to the storage room," Nancy said.

Nancy removed test tubes of various colors, butterfly needles, and a rubber tourniquet from the room. Savannah waited patiently, thinking of her time as a nurse and how demanding some doctors could be. She vowed not to be one of those doctors.

Nancy returned and efficiently inserted the tiny butterfly needle into Savannah's arm, trying to remember which color tube she was supposed to use. Savannah could see she was struggling with her choice.

"Use the lavender and yellow tubes, and while you're at it, use the red one to type and cross-match my blood, just in case she needs a blood transfusion," Savannah said calmly. "I'm sure the phlebotomists do this daily. I know because I was an RN like you."

Nancy relaxed and smiled. "Thank you for understanding. It's been years since I've had to do this, but Dr. Stone gave me his direct order. You don't argue with him." She rolled her eyes.

The nurse labeled the tubes and placed them in a plastic bag to be sent immediately to the lab.

Savannah rejoined her friends, still waiting patiently at the nurses' station. Dr. Stone was down the hall, talking on his cell phone.

Savannah told Cathi, "It could take a few days before we know the results."

She didn't want to raise their hopes, but felt confident she would be a match high enough.

Robert asked, "Savannah, can you explain HPL to us, in layman's terms?"

She smiled. "It's HLA, Robert. It's called Human Leukocyte Antigens. It's a gene found in our DNA. The test helps identify if the donor cells are compatible with the person you donate to. Our bodies recognize foreign objects and go to war like an army of warriors to destroy incompatible cells. I'm sure you've heard of other types of organ transplants that fail because the patient's tissues reject the donor's tissue. So, the higher the matching antigens found with Dani's, the more the donated stem cells will produce new blood cells to replace the unhealthy ones. The red and white blood cells and platelets are manufactured in the bone marrow, and Dani's current counts are very low. So, the higher the number of matching genes, the better the bone marrow transplant will help her start manufacturing the blood cells she needs. There's only a twenty-five percent chance that sibling cells would be compatible, so it doesn't surprise me that your results are low, Michael. You were Noah's step-brother, so you won't share a significant amount of DNA through a DNA test. A child receives one-half of the genes from her father and one-half from her mother, so as her birth mother, I'm hopeful the results will be high enough so I can donate my bone marrow to her."

Dr. Stone approached, "Dr. Hayes, may I have a word in private?"

"Of course."

He walked her to the elevator, carrying the tubes of fresh blood that Nancy had given him. Savannah eyed it suspiciously.

He held up the bag. "I am dropping this off at the lab on my way back to my office. I'll lean on them to rush it through." Savannah nodded.

Savannah asked, "It's not Burkitt's Lymphoma, is it, doctor?"

Absent-mindedly, Dr. Stone, thinking about his disturbing phone conversation, said, "Yes."

Savannah said, "Oh no." She knew Burkitt's Lymphoma was very aggressive.

She thought it odd that he failed to mention this vital information.

Dr. Stone then wondered why the family thought Dr. Hayes would be a match, but he didn't question it, even though he knew she had to be related somehow. He didn't care.

He continued, "Her kidneys are failing. She hasn't tolerated the chemo or steroids well. I debated whether I should order radiation, but at this point, I don't think her body can handle it. Let's hope your antigens match high enough, or we'll lose her. I hope to stabilize her immune system and possibly transplant a kidney. God only knows there have been too many children dying here lately, a couple recently from simple tonsillectomies.

31

Here is my card. Call me anytime," he said as he stepped into the elevator.

Robert joined her at the elevator as the doors for Dr. Stone were closing. She carefully placed the doctor's card in her purse.

Robert said, "Vanna, you always said Dr. Kyle Clark was the best oncologist. Maybe you should call him."

"Robert, he doesn't take children as patients. Besides, didn't he marry Lily Mason?"

"Yes, but divorced her six months later, then remarried her. Dr. Clark may be a brilliant doctor, but he's a fool when it comes to love."

Savannah laughed. "They both got what they deserved, I guess." He hesitated. "Oh my God, being Noah's mother, Dani's only living grandmother, I wonder if Lily would match high enough."

"Let's hope it doesn't come to that. Lily is such an evil bitch. Who knows what she may do if she finds out about Dani? Michael is certain that Lily doesn't know about her or that Noah was the real father."

Robert shook his head, remembering when he and Savannah first learned of the affair between Dr. Clark and Lily Mason.

Savannah had still been running from the police, trying to prove her innocence, when a coincidence brought them all to the same hotel, where they saw the two kissing. That was ten long years ago, but it felt like yesterday.

They rejoined Michael and Cathi, who remained at the nurse's station.

Michael said he had to get back to the office. He asked Robert to stay with Savannah, and they would appreciate it if he would introduce Savannah to Dani.

Cathi said, "She was awake when I left her room to greet you. I need to go home, shower, and get fresh clothes. I'll be back in a couple of hours."

Michael placed his arm around her shoulder. "Come on, love. I'll walk you to your car."

"Of course, we've got you covered," Robert answered.

Cathi hugged Savannah again. "Thank God, you're here. It's so lovely to see you again."

Savannah watched the pair step into the elevator. She admired the couple's genuine love.

Robert looked at Savannah. "You've got this. Just know she doesn't look like herself."

He pulled out his phone and showed her a video of Dani when she was healthy. Savannah saw a beautiful child with dark blond hair, big green eyes, and light olive skin. She was laughing and running around the yard with a puppy chasing her.

"This is who she is. THIS is who I want you to see when you look at her. THIS is who I still see," Robert said sadly.

Savannah watched the video twice. She was excited to meet Dani, but anxious that the girl might not survive this horrible disease. A tear ran down her face as she felt remorse that she had lost ten years of Danielle's life, but she had never wanted to complicate the child's life. She never told anyone she worked with that she had given up a child, mainly out of the shame she felt. Only a handful of people knew about the situation.

She lived her life and kept busy as a doctor to keep her mind off the adoption. She reminded herself, over and over, that Dani was with a loving family, and it was for the best. She was single and childless and would probably remain so. She felt it was too late to have a family of her own now.

Now, after watching the video, for the first time, she acknowledged that this was her beautiful daughter.

She straightened her stature, took a deep breath, and put on the mask and gloves Robert had handed her.

"I'm ready."

Chapter 4

Ten-year-old Danielle Mason was sitting up in her hospital bed, attached to IVs and a cardiac machine, which was being monitored at the nurse's station. She was wearing a light pink hospital gown with pictures of puppies. Her eyes were sunken, and her skin was ashen because of the anemia. She looked ill, but she slightly smiled as Robert entered the room. Savannah tried to imagine the beautiful, healthy girl in the video, but the girl in the bed looked like a skeleton. She felt nauseous and sorry she had to meet her daughter this way, but she had to remain strong and not show the heartache she was feeling.

"Hello, my little lady," Robert said as he kissed her thin hand.

"Hello, Uncle Robert," she said weakly.

Dani stared at the woman standing next to her uncle. She noticed she had green eyes like hers.

"I want to introduce you to my friend, Savannah. She's a doctor who wants to help you. Would you like that?"

"Yes, thank you. I'm afraid no one else has been able to help me so far. I can't even leave this room because the nurses say I'll get sicker if I do. One nurse told me I would die like the other kids in the hospital if I didn't behave myself."

Savannah was stunned. She looked at Robert with wide, unblinking eyes. Her mouth was open under her mask, and she was grateful Dani couldn't see the look of horror on her face.

Savannah spoke up to give Dani more confidence.

"That wasn't nice for that nurse to say to you. Some people can't communicate well. I'm sure she meant to say your body doesn't have the immune system you need to fight off infections right now. But I'm here to help you get stronger, so one day soon, you can leave the room and, better yet, go home."

She knew she might be giving the child false hope, but she had nothing more to offer than support.

Savannah pulled a chair up next to the hospital bed.

"You know, you look like a princess to me. Are you a princess?"

Dani smiled, "No, I'm a regular kid."

"I bet you're a princess to Robert and your parents."

Robert nodded yes, and he wondered where Savannah was going with this.

"Whenever I am scared or anxious, I pretend to put on a tiara. It makes me brave. That's how I got through medical school. Whenever I have doubts or feel stressed, I put on my tiara. Have you ever heard the Queen of England say, 'Carry On'?"

Dani shook her head no.

"Well, she does when the country is fearful of something terrible. She encourages her people to stay strong. She wears her crown proudly as she supports all who listen, even though she may be fearful herself. But, she never shows it."

Savannah reached inside her purse and pulled out a shiny tiara, much like the one Robert had given her ten years prior.

She placed it on the child's head. "I, Dr. Savannah Hayes, dub thee Princess Danielle Mason."

A tear ran down Robert's face, and he quickly wiped it away before Dani could see it. He was so proud of Savannah and happy to hear how the tiara he had gifted her had given her courage.

Dani smiled. "I'm the princess of Children's Hospital and can help keep the other children strong."

Dani reached up to touch the little tiara. Savannah removed a compact mirror from her purse, and Dani admired her reflection. She sat up straighter in her bed. Robert adjusted the pillows.

"I'm not dying like the other children? I hear someone say, 'Code Blue,' and I hear people running down the hallway. I hear people crying. That nurse told me they had been bad children, and God took them off the planet."

Savannah was livid but held her temper. "What is this nurse's name that lies to you?"

"I don't remember."

"Can you describe her?"

"No, she always wears a mask."

"What color hair does she have?"

"It's blond."

"Is she tall or short?"

"She's short."

"Anything else you can remember?"

Dani looked down at her hands, deep in thought, and suddenly, her green eyes opened wide as she looked at Savannah. "She got a phone call once. She answered it, and a man shouted loud enough for me to hear him call her name."

Robert said, "Dani, tell us her name, and your kingdom will punish her for lying."

"I think it was some kind of flower. I'm trying to remember."

"Rose?"

Dani shook her head no.

Savannah and Robert named different flowers, but kept getting a no from Dani.

Robert looked at Savannah and asked, "Was it a lily?"

"Yes, that was it. It was a lily."

Savannah and Robert looked at each other again, wondering if this could possibly be who they thought it was.

"As a doctor and a princess myself, I want you to know that we will find this Lily person, and she will no longer be allowed to lie to you. Was she in your room today?"

"No, she always comes in when my mom leaves to get something to eat."

"So, around lunchtime, then?"

"I guess so."

Robert spoke, "Did I ever tell you I was once a cop?"

Dani looked at him wide-eyed, enjoying this new knowledge.

"Yep, I was a detective. We detectives know how to find people who do bad things. I will stop this even if I must stay here 24/7, but you'll have to scoot over and let me sleep in your bed." Robert teased as he tickled her.

Dani laughed and then coughed, and her face showed fear because she couldn't stop.

Savannah immediately put an oxygen mask on Dani's face and turned the oxygen on at the wall. She didn't have the authority to increase the flow, but she would mention it to Dr. Stone. Savannah removed a pink stethoscope from her purse and listened to Dani's lungs. Dani's breath sounds were diminished, and she could hear faint crackles indicating fluid in the smaller airways in her lungs.

The oxygen helped, and Dani closed her eyes.

Savannah said, "Try not to be afraid. I'll ask Nancy, the head nurse, to call the doctor to order respiratory therapy to help you breathe. You need to rest now. Your Uncle Robert and I will see you tomorrow, and your mom will be here soon. She went home to shower and change her clothes."

They waited silently until Dani was stable and sleeping before quietly leaving the room.

Robert and Savannah sat in comfortable blue leather chairs in the waiting room. They looked toward the hallway at each person passing by the door. They wanted to catch Cathi before she went back to Dani's room. She had to be alerted that Lily Mason-Clark was possibly up to no good again.

Robert was angry and raised his eyebrows, remembering their conversation with Dani.

"Do you think the nurse Dani mentioned was Lily Mason-Clark? How could she know Dani was in the hospital? I don't believe she even knew about Dani."

Savannah quickly answered, "From Dr. Clark, of course. All the oncologists know one another. I'm sure Dr. Stone talked with him about Dani, knowing he married a Mason."

"It's just like Lily to start trouble. She seems to enjoy chaos. You need to talk to the nurses and alert them to watch out for her."

"Good idea. I'll talk to Nancy. She seems competent." Savannah answered.

"Maybe we should put a uniformed security cop at the door for a while. Michael and I can't always be here, and you're leaving us again soon."

"I'm sorry, Robert. I have a good job in the emergency room in a great hospital. I love all the staff. I have a condo overlooking the ocean. The water is aqua blue, just like in the Bahamas. It's so clear that I can watch the dolphins playing. Not like here, where the water is brown."

"Penthouse?"

Savannah was embarrassed, and her face turned red. "Yes, you caught me."

"You never cared about material things before. You've changed."

"Not really. I have nightmares about being chased. I wanted a safe haven where you need a key to get to the upper floor, like Mark's condos in Nassau and Fort Lauderdale."

"Dating anyone?"

"No. I don't have the time or the energy. My job keeps me busy. You?"

"I have gone on several dates but never had chemistry," Robert said, wanting to add that he could never love anyone else but her, but kept silent.

Robert saw Cathi pass by the door and jumped up to catch her before going to Dani's room.

"We need to talk, Cathi." He took her arm and guided her into the waiting room.

As Robert shared the conversation about Lily with Cathi, Savannah took the time to talk to Nancy.

She found Nancy sitting with her back to the door of her office. She was whispering on her cell phone, and Savannah overheard her say, "I can't do this anymore. Please stop calling me."

Savannah had surprised her, and she recognized that Nancy was fearful that she had heard the conversation. Nancy's mouth was downturned, and her eyes were wide open.

Nancy sat still and kept her head down.

"An old boyfriend," she explained.

Savannah wondered why Nancy would be fearful of her hearing that.

Savannah waited for Nancy to gain her composure.

"Is he violent?"

"Who?"

"Your old boyfriend."

"No, I mean, he can be, I guess."

Nancy quickly changed the subject.

"How can I help you, doctor?"

"Do you have a day nurse named Lily?"

"No, why?"

Savannah told her what Dani had said.

Nancy stood up from her chair, quickly dismissing the conversation.

"I'll look into it. Now, excuse me, I have work to do."

"Of course," Savannah said as she left the room. She stood beside the office door, waiting to see if Nancy would make another call. Intuition told her something was amiss. Nancy's demeanor had changed from earlier.

As Savannah suspected, Nancy picked up her phone.

"You need to be more careful. I don't want to be involved in your schemes anymore."

Savannah wondered who Nancy was talking to. She knew she could be too judgmental and suspicious of people. She decided it was none of her business, but she would be careful what she said around Nancy.

Cathi called Michael and told him what had occurred. Michael despised his ex-stepmother and didn't trust her. It's very possible Lily found out about Dani. But why would she care? Unless she wanted to pay him back for kicking her out of his father's mansion, leaving her with only a car and $30,000 after learning of her illicit affair with Dr. Clark. Did she know Dani was the product of her dead son, Noah? Or did she think Dani was his child? He didn't know the answers. He only knew Lily was an evil, conniving bitch.

He Googled private security companies and researched ratings of different companies. He found one and called a company that sounded familiar and had the highest rating with the Better Business Bureau. Once satisfied with their credentials, he hired them on the spot. They were to start immediately.

*****

David Atkins was fifty-six years old and a retired Navy SEAL. He was 6'2" with an athletic body. His security uniform looked too small over his broad shoulders and big chest. His leg muscles were bulging beneath his black pants. He wore a blue and gold badge with the name Rollins Security imprinted on it. Anyone could see this man was a bodybuilder, not to be messed with. He also visibly carried a gun in a holster around his waist.

Robert found a comfortable chair for David and placed it outside Dani's door. Cathi introduced herself and quickly went back into Dani's room.

Robert introduced himself and explained the necessity of having security. He described Lily as short with blond hair, but she had a propensity for wearing wigs to conceal her true identity.

"Don't let anyone in this room unless you know for certain who they are."

He gave the names of the family members along with his and Savannah's.

"Each morning you're here, take note of the staff on duty. Verify any other personnel from the hospital. Danielle's doctor is Dr. Kent Stone. No one else outside the hospital has permission to enter this room. We don't expect you to sit all day, but stay nearby and watch the room closely. Someone will bring you lunch daily and guard the door while you eat. I have arranged for you to eat in the head nurse's office. Her name is Nancy." He pointed to her.

Nancy looked up and smiled at the handsome man. She was interested in getting to know him.

Robert continued, "The woman I described is very cunning. She usually comes when the patient's mother is at lunch. We may need to hire your company around the clock at some point, but for now, eight hours should suffice."

David explained that he had been deployed as a SEAL for four tours in the Middle East. He was retired but still wanted to work.

"No one gets past me, I assure you."

Robert felt comfortable with the man. He admired all military personnel but was a little envious of Navy SEALs, who were, to him, the elite.

A pretty respiratory therapist walked up to the room as they spoke. David gave her the once-over after questioning her. The girl was a new graduate who cowered at his questions. David was satisfied and allowed her entry to the room.

Five minutes later, the girl ran out of the room, asking for assistance from a nurse.

"Help. She's having a seizure," the therapist yelled loudly.

Savannah heard the screams for help from the nurse's station and quickly ran to the room.

Calmly, as she put on her mask, Savannah asked the therapist, "Did you give her albuterol?"

The therapist nodded. "Yes."

"She must be allergic," Savannah said beside Dani's hospital bed.

Cathi entered the room and took Dani's hand. She was obviously anxious, feeling helpless, and did not know what to do.

Dani was twitching, and seeing her mother panicking made her even more anxious.

Cathi trepidatiously asked, "What's happening? Do something."

Savannah looked at the cardiac monitor and noticed Dani was in V-Tach, a potentially life-threatening emergency. Nancy entered the room to provide antiarrhythmic medication through the IV. Another nurse brought a defibrillator, but Savannah noticed Dani's heart rate was stabilizing with the medication, and the twitching lessened; she calmly told the nurses they could leave the room to assure Dani that she had nothing to fear. The nurses looked at Cathi, who gave a nod of approval.

"Make sure to note that Danielle is allergic to albuterol," she told Nancy as she removed Dr. Stone's card from her purse and dialed his number.

Chapter 5

Dr. Kyle Clark stood alone, sipping on scotch at a bar in a private room at a Colonial Williamsburg inn. He was there to attend a monthly meeting with other doctors from Norfolk. They always met in Williamsburg or Virginia Beach, where no one would recognize them.

While he waited for Lily to freshen in the ladies' room, he admired the room's richness. Although he had been at the inn many times, he soaked in soft lighting from sconces and candles that lit the room, designed in the colonial style with a golden oak wood bar and comfortable dark leather chairs around wooden tables. The primitive, wide-planked pine flooring was scuffed from the years of abuse from shoes. However, it gave the room an ambiance of antiquity. The walls were adorned with royal blue embossed damask wallpaper. Large 18th-century paintings with beautiful, gold, ornate frames surrounded the paintings of men in red hunting clothes. The hunters followed their hounds on horseback. The paintings were strategically placed around the room.

He loved the hunt scenes and wished he had lived back when men shared their passion for hunting. The room reminded him of an old gentleman's club, and he envisioned men sitting at the tables smoking from long-stem clay tavern pipes, talking about hunting or political news of the day. The quaint room had a slight musty smell, released by decaying biological matter since the 18th century. He loved the old colonial room.

His wife, Lily, interrupted his train of thought. She approached with the three doctors who had come to the inn for their monthly meeting.

Lily said, "Doctors, we have much to discuss. Our little side business has made us all very rich, and we must continue our plans."

Lily looked proud, and her smile beamed from ear to ear. She was enthusiastic tonight. Her plans had gone without a hitch for the last two years.

Kyle Clark was visibly uncomfortable. He downed his scotch, which gave him the courage to disagree with his wife.

"Lily, we need to stop. We have enough money. We don't need to continue. I didn't want to do this in the first place."

The men ordered a round of drinks. The lone bartender worked swiftly, knowing he would receive a generous tip from the group. He had always volunteered to work the private function, knowing he would be paid more in just a couple of hours than his eight-hour shift at another inn.

While waiting for the drinks, Dr. Roy Hart, a seventy-four-year-old thoracic surgeon, said, "I'm not ready to throw in the towel just yet. I have one year left before retirement, and all my damn children have nickel-and-dimed me to death. I need that money. My wife has Alzheimer's, and her care is costing me a bundle. I have been doing the heart transplants."

Dr. Paul Wilson, a nephrologist, was sixty years old and the youngest and newest member of the group. "I'd like to hear what Lily has to say. My wife has asked for a divorce and is trying to take me to the cleaners. Besides, I'm the one who has been transplanting all the kidneys recently. I want to discuss money and how it's split."

Dr. Kent Stone said, "You have only operated on the adults; I have assisted you in the operating room on the children. Don't act like you're doing all the work here, Paul. And you're not a surgeon, Kyle. What is your part in this?"

Kyle looked embarrassed. He kept his head down, staring at the floor. He wanted to say, "I'm the one married to the bitch." Instead, he said, "I falsify records so some of my patients and your patients can receive or donate the kidneys for transplantation. I don't feel comfortable with what we are doing. We took an oath to do no harm, for God's sake."

After the drinks were served, Lily motioned for the men to move to a table in the far corner of the room.

"Gentlemen, we mustn't let prying eyes or ears hear our conversation. Let's move to the table."

They followed Lily to a large round table.

62-year-old Lily was a five-foot-two spitball, all polish and shine. She dressed immaculately, and not one blond hair on her head was out of place. She dripped in jewels.

All the men except Kyle admired her energy and intelligence because she was a master planner, although they all mainly feared her. She was devious, and they were too afraid of how she would scheme against them. They were all guilty and too involved in Lily's organization.

Kyle Clark hated his wife. He understood why Michael Mason disowned his stepmother ten years ago after his father had been murdered. Kyle didn't understand it then because he was in love with her. Kyle had divorced his first wife to marry her, and it didn't take long before the real Lily showed up and bared her teeth. He divorced her within six months, but she somehow swindled attorneys and finagled her way into becoming his business partner. She threatened to ruin his reputation in the community. He remarried her to keep his good reputation and the medical clinic he owned and loved. He had worked too hard to let Lily destroy it all.

He eventually forced her into signing a prenuptial agreement a day before the second wedding. She had been hungover from drinking too much wine the night before, and probably didn't realize what she was signing.

"Listen up, men. Luck is on our side. I recently found another partner, Jesús Rodríguez, from Mexico. He has the means to triple our business." Lily said.

"Wait, wait, just a minute. Isn't Jesús the head of a drug cartel? You can't be serious. He's infamous." Kent Stone said as he squirmed in his seat.

"Yes, so what?" Lily quickly answered and squinted her eyes as she looked at the doctors.

Kent Stone answered, "Look, harvesting kidneys is one thing, but human trafficking and drugs are another. I involved myself in saving lives to give children a chance at life. I thought your organization was legal, but I won't be involved in another one of your schemes. I'm out."

None of them had ever questioned Lily, even though they all wondered if Lily's organization, A Lil Help, was legitimate.

The doctors knew that the trading of human organs and tissues for commercial transplantation was illegal. They were too afraid to ask where the donated organs came from, and didn't ask. There was a need, but this was getting out of hand.

Lily spoke, "Commercial trade in human organs is illegal, as you probably know, and it's getting too hard for me to find donors. Jesús and a dozen of his men will ensure we have plenty of organs to transplant. We'll have more hearts, livers, pancreases, and, of course, kidneys. Isn't it exciting?"

"I'm out too," Paul Wilson said. "I transplanted most of those kidneys. And now you are talking about murdering people for their organs."

Lily stood and pointed her fingers at the men.

"And you have all been paid very handsomely. Kent, you falsified Danielle Mason's records to show her kidneys are failing. Now, I want her kidneys removed and for you to replace them with bad ones. You will be paid a great sum, I assure you. If you choose not to do the surgery," she hesitated before finishing her sentence and took a drink of water.

She glared at the men and warned, "Or Jesús will pay your families a visit."

"LILY," Kyle shouted, "Surely, you don't mean that. We all got involved in this, thinking we could help people, but now you are threatening lives and asking us to commit murder."

He pulled her back down into her seat.

A look of pure evil contorted her face.

"As sure as my name is Lily Mason-Clark, I will see Danielle Mason dead."

"But why, Lily, why do you want to keep up this charade? You are talking about murder. I want no part of it." Dr. Stone stood to leave.

"Sit your ass back down," Lily growled. He abided because he feared her, and a part of him wanted to know her reasoning.

"Because she is Michael Mason's child, and I will punish him just like he punished me. I want him to suffer as I have suffered. I have been waiting ten long, agonizing years to get my revenge. I guarantee I will have it. I have put in all the grunt work for us all to become very wealthy. I agree that harvesting kidneys and falsifying medical records have helped save lives, and I'm telling you that human trafficking will bring in more organs. Leave the human trafficking and drugs to me and Jesùs. We'll all be rich beyond our wildest dreams."

She hesitated to get the feel of the room before continuing.

"And you, Dr. Stone, will do as I say. Whatever Dr. Savannah Hayes is doing to help the child must stop immediately! Why is she here anyway?"

"How do you know about her, Lily?" Kent asked anxiously.

"I have my spies. They are my little birdies that whisper in my ears."

Kyle Clark's mouth dropped open upon hearing Savannah's name. Lily said she was a doctor. Could that be true?

"Answer me, Kent," she demanded.

Kent Stone sighed. "She had her blood drawn to see if she's a match for a bone marrow transplant because the unnecessary chemo has destroyed the child's blood cells, but I know she doesn't need a transplant. All I need to do is discontinue the chemo and treatments. I falsified all the tests from her parents and Miss Hayes to ensure they didn't match. But Savannah Hayes is a doctor, Lily. She'll find out the girl doesn't have any cancer markers, and I misdiagnosed her with lymphoma. We can't fool her for too long. Danielle Mason's kidneys are failing because of the chemo. You originally said you wanted to transplant one kidney, but now you're asking me to order the kidneys removed to kill the child. That girl is innocent. She has never done anything to you."

"She's a product of Michael. I want to destroy him. I want to hurt him to his core. I want to see him on his knees, begging for his little girl's life. I want the girl dead. I tried to destroy his business but failed. I won't fail this time."

Kent Stone questioned her, "But that little girl is your granddaughter, isn't she?"

"I dare you to question me. But to answer you, Michael is not my biological son. He was seven when I married his father. Michael killed my biological son by putting him on an airplane that he knew was having mechanical problems. I haven't been able to prove it, so I want his child to die, just like my son, Noah, died. Tit for tat."

Lily, the ultimate narcissist, was growing impatient with the men defying her. She didn't comprehend their apprehension and thought they should all be appreciative.

Her demeanor changed as the men stared at her with fear in their eyes. She was enjoying her power.

She spoke gleefully, "Now, back to business. Jesús will be available only to me. I will bring you all healthier organs. I'll ask you again, isn't it exciting?" Lily glared at the men.

"NO," the doctors said in unison.

Kyle Clark stood to leave. "Meeting adjourned. Get up, Lily, we're leaving."

"We'll leave when I say we leave. But I have said my piece. You will all abide, or remember, Jesús won't be far behind. You'll all need to move to another country to get out of this. You think I'm evil? You haven't seen anything yet."

She laughed an evil laugh, and her mouth twisted in satisfaction. She owned these doctors because she had them over a barrel.

She stood up and said, "And if you run, you must keep running. I will find you. Don't think you can outsmart or harm me in any way. Jesús Rodríguez is being paid to protect me. If anything happens to me, he'll kill you all, including you, my dear, stupid husband."

The men sat silently, knowing Lily was evil enough to follow through on her threats.

Lily picked up her purse and spoke to her husband, who sat motionless in his chair as he thought, "Who is this evil bitch?"

"Come, Kyle, I want to go home. I have already paid for the room; now you doctors can pay the bartender's tip."

Kyle followed his wife meekly out the door as directed. The other men remained in their seats.

After the remaining doctors were confident Lily was leaving the inn, Dr. Stone whispered, "We have to find a way out of this. We can't go to the police. She may have bugged our phones, so be careful when calling each other. We may need to involve our nurses somehow, like having them text the nurses in your offices or calling your office lines on the ruse that we need to discuss a patient. When one of us gets a call, we all get the call except for Kyle. Tonight's meeting stays between the three of us. We'll meet somewhere safe to discuss the matter if one of us has an idea that won't incriminate us. Let's meet at the Hilton, downtown Norfolk, at 7 p.m. on a Wednesday if we all get the call."

Before leaving the inn, they worked out a satisfactory arrangement.

They left a hefty tip for the bartender, who had overheard portions of their conversation with Lily. The bartender didn't look up and didn't want to be involved.

Chapter 6

Traveling home from Williamsburg meant driving through the Hampton Bay Bridge tunnel.

Kyle cursed under his breath because there had been an accident. That meant he had no choice but to sit in the car with the evil bitch in the passenger seat. He turned on the radio to listen to the traffic report. With any luck, it wouldn't be hours of sitting in a long line of traffic, waiting for the accident to clear. He was too close to the tunnel to exit the highway.

Besides, it was the fastest route home. If he chose another direction, he'd still need to drive through another tunnel in Chesapeake, which could still take hours. He looked at the gas gauge and was thankful he still had a tank half full of fuel.

Lily was silent, busy texting away. He ventured she was cooking up another scheme. God, how he hated her. He kicked himself for being so stupid for getting involved with a patient's wife in the first place. That had been his first big mistake. His second mistake was falling in love with her. She pretended to be a sweet, caring woman. The sex had been great, something that neither of them got at home. Her then husband, Daniel Mason, was always traveling on his yacht. Now he understood why Daniel chose to live away for months. He felt depressed as remorse set in, and he wanted to flee, but he was caught in her web of lies and deceit. He had to find a way out, for the doctor's sake.

He thought about Savannah. It had been over ten years since he last saw her when he obtained a job for her on the yacht with Daniel Mason. He had no idea she had reached her goal of becoming a doctor. He felt his chest swell with pride. He always knew she was someone special.

He tried to remember what was said back at the inn. Kent Stone mentioned a blood test for a bone marrow transplant. Why was Savannah giving blood for an HLA test? Only relatives usually would be a good match. What other test could it possibly be?

The cars started slowly moving, and he concentrated on the taillights ahead of him, being careful with the stop-and-go of the vehicles in front of him. He was anxious to get home so he could shower, go to his bedroom, and lock the door. He needed to get away from Lily. Every moment with her was agonizingly difficult. A thought entered his head. He would visit Dr. Stone at the Children's Hospital this week. He hoped he would get a chance to run into Savannah there. He had to scheme how he could manage not to get caught by Lily and her spies.

It was half past ten at night when they arrived at their house in Norfolk. He hurriedly pulled the car into the garage. He didn't bother to wait for Lily to exit the vehicle, but walked directly up the stairs to the guest room, which was his sanctuary in his home. He showered, allowing the hot water to soothe his aching body, and he wished he could open up his skull and let the water wash away all the bad memories of the night's meeting from his brain. He was now seventy-two years old. He wondered what the rest of his life would be like, especially if he had to spend the time he had left rotting in a prison cell. He turned off the sadness as he turned off the water because a plan was formulating. He would sleep on it. He finally crawled into bed, hoping sleep would overtake him soon and alleviate his misery.

Lily removed her makeup, dressed for bed in the downstairs primary bedroom, and entered the kitchen in the back of the house. She turned on the stereo to listen to music and opened a bottle of chilled wine. The music was upbeat as she danced around the kitchen in her lacy nightgown. As she drank, the music got louder.

The bottle was soon empty. Lily was feeling more powerful with each glass of alcohol. She felt influential and ecstatic and was utterly satisfied with the meeting. She patted herself on the back as she finished the last glass of wine. She laughed out loud when she stumbled and hit her toe on the edge of a chair at the center island.

Another bottle beckoned to be opened, but Kyle bolted down the stairs as she held the opener on top of it, trying to twist it.

"God damn it, Lily. Turn the fucking music off and go to bed," he growled. He turned off the music.

She stared at him and burst into laughter.

Kyle reached for the unopened bottle she was attempting to open. She pushed him away and screamed so loudly that he was sure the neighbors could hear. She was like a wild animal, scratching and clawing at his face.

As they wrestled and struggled with the bottle, it flew out of her hands and crashed onto the tile floor, spilling its contents.

Broken glass was everywhere. They were both barefoot, but he didn't care. He cut his foot on a small piece of broken glass and hobbled toward her. He scooped her into his arms, dripping blood on the tiles as he forcefully carried her to the nearby bedroom. He threw her on the bed with all his strength.

She cried out, "Rape, rape," as she continued to laugh in his face.

He turned his back on her to leave the room and heard a gunshot when he was at the doorway. The bullet felt like a hard punch to his right shoulder, and he stumbled to the phone lying on the kitchen counter to dial 9-1-1 while stepping on more broken glass.

He saw blood oozing from his right foot. He put his left hand on his right shoulder, but couldn't reach the wound where the bullet had entered. He saw more blood dripping on the floor, and he knew it was draining down his naked back.

Lily stood in the doorway, laughing hysterically, holding the pistol and pointing it at him.

He grabbed a clean dish towel and threw it over his right shoulder. He ran up the stairs to change his clothes and try to stop the bleeding, leaving drops of blood along the way.

He removed his pajama bottoms and stood in front of the bathroom mirror. He wrapped gauze around his bleeding foot. He examined the scratches on his face and neck. He decided they would heal quickly as he turned his attention to his shoulder.

He knew the bullet was lodged in his scapula because he couldn't find an exit wound. Blood was still dripping down his back. He grabbed an old shirt and a pair of pants from the closet and grimaced as he slowly climbed into the clean clothes. The back of his shirt was soon soaked in blood. He slipped into a pair of house slippers. He cried out when he put his weight on his right foot. He hopped to the bathroom to replace the bandages and wrapped an elastic compression bandage around the new gauze.

He noticed he had dripped blood onto the white wool carpet, but was happy because Lily loved the expensive rug she had chosen for the room.

He sat on the bed's edge, hiding behind the locked bedroom door, waiting for the ambulance.

He needed to make up a story.

He felt lucky to be alive, yet at the same time, he almost wished she had killed him to end his misery.

Fifteen minutes later, Lily answered the doorbell, dressed to the nines as if nothing had happened. She had sobered up some and began telling her lies.

The EMT could smell the sweet stench of alcohol on her breath.

"My husband tried to rape me. I had no choice but to shoot him in the shoulder to protect myself."

Kyle slowly walked down the steps, taking small steps as he ascended the stairs, holding onto the wooden railing attached to the wall with both hands. One of the EMTs ran to help him down into the foyer.

They examined the wound. More blood dripped onto the black and white marble floor.

The driver turned to Lily and said, "You shot him in the back? How could he rape you when he was walking away?"

"Just an unfortunate quarrel between an old married couple," Kyle said calmly to the ambulance driver. "I'm okay, but I have lost a lot of blood, so if you'll be so kind, please take me to the hospital."

Lily slammed and locked the front door as Kyle was being carried on a stretcher to the waiting ambulance. She returned to the kitchen, turned up the music, and opened another bottle of wine. Stepping over the broken glass on the floor, she began dancing.

When the ambulance arrived at the hospital, Dr. Clark, bleeding profusely, barely had a pulse or blood pressure, and was rushed into surgery.

The ambulance driver called the police.

Chapter 7

Savannah and Robert had spent the evening at his comfortable home. Ana was pleased to sit quietly beside them as they sat on the back deck, listening to music and the ocean waves gently rolling onto the beach. Robert had cooked a delicious meal and shared a bottle of Chardonnay. Robert smoked a cigar. They reminisced about their time together and laughed. They caught up on the last ten years apart, except they didn't want to talk about when they had been together four years ago in Boston because it hadn't ended well.

Time flew by quickly, and Ana began snoring.

"It's eleven. I guess it's time to hit the hay." Savannah yawned.

"Get some sleep. We'll have a nice breakfast and pick up lunch for David Atkins on our way to the hospital tomorrow. We should be there before noon, so take your time in the morning. I'm sure you don't often get to sleep in."

"You've got that right. Your bed is very comfortable, and I may sleep for a week."

Robert refrained from inviting her to his bedroom. He knew whatever they had ten years ago was over. They couldn't make up for lost time. It was too late to start another relationship because they had different lives in different states.

Savannah said goodnight and hurried off to bed. She wondered what it would be like to kiss him once more and kicked herself for asking herself such a silly question.

Ana positioned herself on the floor next to Savannah's bed once again.

*****

Savannah and Ana slept in until 9 a.m.

Robert could hear the shower running upstairs from the kitchen. He was making pancakes when she finally entered the room dressed for the day. They talked while they ate and played with Ana until it was time to leave at eleven.

Robert called his neighbor, whom he paid weekly to watch and feed Ana when he knew he would be gone for the day. He felt happy that he had installed a doggie door when he had remodeled the house. He had also installed a latched gate in the fence between his and his neighbor's house, so the woman didn't need to walk over to get Ana.

Robert watched his neighbor open the gate and saw Ana walk excitedly next to her, entering her house through the back door.

Robert teased Savannah, "Do you own any shoes other than white tennis shoes?"

"Nope. Why? Do they make my feet look too big?"

Robert knew this was like asking him if her pants made her butt look too big. He knew he had to tread lightly.

"Of course not. I just noticed you only wear white tennis shoes, just like you only wear light pink lipstick. That's all."

She straightened her back, ready for a fight, but had to laugh at herself.

"Hey, they're comfortable. I'm on my feet all day."

He laughed and asked sheepishly, "So, how many pairs do you own?"

She threw a dish towel at him and admitted, in a low voice, "Ten."

"Exactly the same?"

Savannah blushed, "Exactly the same."

They both laughed.

When they arrived at the hospital, Dr. Stone was patiently waiting for Savannah at the nurse's station. He was behind schedule, but he didn't want to miss her. He thought about calling, but he knew that was inappropriate because his friend, Kyle, had explicitly asked him to speak to her in person.

"What's wrong?" Savannah could tell he was anxious about something and worried Dani's health had worsened.

"Dr. Hayes, there's been an accident. Kyle Clark was shot last night in his home. He underwent surgery but should have a full recovery. He knows you're in town and wants to see you."

Robert immediately said, "Did Lily shoot him?"

Dr. Stone answered, "Yes, but I don't know the entire story. I heard it on the news this morning, and I visited Dr. Clark in the hospital before making my rounds."

"So Danielle is stable?"

"Yes, she's feeling better. She's wearing a little tiara and said she's a princess now." He laughed.

Savannah smiled, happy that Dani liked her gift.

"Is Dr. Clark at his hospital or somewhere else?"

"He's at Norfolk General East, where he has his clinic, because it's the closest to his house."

"Okay, thank you, doctor. By the way, you ordered a different medication for Danielle's breathing treatments, correct?"

As Savannah looked him in the eyes, Dr. Stone felt like she knew his secrets. He wanted to tell her everything Lily was forcing him to do. He was embarrassed because he sensed Savannah didn't trust his medical judgment, and for good reason. He knew he was a good doctor, but in Danielle Mason's case, he was screwing up royally because of Lily's orders. His goal wasn't to harm the girl to this point; he felt he could make things right. The child had been healthy except for a mild case of one kidney not functioning correctly. He had diagnosed her with fraudulent non-Hodgkin lymphoma to admit her to the hospital under his care. He had no intention of losing his medical license for Lily or anyone. He had no clue he would be under the microscope of another doctor because his buddy in the lab and the other doctors in Danielle's care were in on the scheme. Now, he wondered who he should be more afraid of, Lily Mason-Clark or Dr. Savannah Hayes. He realized Savannah was questioning him and paid attention.

"What medication? Oh, you mean the albuterol? Yes, I changed that."

Savannah lied, "The parents prefer you discontinue the chemo for now. Let's try a different approach and give her a blood transfusion to bring up her blood counts. Let's see if her bone marrow can start manufacturing its own after the transfusion. Also, you should begin the proper medications for

71

her platelets and white blood cells. I didn't see orders for any of that in her chart. Hopefully, stopping the chemo will help her kidneys, too."

Dr. Stone was actually relieved. Certainly, Lily couldn't deny the family their rights as parents. His hands would be tied. She wasn't stupid. She knew the Masons would fire him; then Lily wouldn't have any chance of getting close to the girl.

Robert stood quietly as Savannah gave the doctor orders. He was beyond proud.

"I agree with you, Dr. Hayes. I'll write the orders now."

"Please, call me Dr. Savannah. Everyone else does."

Nancy listened behind the desk, pretending to be busy, but Robert noticed that she was acting strangely. She behaved as if they didn't exist and refused to look at them.

However, Nancy exchanged glances with Dr. Stone. They both knew Savannah Hayes was now in charge.

"We'll visit Dr. Clark this afternoon. First, I want to check on Danielle," Savannah said.

Dr. Stone nodded and wrote the orders. He couldn't help but wonder if the families' prayers were finally being answered. Savannah Hayes was a God-send to them and, frankly, to himself. He felt hopeful for the first time since meeting Lily Mason-Clark.

Robert offered David, the guard, a sack full of different foods. He wasn't sure what bodybuilders ate, so he had purchased a variety of proteins, fruits, and nuts.

He sat in the chair outside Dani's room so David could eat his lunch.

Nancy made excuses to come and go out of her office to get David's undivided attention until he mentioned his wife. Disappointed, she walked to the private nurse's restroom to call Lily.

*****

Lily was angry. First, the cops showed up at her damn door and questioned her about the shooting. Thankfully, her asshole husband refused to put a warrant out for her arrest. And now the bad news about the family's wishes. She was going to do something about Savannah Hayes!

*****

While Robert stood guard, Savannah donned a mask and gloves and entered Dani's room. She was pleased to see some color on the little girl's face. She listened to the child's lungs and was relieved that the breathing treatments were working. Giving Dani encouragement always to keep the oxygen cannula in her nose, she clapped her hands and said, "Good job, princess."

Cathi thanked Savannah as she motioned for Cathi to step outside the room.

When David returned from his lunch break, Robert talked to him and explained that he used to be a detective. Without going into too much detail, Robert gave a short synopsis: Robert felt David was a brother in arms, albeit a different kind of brother. They had once protected the United States's citizens from thugs of all kinds.

Robert continued, "David, Dr. Savannah, and I feel something peculiar is happening in the hospital. Keep an eye on Nancy. She's acting strangely. I don't trust her. Pay attention if she's in Dani's room when Mrs. Mason isn't there. If she lingers too long, wear a mask and enter the room to see what she's doing. Savannah explained that most head nurses don't typically provide patient care. She shouldn't be in Dani's room unless it's an emergency."

Robert handed him a DM Yacht, Inc. business card on which he had written phone numbers on the back.

"Here are mine and Dr. Savannah's cell phone numbers. Call us if you see or hear anything unusual. There is no need to upset the Masons for suspicious activity. I'll take care of any problems."

David understood it was his duty to protect the girl by any means. David had been the team leader of SEAL Team Six,

74

based out of Norfolk. He had PTSD from the horrors he had witnessed, but he was functional.

Once back outside in the hallway, Savannah explained to Cathi how she had lied to Dr. Stone as they stood beside Robert and David.

"I'm not completely sure Dr. Stone is following hospital protocols, but I'm uncomfortable with his medical procedures and treatments. As you know, I worked for Dr. Clark for several years. His treatments were entirely different than Dr. Stone's. I advise you to get a second opinion."

Cathi nodded, "I'll talk to Michael when he comes to visit Dani after work today."

"Maybe it's the hospital's protocol, or he isn't a very good doctor, but something isn't right here, Cathi. I can't reiterate my fears enough."

Robert listened and spoke to Cathi after being satisfied that the conversation had ended.

"And guess who shot Dr. Clark last night?" Robert said excitedly.

Cathi stepped backward, saying, "No way! Lily? Unbelievable. Wait until I tell Michael; he's going to freak out. Oh, is Dr. Clark okay?"

"We think so. Robert and I are going to visit him shortly. I don't think Lily will be coming around here today. Maybe you should take the opportunity to go home and get some rest. Doctor's orders. David seems to be competent, and you can relax." Savannah smiled at the large man sitting in the chair.

David informally saluted her.

Cathi was so grateful that she cried.

"I'm sorry to cry. It's been a rough few weeks. I think I'll do as you suggest. Thank you both so much."

When Cathi returned to the room, Savannah and Robert walked to the elevators and past the nurses' station. Nancy saw them and quickly looked down. Robert thought it odd. How could she be so friendly one minute and so cold the next? Something wasn't right in the neighborhood. He and David would observe her more carefully.

Robert was relieved they had more eyes watching the visitors to Dani's room.

They rode the elevator to the first floor when they heard a warning over the intercom, "Code Blue, Code Blue, 5th floor."

The pair rushed up the five flights of the hospital stairs instead of waiting for the elevator. Once on the fifth floor, they relaxed when they saw four nurses running with equipment past

Dani's room. Their hearts were beating fast, and they were both out of breath, so they decided to wait for the elevator again.

Savannah was still breathing hard from the physical and mental activity and unconsciously leaned her head on Robert's shoulder for support. His heart quickened from her touch. He placed his arm around her waist. When she realized what she was doing, she quickly lifted her head and removed his arm.

Robert was confused.

He thought to himself, "Women! I'll never understand them."

Chapter 8

Robert pulled into the parking lot of his favorite diner.

"How long has it been since you've eaten she-crab soup?"

He knew most Florida restaurants didn't serve the delicious soup.

Savannah wasn't hungry but could always make room for her favorite foods.

"Forever," she excitedly answered.

"Charlie's Diner makes the best in town. Let's eat before going to see Dr. Clark."

Savannah jumped out of the parked car and raced Robert to the door of the small restaurant. They laughed like two teenagers. It had once been their game. Whoever lost the race had to pay for the meal.

"You lost, buddy," She said teasingly.

"Actually, I think you lost, but I'll buy it anyway because it was my idea to come here."

"One way or the other, I still win." She winked at him and laughed.

Robert was over the moon to be with her again. People were staring at the good-looking couple enjoying themselves. One woman hit her husband in the arm for staring at Savannah too long.

Savannah groaned as she slurped the delicious soup. She pretended to have a foodgasm, an intense pleasure from each bite. Robert was pleased and joined in with his own groans of pleasure. They laughed and continued to finish their bowls.

"Another round? Let's see if you can still eat more than I can," he teased.

"Yes, please."

They ate until she couldn't take another bite, but Robert noticed she had almost finished the second bowl of soup.

Savannah sat back and held her abdomen with her right hand. She extended her open palm toward Robert as she surrendered.

"I give. You win," she laughed, and noticed he had finished his bowl and pretended to lick the spoon.

Robert paid the bill and helped Savannah to her feet. She waddled back to the car holding her belly as if she were nine months pregnant with twins. Robert doubled over in laughter, watching her antics. He couldn't remember the last time he had laughed so much.

Once they reached his car, Savannah strapped herself in with the seatbelt.

"Thank you, kind sir, for the enjoyable meal."

He kissed her left hand. "You're very welcome, my Lady."

Savannah smiled. It seemed like the old days again when he treated her like a queen. She tingled at his touch, and it scared her because she felt vulnerable, so she withdrew her hand while saying, "Okay, fun's over; I guess we should go see Dr. Clark. It seems I live my life in hospitals."

Robert drove to Norfolk General East Hospital and parked near the entrance. It had started to rain, and they raced to the door again. Robert got to the door first and said, "Open," as he extended his arms as if he had magically opened the automated door. He bowed and extended his right arm to let her walk through first. She curtsied, raised her right hand, and held her hand vertically, twisting her wrist, waving to the people inside, much like Queen Elizabeth had waved.

Savannah knew she was acting silly. She also knew she had to put on her professional game face, but she couldn't help herself. She enjoyed her little game with Robert.

They went to the information desk, presented their IDs, and had their pictures taken. Then, they slapped the grey and white stickers onto their shirts, showing their distorted faces and names.

As they rode the elevator to the medical-surgical floor, Savannah removed a hair scrunchie from her purse and pulled her hair into a ponytail. Dr. Clark had never seen her with her hair down.

They waited outside the open door to Dr. Clark's room, where two uniformed police officers were questioning the patient. They strained their ears to listen to the questions and answers. They heard Dr. Clark refuse to press charges against his wife, explaining it was an accident and that Lily meant no harm. He asked the officers to leave due to the pain he was experiencing from the gunshot wound and the two-hour surgery.

The officers left disappointed because they didn't believe the shooting was an accident, but without a criminal charge, their hands were tied, and they knew the case wouldn't go any further. They were only left with more questions and the knowledge that they were stuck with a lot of unnecessary paperwork.

Dr. Clark saw the two visitors at his door and beckoned them inside the room. He didn't think Savannah could look more beautiful than he remembered, but as she stood in front of the glass windows beside him, the light filtered through, glowing around her. He swore he saw a halo over her head.

She smiled like an angel and leaned over to give him a sweet kiss on his right cheek, careful not to disturb his injured shoulder.

Dr. Clark took her hand. "Thank you for coming, Savannah. It's wonderful to see you again after all these years. I was so surprised when Dr. Stone told me you're back in town. And you're a doctor now. I can't tell you how proud I am of you."

"It's nice to see you, too, Dr. Clark. The man standing here is my friend, Robert Malone."

"Call me Kyle, please."

He looked at Robert standing on the other side of the bed and smiled. He turned back to Savannah.

"I remember the day I suggested you take a private duty position with Daniel Mason. You almost cried when you had to hand over your pink stethoscope to be placed with the supplies I was sending to Nassau with you."

Savannah reached into her purse and pulled out the instrument.

"I still have it," she laughed.

Savannah pointed to Kyle's right shoulder, wrapped in bandages. "How much damage did the bullet cause?"

"First of all, I'm glad it was my shoulder and not my chest or abdomen, which could have been much worse. I have some nerve and muscle damage, along with a fractured scapula. The broken blood vessels caused a lot of bleeding."

Kyle put on a brave face and smiled. "Other than that, I'll be fine with some rehabilitation. But…" He hesitated.

"There always seems to be a but," Savannah said.

"Is it a good but or a bad but?"

"Depends on your answer to my question, I suppose," Kyle said as he pushed the bedside button to raise the head of his bed.

"I'm listening."

Robert was also interested in what Dr. Clark would ask of her.

"As you probably already know, Lily was drunk when she shot me. You also probably know the woman is an evil schemer. I think everyone knows the truth about her now. Anyway, she once told me you somehow managed to get Daniel Mason's will and took it to his attorney in Virginia Beach. Did she lie?"

"No, even though she omitted much of the long story, the bottom line is that it is true."

"Okay, then I have a much-needed favor."

"Oh God, now what?" Robert thought.

"I think I need to sit," Savannah said as she pulled up a chair beside the bed.

"I'm listening."

"I hate to ask you this, but Lily is trying to blackmail me. You don't need to know why. She may even try to finish me off by sneaking in here and putting potassium in my IV. She once asked me to put potassium in the chemo I sent to Daniel to kill him for the money, saying we could run away together. Of course, I refused. When she saw the horrified look on my face, she backed down and said she was only kidding. I don't put anything past her anymore."

Savannah interrupted, "So she must have researched that interpreting potassium levels is difficult and complex when trying to determine the cause of death or time of death postmortem. She is evil! Wow!"

"That's just one example, but I digress. I have a handwritten addendum that I signed to my will. She was with me at her attorney's when we changed the will from my ex-wife to her, leaving her all my worldly possessions. I don't care about the house or cars, and I don't have children, but that clinic is my baby. I would roll over in my grave if Lily destroyed it. The

84

original will and addendum are in my office safe, along with a prenup she signed before we married the second time. I have them hidden behind a painting. I want to give you the code so you can take the will and the prenup to Brett Edwards, Daniel's attorney in Virginia Beach. I have already talked with him about the changes I made. I want him to safeguard the prenup. The prenup says she can't have the clinic when I pass, but the will leaves everything else to her. There are slight changes to the will regarding the clinic, but you don't need to know the specifics. Mr. Edwards would like to see a copy of my will, but there is only one. That's the original. I destroyed all the other copies of the will and the prenup because Lily could destroy the prenup after I pass. Virginia law is complicated, and I won't go into the particulars."

Savannah sighed, "Surely, there must be copies of the will and prenup at the attorney's office where the documents were originally drawn."

Kyle Clark smiled. "I assure you that isn't the case. The less you know, the better, but it's vital that Mr. Edwards receives the documents as soon as possible. When I'm discharged and can drive, I'll go to his office and sign the new will. I have already signed the handwritten addendum and had it notarized. Revising the documents may take several weeks, so the attorney must start immediately. For this favor, I am leaving the clinic to you."

Savannah almost fell out of the chair.

"What? Why me?"

"You deserve a break in life. I know your parents were killed in an automobile accident when you were a teenager. You're a hard worker and kind. I saw how you treated our patients. The staff loved you. Cindy and JoAnn are still working there."

"I'll take the will and the prenup, as a favor to you, but I'm not an oncologist, Dr. Clark. I work in an emergency room."

"Then hire an oncologist and oversee the operation. Hire two oncologists; I don't care as long as they're qualified. You sometimes recognized symptoms in our patients before I did. You're smart, and you are qualified. Or you can go back to medical school to specialize in Oncology. Your choice, as long as I can die a happy man, knowing you will safeguard my clinic."

Savannah and Robert were speechless. He, for one, wanted Savannah back in Norfolk.

Begrudgingly, she answered, "Okay, give me the code. I will help you because you were such a great boss when I worked for you. Robert and I will go to the clinic when we leave you. Please call Brett Edwards to tell him we will be there when he opens at eight-thirty in the morning. That is about all I can do for you."

Kyle whispered the six-number combination as Savannah wrote down the numbers on a piece of paper. She folded the paper and placed it in her purse.

"Please consider my offer, Savannah." He took her hand, and tears formed in his blue eyes as he pleaded with her.

"I'll give you my answer tomorrow," Savannah said as she withdrew her hand.

Robert knew she wouldn't answer him tomorrow because that's what she said when he had asked her to marry him. She never gave him a verbal answer. Instead, she left him to go to medical school.

Savannah stood and thanked Kyle for his trust in her.

Before exiting the room, she turned at the doorway and teased, "We'll see you tomorrow. Don't give the nurses a hard time."

Kyle pushed the control button on the bed to recline so he could nap. He felt exhausted yet worried about Lily, the doctors she had threatened with their lives, and his clinic. The weight of the world was on his shoulders, ironically, in more ways than one. He touched his right shoulder, grimaced, and pushed the button on the automated pain pump to deliver him morphine.

Chapter 9

Savannah led Robert through a corridor in the hospital attached to Dr. Clark's oncology clinic.

She opened one of the double doors and entered the familiar foyer. She opened a door that led to the clinic. She felt like she was home. Memories of patients and the staff flooded her brain. She felt overwhelmed and grabbed Robert's hand for comfort. She led him into a large open room with five chairs on both sides. The ten patients were seated in leather recliners receiving chemotherapy treatments. She also noticed that the cheap linoleum flooring had been replaced with warm brown, rustic laminate flooring that looked like it belonged in a tavern. She knew Kyle Clark's taste. She wondered if his home was filled with antiques or shabby chic furnishings. Then she realized Lily would not allow it.

Cindy, a heavy-set woman of about fifty, was checking an IV when she looked up to see who was intruding. She immediately recognized Savannah and rushed up to her, throwing her big arms around the much thinner Savannah.

"Oh my God, look who it is," she declared in her southern accent.

"JoAnn, JoAnn, come see who's here," she hollered.

The patients all looked up to see a beautiful woman and a handsome man holding hands.

JoAnn ran out of a room that Savannah knew to be the kitchen and lounge area.

"What's all the fuss?" she said as she dried her hands on brown paper towels dispensed from one of the machines hanging on the walls near each sink.

"Lordy, child, you look like an angel. Come here and let me get a good look at you."

She turned Savannah around.

"Aha, child, you as pretty as a new shiny penny. You ain't changed a bit."

The staff called her Mother JoAnn. She was the office manager, a sweet, heavy-set, practical black woman with gray hair who had worked for Dr. Clark for over thirty years. She took no nonsense from anyone. She was a hard worker and expected the staff to work just as hard.

She now eyed Savannah suspiciously, "Why you here? You come to get your job back or just show off your pretty man whose hand you holding?"

Savannah hugged her.

"We just came from visiting Dr. Clark in his room. He sent me here on an errand. He wants me to bring him a file he left in his office," she lied.

"Mm-hmm. He don't trust Miss Lily, then?" she stated, more as a fact than a question.

"No, and please don't tell her I've been here. She scares me, Mother JoAnn."

"Speak of the devil. Look who just waltzed through the door."

Everyone turned to look at Lily. She pushed a nurse away who got too close. "Get out of my way."

Lily started walking to Kyle's office, ignoring everyone except Mother JoAnn, who towered at least seven inches over her.

JoAnn stood her ground in front of Lily. "Now, you git Miss Lily. You ain't got reason to be here. You in my territory now, girl, and what I say goes when Dr. C ain't here."

Savannah laughed inside because she knew JoAnn was an educated woman who liked to put on a show pretending to be Madea, a character that Tyler Perry made famous in movies.

Robert was enjoying the action. He held Savannah's hand and squeezed it when Lily walked in.

Lily wasn't impressed. "Get out of my way, JoAnn. This will be my clinic someday, and you'll be fired."

"Don't care, Miss Lily. I'll be dead and gone before that happens."

JoAnn picked up an IV pole and pretended to jab Lily with it, moving it back and forth. Robert wanted to hand Lily a pole because he envisioned a sword fight between the two.

"Don't you dare touch me," Lily screamed.

JoAnn put down the pole and pretended to be a bull, scraping the ground with her feet. She placed her fingers against her head like horns and flared her nostrils as if ready to charge.

"Back away, bitch. Don't you dare touch me," Lily screeched.

"Oh, I'm touching you, alright. See this hand? Ain't it bigger than your face?"

Lily looked at the black woman's hand, which JoAnn had held up in the air. She suddenly became fearful.

Lily took her word and began walking backward, not taking her eyes off the hand.

"Now git, and don't you come back here, ya hear me, woman?"

Lily turned to look at Savannah. "Why are you here?"

JoAnn moved closer to Lily. "Git, I said."

Lily walked backwards out of the clinic.

Everyone clapped for the performance. JoAnn bowed to her audience.

She walked back to Savannah and, in her normal voice, said, "Now, where were we? How can I help you?"

Robert fell in love with this brave, funny woman.

"Like I said, I need to get a file from the doctor's office. He gave me the combination to his safe. It's imperative I get it. I believe there's something in there that will protect him from Lily. I believe he's afraid of her now. You know she shot him, right?"

"Yes, I visited him this morning. I put the fear of God in the nursing staff, warning them that they had better tell me if the witch came near him. Go do what Dr. Clark asked you to do," JoAnn said as she walked toward the front door.

"Where are you going, JoAnn?" Cindy asked.

"To see where Lily went. I will kick her butt from here to kingdom come if she goes around poor Dr. Clark."

As JoAnn left the clinic, Savannah led Robert into Kyle's office, which overlooked the Elizabeth River. Several paintings hung on the walls, along with his physician's diplomas and awards.

Robert studied each painting, guessing which painting the safe was under.

She laughed as Robert teased, "I'll take door number one for one hundred." He lifted one close to the door.

"Bzzz, wrong," Savannah teased. "Would you like to try again for two hundred, Mr. Malone?"

"Yes, Ma'am. I'll take this pretty one here." He pointed to a colorful landscape painting and lifted it off the wall.

"Wrong again, Mr. Malone."

Robert continued lifting paintings until there was only one painting left. It was a hunt scene of men in hunting clothes riding horses in an open field.

He looked at Savannah. "I bet it's this one," he winked as he teased.

"It better be; it's the last one," she said as she laughed.

Robert lifted the painting. "Bingo."

Savannah reached into her purse and pulled out the folded paper containing the safe's combination.

She handed it to Robert. "Thank God this isn't a burglary, or we would have been caught by now."

Savannah rifled through several documents in the safe until she found the will secured in a manila envelope.

"This must be it. Dr. Clark said it was in a legal-sized envelope, and it's the only one in the safe, but there's no name or what it says it is."

She carefully removed the envelope and shut the safe's door, ensuring it was locked. Robert rehung the painting.

Before they left the clinic, Savannah hugged and said goodbye to Cindy.

"Don't be a stranger."

Savannah nodded, thinking, "I may be the clinic owner someday."

She was still mulling it over. Although she was grateful Kyle trusted her with the clinic, she wasn't sure she wanted the responsibility.

When they exited the hospital, it was five o'clock. The rain had stopped, so they didn't race back to Robert's Mercedes.

"Let's eat dinner out. What do you feel like having?" Robert asked.

Savannah licked her lips. "Let's go back to the diner. I noticed they had fried green tomatoes on the menu. I haven't eaten that in ten years. I could eat another bowl of that delicious she-crap soup again."

"You're a glutton for punishment, you know that?" he laughed.

As Robert drove to the diner, he noticed a black SUV following them.

"Savannah, don't look, but we're being followed. The same SUV followed us out of the hospital's parking lot."

Twenty minutes later, Robert pulled up to the diner. He noticed the same SUV parked across the street. The windows were tinted dark black, and he couldn't see the occupants in the vehicle.

"It has to be Lily," Savannah said as she guarded the paperwork she was carrying.

They noticed the SUV had remained stationary across the street as they ate.

"The car must be from out of town. Blackout windows tinted that dark are prohibited in Virginia, and it doesn't have a license plate on the front bumper like we are required to have in

Virginia. Lily doesn't know where I live. I can't let whoever is driving follow us home. Are you up for a drive to Virginia Beach? We can stay in one of the hotels on the boardwalk. That way, we'll be closer to Brett Edwards's office in the morning. I'll call my neighbor to watch Ana."

Savannah was getting nervous. She twisted her ponytail, and Robert removed her hand from her mouth. She was absent-mindedly chewing on her index fingernail.

When they left the diner, Robert stayed close to Savannah and opened the passenger's door. Once she was seated, he quickly walked to the driver's seat.

"Let's see if the SUV follows us," he said as he pulled out of the parking lot.

The black SUV followed. Robert drove to the nearest police station, and the SUV continued to drive.

Robert didn't turn off the engine to let the car idle, and once he figured they had ditched the SUV, he drove to I-264, heading to Virginia Beach. When they hit Newtown Road, he looked in his rearview mirror and saw the black SUV following two cars behind. He didn't want to scare Savannah, so he didn't bother to mention it.

Robert sped up to eighty miles per hour as he weaved in and out of traffic. He prayed for a cop to stop them.

Savannah said, "They're following us, aren't they?" as she pretended to straighten her invisible tiara on her head.

Robert knew she was frightened. He knew her habit of putting her hands to the front of her head meant she was adjusting her invisible crown, trying to stay strong.

Savannah was relieved when she knew they were getting close to the oceanfront in Virginia Beach, where the interstate ended. She had grown up in the area and wanted to enjoy and share the many restaurants and the view of the ocean while they strolled along the boardwalk.

Nearing the end of the interstate, yellow blinking lights warned drivers to slow their speed to thirty-five mph from fifty-five mph.

Robert slowed and stayed in the right-hand lane, and the SUV drove beside them on their left on the four-lane highway. The passenger's window rolled down, and a man pointed a gun at Robert. Robert floored the gas pedal, running a red light. The SUV didn't have the power of the Mercedes and was slow to accelerate...it didn't make it through the red light and was broadsided by a car with the right-of-way.

A woman got out of her car to inspect the damage. She stumbled out of the sedan, holding her face, which was hurt when the airbags deployed. She raised her right fist and cursed at the driver for running the red light. The man in the passenger's seat of the SUV stepped out of the vehicle and shot her, leaving her bleeding in the middle of the street.

Savannah had turned in her seat and watched the incident as it occurred.

"Hurry, Robert, the man just shot a woman," as she dialed 9-1-1, praying the woman wasn't dead.

Robert quickly drove to the Hilton Hotel on the oceanfront. He gave the valet a $100 bill and asked the young man to park the car out of sight.

"I don't want my wife to see my car here if you know what I mean."

Savannah remained in the car, and the young man nodded as he handed Robert a ticket stub.

When Savannah exited the car, the young valet wished he could get that lucky.

Once safely inside the hotel, Robert asked for an ocean view with double beds.

Savannah sat on the edge of the bed closest to the window.

Robert called the Virginia Beach Police Department. He stood by the window with his back to her, looking at the ocean. The operator transferred the call to a detective, John Perry, who answered the phone.

Robert explained how they were hiding from the black SUV and were too afraid to leave the hotel room. He described the SUV and how the man had shot and possibly killed a woman who had T-boned the driver's side of the vehicle. He explained he didn't know why the SUV was following them. He couldn't provide license plate numbers because the front bumper didn't have one. He never saw the back bumper.

Robert hung up after giving the detective his full name and phone number, mentioning he was an ex-detective.

"Oh my God, Robert, why does trouble always seem to follow me?"

She placed her face in her hands and tried not to cry.

"Well, I can definitely say you're not boring, that's for sure," he said, sitting on the bed beside her and patting her arm.

Savannah didn't know if she should laugh or cry.

"If this is Lily's doing, why would she want to harm us? Did someone tell her we have Kyle's will and prenup? Or does she think I killed Daniel?"

"I don't know the answers, Vanna, but she is destructive. She destroys everything and everyone around her. She could have killed her husband. She wouldn't think twice about killing us. I guarantee you, I'll find out why if she truly is trying to harm us. In the meantime, we need to stay vigilant."

Robert turned on the local news. They were saddened when the newscaster reported that a woman with three young children was shot and killed after experiencing a car crash in Virginia Beach.

"Oh, my God, they killed that poor woman." Savannah's salty tears ran down her face. She placed her hands together to try to stop them from shaking.

Robert was angry and tried not to show it, but he knew they were both in danger. The bullet was meant for him, or Savannah, or both. But why?

Savannah said, "I wonder if Lily was having us followed because she assumed we had been to the clinic looking for Dr. Clark's will."

Robert tried to control his temper, softly answering, "Who knows? I can guarantee that was the reason why Lily was there, though. Thank God she came to the clinic before we opened the safe."

They decided to order room service and hide out in their hotel room. They continued asking questions and giving what-if scenarios. They came to two conclusions. First and foremost, they agreed Lily was dangerous and had hired men who were killers. Secondly, she would kill to find the will and prenup.

But why was she so interested in Dr. Clark's clinic? They had no answers.

At the end of the evening, they climbed into the double beds, turned off the light, and continued talking in the dark until they were both too exhausted to speak.

Chapter 10

The following morning, Robert carefully drove the speed limit to Brett Edwards's office from the hotel while Savannah looked for the black SUV. They had checked out of the hotel early, giving themselves enough time to drive down side streets instead of taking main roads. When they sensed they weren't followed, Robert pulled into the front of the attorney's building and parked the car by the front entrance.

"I'll run the paperwork into Mr. Edwards's office. There's no need for both of us to go. I don't need to see him, so I'll just be a few minutes." Savannah said as she exited the Mercedes.

"I'll be right back."

Once inside the building, Savannah waited in the empty lobby on the ground floor for the elevator to take her to the second floor.

Two masked men dressed in black exited a doorway leading to the stairwell and forcefully grabbed Savannah by her arms. One man put his hand over Savannah's mouth as she screamed.

She bit his hand and kicked him in the groin, so the man struck her with her fist. She slumped to the floor, and the paperwork fell from her hands. The men dragged her by her feet out the back door of the building, shoved her into a van, and slammed the door.

Savannah was stunned but alert enough to realize she was being kidnapped.

She angrily asked, "Who are you? What do you want?"

No one answered, but one of the four men in the vehicle inserted a needle into her vein at the crook of her arm to sedate her.

The driver picked up his cell phone.

"We have the package. We're on our way."

Robert waited patiently in the car, listening to music. After fifteen minutes, he began worrying when Savannah hadn't returned. He noticed Savannah had left her purse in the car. He saw her phone in a side pocket and knew he couldn't call her.

He locked the car and ran into the building to an open elevator, hoping Brett Edwards had kept her waiting. He stepped into the elevator and rode it to the second floor.

A receptionist looked up from her desk when Robert entered the office.

"May I help you?"

"I have been waiting for my friend, Savannah. Is she with Mr. Edwards?"

"Sir, no one has been here by that name. Is she a client?"

"She was dropping off paperwork for Dr. Kyle Clark. Maybe she's in his office, and you didn't see her come in."

He didn't wait for a reply. He ran down a hallway and opened the attorney's door to his office. Savannah wasn't there.

The attorney looked up from his desk and growled, "What the hell do you think you're doing, storming into my office?"

"Sir, you must remember me. I'm with Savannah Hayes. Did she drop off the will to you?"

"I haven't seen her or a will. Do you mean Dr. Clark's will? I've been expecting it."

Robert was now frantic. He ran out of the office, checked the bathroom in the hallway, looked around the empty stalls, flew open the door, turned right in the hallway when he exited the bathroom, and began running down the stairs.

He raced back to his car, hoping to see her there.

He sat inside his car, gathering his thoughts. He decided against calling the Virginia Beach police and would talk to David Atkins instead.

He drove like a madman, traveling at high speeds, darting in and around the slower traffic to get back to Norfolk.

He parked his car at the Children's Hospital, ran inside the building, and rushed up five flights, taking two stairs at a time.

Michael Mason stood outside Dani's room, talking with David, sitting in his designated chair.

"Robert, why the rush? What's wrong?" Michael asked anxiously.

He had never seen his friend so frazzled. It scared him.

Robert said breathlessly, "They took her. We have to do something."

"Calm down. Took who?"

"Savannah, they took Savannah. We have to do something."

Robert leaned over and placed his hands on his knees, drawing in deep breaths and slowly blowing out. He calmed himself and quickly told the two men the story and all he knew, which wasn't much.

"Who are they? Why would anyone want to kidnap Dr. Savannah?" David asked.

"It has to be Lily," Michael concluded.

They saw Dr. Stone heading down the hallway toward them as they pondered who could have taken Savannah.

The hairs on Dr. Stone's arm went up, alerting him to danger. He approached the three men, who became quiet as they stared at him.

"Why do you have an armed guard at the door? What has happened?"

He knew it had to be Lily, but the men had no idea he knew about the bitch.

As the doctor put on his mask to check on Dani, he suddenly removed it. He couldn't take the drama any longer. Lily was getting out of control.

"Maybe I can be of some assistance. Tell me what is happening."

Michael answered, "It's nothing of concern to you, doctor, but my ex-stepmother is evil and always causing trouble. The guard is here to keep her away from Danielle. We believe she has been entering Danielle's room and scaring her. I just want to talk to her to understand why she insists on her bad behavior."

"I know Lily. She's married to my friend, Dr. Clark. If you're looking for her, she has an office and a warehouse off Lang Avenue in Norfolk. But be careful; she has security alarms and won't let anyone inside the building. I was there once with Dr. Clark; she wouldn't even allow us entry. Can you imagine?

She didn't allow her own husband inside, although he said he was there once when they first bought the abandoned building."

The three men listened attentively.

"What kind of security?" David asked.

"Cameras, alarm systems, men with guns, that sort of security."

Dr. Stone wished he could tell them his secrets, but he had said too much.

"Why would she need all that? It sounds like she thinks she's Fort Knox or something. What is she protecting? It has to be illegal, knowing Lily," Michael said anxiously.

"I don't know. Just be careful." Dr. Stone answered.

He put on his mask, and as he placed his hand on the door to enter the room, he said, "She shot her husband, you know. She's dangerous."

When the doctor entered Danielle's room, Robert looked at David, who was standing. "Do you have buddies who can help?"

Michael's mouth dropped. "You aren't Liam Neeson, and this isn't *Taken*, for God's sake. Let the police handle this, Robert."

"No, it's more like Denzel Washington in *The Equalizer*. The cops would take too long. I will find Lily, and if she has harmed Savannah, I will kill the bitch." Robert said with fury. He began pacing, thinking about what to do next.

David chuckled, "Well, you do sound like Liam Neeson."

Robert didn't laugh but looked at David. "You in?"

"I'm in. Let me make some phone calls."

I'm sorry, Mr. Mason. You need to call my company and get someone to take my place. Duty calls." David was happy to get back into action. He was bored to death.

Michael couldn't believe what was happening. He hated drama but picked up his cell phone to request an immediate replacement. He trusted Robert, knowing if anyone could find Savannah, he could.

The men waited while Michael made the call. Once he was satisfied a replacement would be sent within the hour, Michael said, "Done! Now, what do we do? I'm going with you. Who's driving?"

Robert nodded, "No, don't get involved, Michael."

Michael ignored Robert and looked at David. "These friends of yours, I assume they would appreciate being paid handsomely?" He asked.

"Uh, yes, sir, it would help."

"Call your buddies and ask anyone interested in helping to meet us at DM Yachts when the staff leaves at five o'clock. We have security cameras too, so tell them to ring from the main gate. I'll tell the guard to expect all of you. Once everyone is there, we'll make a plan of action."

Robert felt proud of Michael.

"And here you always said you hated drama of any kind, Michael."

"I do, but I have always wanted to be like Liam and Denzel." He smiled.

"You've heard the saying that the pen is mightier than the sword? My pen can write and sign big checks."

The three men chuckled.

David walked down the end of the hallway, where he could have privacy, and dialed his first number. He remained there until four of his buddies, all ex-Navy SEALs, agreed to assist him.

Dr. Stone exited Dani's room and was relieved to update Michael.

"Danielle is coming around. She feels much better now that we have discontinued the chemo. Her kidneys are functioning better, too. We'll take another route to get her into remission of the lymphoma," he lied. He knew she didn't have cancer, but he had to continue with the lie. However, Lily was still trying to force him into operating to remove one of her kidneys to harvest.

Dr. Stone sensed something more was happening. Were the men aware of Lily's schemes? Because Lily had prompted the men to talk about her. But about what, he wasn't sure. He prayed no one would ever discover his involvement with Lily's schemes. Maybe these men could be of valuable help, and he could back out of Lily's stronghold.

"I can't help but sense Lily Clark has done something to anger you. Do you mind sharing?" he asked.

Michael spoke first, "I'm concerned she is upsetting my daughter. I need to talk to her."

The other two men kept quiet and stared at the doctor.

Dr. Stone instinctively knew there was more to the story. He also knew he wasn't privy to any information they could provide, so he had to talk with the other doctors as soon as possible.

He feared something bad was about to happen, and he had to find a way out of their mess. Maybe giving the men the location of the warehouse was a good start. He just hoped Lily was smart enough not to keep records that could incriminate them all.

With that thought, he left the men still staring at him, walked down the hallway toward the elevator, and dialed Dr. Paul Wilson's phone number.

Chapter 11

Savannah woke up lying on a thin, dirty mattress on a metal bed. The twin bed creaked when she moved. The mattress reminded her of the old feather tick mattress with blue stripes that her grandmother used to have. She was upset that the bed didn't have a sheet or blanket. She wondered how many dead cells she had been sleeping on and became angry. She flinched when she touched her bruised face. She sat up facing the door and looked around the room. Cement block walls and concrete floors encased her on four sides in the darkened room. The grey walls were very dingy. A large metal ring was embedded in the wall ahead of the bed. A pair of handcuffs dangled from the ring. There were no windows and only one metal door across the room in front of the bed.

An old, armless, wooden chair with straight legs sat to Savannah's left. A black plastic bucket sat beneath it. She noticed the chair had a seat that lifted and assumed this was a makeshift, portable toilet. An old, rusty pedestal sink was attached to the wall next to the chair. It contained a bar of soap and a toothbrush in a cup. A roll of toilet paper and paper towels sat on the floor to the right of the chair. There was no wastebasket. One Edison-type lightbulb hung down from the metal rafters in the twelve-foot ceiling. She saw a large, black metal speaker and a camera aimed down into the room. She noticed the camera moved and followed her as she stumbled to the door. The door was locked. She placed her ear against the door but didn't hear anything.

"Hello," she screamed.

She looked at the camera. "Who are you, and what do you want?"

Silence greeted her.

She carefully sat on the side of the mattress and studied the chair. She had to pee, but didn't want to remove her pants in front of the person behind the camera watching her. She lifted the thin, wobbly mattress and held it vertically, shielding herself from the camera. She dragged it to the farthest wall, where there wasn't any furniture, and held the mattress upright with one hand while balancing it with her head against it. She hid behind the mattress from the camera. She carefully lowered her jeans and her panties with her free hand. She removed one pant leg, shifted the clothing to the side, spread her legs, and peed standing up. She pulled up her clothing and let the mattress fall as she buttoned her white jeans. She kicked the mattress with her foot, angry that one of her white tennis shoes was wet from her urine. She decided she would use the damn handmade toilet next time, even if it cost all her pride.

She doubled the thin mattress on the bed and sat on it, turning her back to the camera.

She adjusted her invisible tiara with both hands and waited. She stretched her arms and legs. She refused to look at the camera or show any signs of fear. She sat cross-legged like a Buddha, folding her fingers in circles with the tips of her thumbs lightly touching. She placed them near her navel and rested them on her lap. She hoped she was doing the mudra correctly. She tried to relax.

"What the fuck is she doing?" The man watching the camera said out loud.

A second man walked to the monitor to watch.

"How the hell should I know? Maybe it's some kind of ritual."

"Miss Lily gave orders to let her know when the woman was awake. We're to take her a sandwich and water." The first man said.

The second man was superstitious. "You do it; she's probably some voodoo priestess. I don't want her placing a curse on me."

"She looks harmless."

"Yeah, you think?"

He showed the man his hand where Savannah had bitten him. She had punctured his skin, and his hand was bruised from the broken blood vessels.

"She's a she-devil. She has a red owl tattoo on her shoulder. You know owls represent death and witchcraft."

"You're stupid. It's a red rose."

"No, it's an owl. The woman will give us the evil eye if we look at her. Miss Lily said she was a witch."

"I think she called her a bitch, not a witch. You need to learn English."

The second man pulled a gun that had been tucked inside his pants and aimed it at the first man. "Yeah? And you need to keep your fucking mouth shut."

The first man looked back at the monitor. Savannah had moved from the bed and was now standing on her head on the floor, supporting herself against the wall. She pushed her legs off the wall to stand upright and began doing jumping jacks with wild, exaggerated movements.

"Better take her the sandwich before she turns herself into a Mexican jumping bean and turns into a moth. She might fly away." The first man laughed.

"Ha, ha. You're a funny man, yet why am I not laughing?"

"Jesús will be here shortly. Do as you're told."

Savannah was startled when the metal door opened with a clang. She looked up at the camera and watched it move toward the door. She sat back on the bed. She then knew there was more than just one man.

A man with a black mask on his face wore a black T-shirt and black pants. He also had long, greasy black hair and brown eyes. She wondered if he was Latino and knew for sure when he spoke in broken English.

"Eat this, she-devil. You worship the owl."

He carefully laid the paper plate with a peanut butter and jelly sandwich on the floor by the door, along with a bottle of water. He never took his eyes off her, afraid she would put a spell on him. He leaned over and shoved the plate close to where she sat on the mattress.

Savannah sensed his fear.

She looked at the sandwich. "I'm allergic to nuts. Are you trying to kill me before your boss gets a chance to torture me? Fine," she lied, grabbed the sandwich, and took a big bite.

The man was even more fearful of his boss than the woman dying from a nut allergy. He walked close to her, leaned down, and grabbed the sandwich from her. As he did, she grabbed his legs and knocked him off his feet. He landed on his butt and yelled, "You bitch."

She ran to the open door. The man quickly got to his feet and caught her before she exited the room. He grabbed her around her waist and threw her back inside the room.

She tumbled as she hit the floor and hissed at him like a snake, and he backed away quickly, stepping on the sandwich, slipping and falling backward. He hurriedly crawled like a spider with his front side up, his knees and elbows bent, but kept his head up. He continued crawling back through the open door, never taking his eyes off her, fearful of the witch.

All the while, Savannah was screaming, "Hoo, hoo, hoo, hoo," knowing that owls scared some people like the Mexicans.

She had once cared for a patient in the emergency room who was strung out on drugs, screaming that a witch named La Lechuza had turned herself into a giant owl and was trying to kill him.

However, Savannah was glad that she had taken the chance to glimpse what was on the other side of the door. She had looked left and saw what looked to be a warehouse with large metal gambrels and meat hooks hanging from the rafters. She wondered if she was in a meat market where carcasses were once hung. Little did she know that Lily hung blindfolded people from the hooks until they agreed to give up one of their kidneys or die.

Chapter 12

Five men in a white van stopped at the guard gate at DM Yachts, Inc. at a quarter after five.

David Atkins gave the guard his name and driver's license. The guard had expected him, waved him through the gates, and picked up the phone to alert Michael Mason that his guests had arrived.

Michael greeted the men dressed in fatigues in the lobby of the building. He led them to the elevator and to the third floor, where the conference room was. The men chose their chairs and sat around the large table. Robert Malone and Adam Jordan were also seated at the table.

Michael stood at the head of the table, thanked the men for coming, and introduced himself.

David stood and introduced his friends, who were his team from his military days.

"There isn't a need for real names, but we 'frogmen' go by our nicknames."

He stood behind each man as he introduced them.

"This is Knuckles. He can knock a man out with just one blow."

The man showed them his large hands and made a fist with his right hand.

David moved to the second man.

"This is Crusher. He can crush a man's bones to pieces. Don't let him give you a bear hug."

Crusher flexed his large biceps as he sat stone-faced.

David stood behind the third man.

"This is Spudrucker. He can run for miles while carrying heavy backpacks for long distances for hours without tiring. You can call him Spud for short. He also loves potatoes."

The men teasingly laughed when Spudrucker rolled his eyes.

David moved to the fourth man.

"Last but not least is Gizmo. He may only be 5'7", but he is lethal and gets the job done."

"You can call me Giz, for short."

Knuckles laughed, "You got that right, shorty."

After the laughter stopped, David continued, "And you can call me David since you know my real name. My men call me Atlas because of my height and the size of my muscles."

Robert estimated all their ages to be around their early 50s, like himself, but he noticed they were much more physically fit.

Michael began explaining why they were all there.

"Men, Robert, and I believe we are dealing with a very evil woman. For some unknown reason, she has kidnapped our friend, Dr. Savannah Hayes. She sent men in a black SUV to follow Robert and her to Virginia Beach. A passenger in the SUV aimed a gun at Robert when they drove up next to him. They murdered a woman in cold blood after she accidentally broadsided their car when they ran a red light. These men are dangerous. We don't know much right now, but we do know that the woman has a warehouse here in Norfolk with guards who are probably armed. We believe Savannah is being held in this warehouse. I can't guarantee anything except that I will pay each of you two thousand dollars a day until we get Savannah back safely, more if it gets dangerous or if one of you gets hurt. I don't want to put you in harm's way, but we don't know the extent of what this crazy woman is capable of. We don't want the police involved because they may take too long to save our friend. So I'm asking you, brave men, are you up to some danger?"

"Hooyah," they all yelled in unison.

Michael continued, "Okay then. The woman's name is Lily Mason-Clark, my ex-stepmother. I assure you, she is cunning and evil. She shot and almost killed her husband, who is presently recuperating in the hospital. Robert will visit him there tomorrow to question him and get more answers. Once we know precisely where the warehouse is and how to get inside, David will let you know when and where to meet. Robert was a detective in Florida and knew how to handle guns. Adam is my CPA; his only involvement will be writing the checks. I, myself, have never touched a gun, but I will pay for any equipment you may need to get into the warehouse and rescue Dr. Hayes. Any questions?"

The men all looked at each other. They shook their heads no.

"Negative, sir," David answered. "We had long discussions before the meeting today. We all have guns, so we don't need those. We may need other equipment, though. We'll know more when we find out the layout of the warehouse, which can help us get in."

"Okay, meeting adjourned. Time is of the essence, men. So, we will see you soon."

The men stood. As the five ex-military men walked through the door, Robert overheard one of the conversations.

Crusher said, "Do you guys remember when we were in Afghanistan, and I crushed the Pashtun's hand? He told us his secrets really fast, didn't he?"

Gizmo answered, "Yeah, he squealed like a stuffed pig."

They all started sharing other memories, which fascinated Robert.

"Remember when Giz skirted up the wall so fast we almost renamed him Spider-Man?"

They heartily laughed as they shared memories until they stepped into the elevator. He heard the men shouting "Hooyah" again as the elevator door closed.

Robert was grateful for these warriors. He admired the five brave, experienced men and enjoyed their camaraderie. He hoped the five men would be enough to save Savannah. He was anxious to talk to Dr. Clark tomorrow morning.

Chapter 13

Dr. Clark was sitting in a bedside chair in his hospital room, watching the local news. He watched as a man tearfully asked if anyone had any information about who had seen the car accident or who had killed his wife in cold blood, and to please call the Virginia Beach police with any information.

Robert entered Dr. Clark's room.

"I know who killed that woman," Robert said gruffly as he pointed to the television set.

Kyle looked at him. "Who, what? Who killed whom?"

"Your fucking wife." Robert retorted.

"What are you talking about?"

"You put Savannah in danger, you selfish son of a bitch. She's been kidnapped. Lily had us followed to Virginia Beach. They took her and your will before she could deliver your precious paperwork. Were you part of the plan?"

"No, no, of course not. I have no idea what you're talking about. Who are they you speak about?"

Robert approached Kyle, leaning hard on his right shoulder, which was still healing from surgery. Kyle grimaced in pain.

"Tell me, doctor, how do I get into the warehouse? Don't tell me you know nothing about it."

Dr. Stone tried removing Robert's hand, wondering how he knew about the warehouse, but Robert leaned harder, making the doctor cry out in pain.

"Robert, is it?"

Robert nodded. "My name is Robert Malone."

"I swear, Robert, I had nothing to do with this. I only wanted to change my will before Lily could get her hands on it. How did Lily murder someone or kidnap Savannah? Calm down and tell me what you know. Maybe I can be of assistance."

Robert released his grip from Kyle's shoulder.

Robert told him about the black SUV, how they witnessed the woman's murder, how they took the will to the attorneys, and how Savannah never returned to the car.

Kyle sat, soaking in all the new information. He never doubted Robert once. After a few moments, he looked at Robert.

"I'll help you if you help me first."

"I think I've already tried to help you once. The answer is no. But if you help me find Savannah, I'll think about helping you."

"I may be dead by then, and it'll be too late to help you. Lily has my original will and the prenup by now. She has no reason to keep me alive."

Robert walked to the door, looked in the hallway to see if anyone was listening, and shut the door.

"What do you want?"

"Get me out of here. I have a cabin in the woods along a lake. Lily doesn't know about it, and I'll be safe there until I heal. Please."

Kyle removed the oxygen cannula from his nose and pulled out his IV from his left arm. He stood from the chair and walked to the bathroom to grab a washcloth to hold against his bleeding arm until it clotted. He opened the small closet and found his bag of clothing that he had worn the night of the shooting.

He noticed the shirt was stained with dried blood as he carefully put his left arm through the shirt's sleeve. Robert draped the other side of the shirt over Kyle's right shoulder, which was thick with bandages over his shoulder that extended halfway down his back and front of his chest. His right arm was stabilized in a blue sling. Kyle grimaced as Robert managed to button a couple of buttons on his shirt. Robert helped him put on his slippers after Kyle had managed to slide into his pants. Inside the pants pocket were his cell phone, the keys to his Bentley, and several hundred dollars.

Suddenly, the door opened into his room. JoAnn walked in and gasped.

"Just what do you think you're doing, doctor?"

She looked at Robert, and before she could say another word, Kyle said,

"Lily has the will, JoAnn. Robert says she had men follow them to Virginia Beach and ended up murdering a woman."

"Oh Lord, we have to get you out of here." She knew exactly what that meant.

"Stand guard, JoAnn, while Robert takes me someplace safe. Please take care of the clinic until I get back."

"Yes, sir. Take care of yourself."

She folded the sheet from the hospital bed and professionally draped it over the sling to hide the blood stains on the shirt.

"Call me if you need anything. I mean, anything, you know, like a gun. My Henry has several. I can bring you one."

"I don't think I will need that, but thank you, JoAnn."

Kyle knew he had shotguns and ammunition hidden in an upstairs bedroom behind a locked door at the cabin.

JoAnn stood guarding the door until she was sure the coast was clear and waved them outside the room.

Robert helped Kyle to the stairwell close to his hospital room.

"We can't take the chance of anyone seeing us," Robert said, and Kyle nodded.

Kyle waited at the first-floor stairwell, sitting on the steps while Robert pulled up the Mercedes, where the nurses usually drop off patients in wheelchairs to send them home. Kyle strolled to the car and sat in the passenger seat.

Robert strapped on their seatbelts.

Robert said, "Now, tell me how to get into the warehouse."

"With the key on my keyring."

Kyle reached into his left pocket, pulled out his car keys, dangled them in front of Robert, and replaced them in his pant pocket.

"I'll tell you the layout of the warehouses and Lily's office on the way to my car in my garage at home."

"Oh, no, you don't. I'm taking you to the cabin. Where do I go?"

Kyle was too weak to argue. "Head toward Suffolk. I'll tell you everything I know. There's a grocery store not too far from the cabin. I need to stock up."

Robert asked, "Do you have any protection in case Lily finds you at the cabin?"

"I have rifles locked in an upstairs bedroom. But Lily has no clue about the cabin. My phone needs charging, though. Do you mind charging it as we drive?"

Kyle handed him his phone, and Robert laid it on the built-in wireless charger in the Mercedes as he headed west on I-64.

As Robert drove, he constantly looked for the black SUV and listened intently to Kyle's words. He shook his head because he couldn't believe everything he was being told.

Robert kept checking to make sure they weren't being followed. His heart quickened with every black SUV he saw.

It was now day two since Savannah had been kidnapped. He prayed for her safety. He knew now that Lily was involved with the cartel, even though he didn't exactly know why, except that she was interested in human trafficking and fentanyl. That explained the black SUVs.

He now knew of the location and the layout of the warehouses. Kyle couldn't or wouldn't explain exactly why that had anything to do with Savannah.

Kyle lied, not wanting to implicate himself and the other doctors. "Possibly, someone in the organization was hurt, and they needed a doctor. Lily also knew you two were at the clinic and followed you to see if you had my will. That's my best guess," Kyle lied.

"And she tried to kill you and us because of your will?" Robert asked.

"Yes, and now she will try to kill me again. She doesn't have a soul. She's as evil as evil gets. You need to be careful. I fear for Savannah's safety, so don't go to the warehouse alone. Lily doesn't stay there in the evenings because she's usually home to drink her dinner. She gets drunk every night."

When Robert hit the four-lane highway on I-58, a black sedan drove up next to them on the right.

"DUCK!" Robert shouted as a bullet crashed through the passenger's window, hitting Kyle in the side of the head. He died instantly.

Robert swerved hard to the right, hitting the sedan, causing the driver to lose control. The sedan hit a guardrail, which acted like a serrated knife, slicing easily through the middle of the car's metal.

A driver of an 18-wheeler truck slammed on his brakes and ran on top of the sedan to avoid hitting Robert's Mercedes.

The weight of the truck compressed the sedan, crushing the two passengers inside. The semi teetered on top of the mangled car, its front wheels still slowly turning.

Now, at a standstill, Robert nimbly watched the action, giving thanks to God that his life had been spared.

He removed his seatbelt, trying to get his head together. He noticed that the Mercedes had ended up sideways on the highway. He watched in horror as he saw a black SUV approaching him, driving at least fifty miles an hour. He quickly jumped out of his car and rolled under the truck's suspended wheels.

The SUV broadsided the Mercedes so hard that it flipped twice before landing upside down.

The black SUV swerved, squealing its tires, but regained control and continued driving.

All other traffic had stopped on the sides of the road.

Witnesses ran to help Robert out from under the truck. The unharmed semi-truck driver jumped out of his cab after he called the police.

Robert sprinted to his Mercedes to pull Kyle from the wreckage. Another man helped loosen the seatbelt as the dead body slumped into Robert's arms. He gently laid Kyle Clark's body on the ground, reached into Kyle's pants pocket, and took the keyring. He searched the Mercedes for Kyle's phone and finally found it lying on the floor, which was once the sunroof. He squirmed out of the car.

He removed the sheet from Kyle's shoulder, which JoAnn had carefully wrapped around his sling that once hid the blood-stained shirt, and laid it over the body.

He closed Kyle's open, empty eyes, staring at him. The light in his pupils, once there, was suddenly gone.

Robert wasn't sure why he needed to close Kyle's eyes, knowing he wasn't seeing anything in this world. He did it out of respect.

He covered the body with the sheet to protect Kyle from curious eyes staring at the dead body. He was amazed at how quickly dead men's blood darkened and thickened after death. He sat on the ground next to Kyle, protecting his dead body, traumatized.

His next thought was of Savannah. He had to save her.

While waiting for the police, Robert thanked the strangers for their help and asked for privacy to say goodbye to his friend.

He withdrew his phone from his pants pocket and pushed 'send' on one of his emergency phone numbers.

Mark Jenkins's friendly voice answered, "Hey, buddy."

"Mark, I need help; Savannah has been kidnapped. Gather some of your elite friends and come quickly. Bring guns."

Mark didn't ask any questions. He instinctively knew he was being summoned out of desperation.

"We'll be there tomorrow, Buddy. Hang tight."

Chapter 14

Sirens echoed in the silence, screaming down the highway until the drivers of ambulances and a firetruck found their way to the wreckage. Robert was thankful when the noisy sirens turned off, and only the red lights flashed quietly on the vehicles as EMTs picked up the dead body of Dr. Kyle Clark. Robert's legs were shaky, but he stood by his wrecked car while the ambulance whisked Kyle's lifeless body away to the nearest morgue. He watched as it slowly drove away and disappeared down the highway.

He waited patiently, sitting on the side of a deadly road, awaiting the arrival of authorities and a tow truck.

He had time to think. How could he explain Dr. Clark's murder?

He thought about running into the nearby woods, but realized that would be stupid and make him look guilty. Besides, the police could find him by the Mercedes license plate. His registration was still in the glovebox. He shook his head and ran his fingers through his hair, trying to think clearly.

He stood and walked around to the back of the semi-truck and leaned down to see if he could read the license plate on the crushed sedan. The damaged plate was barely legible, but he recognized the Florida plates, barely making out the green writing. He didn't need the missing letters and numbers to realize that the license would read Florida if he could combine all the letters.

Who were these men? Why were they trying to kill him? Why did they kill poor Dr. Clark? He felt no sorrow for the men lying dead under the semi-truck. It would be a while before the fire department or EMTs could retrieve the dead bodies. He wanted them out of his sight. Anger overwhelmed him. His jaw tightened. He clenched and unclenched his sore hands. His shoulders ached and tightened, and he developed a headache that tightened his temples. He silently cursed Lily and her evil men. He thought about Dr. Clark and how he didn't deserve to die.

Then, a disturbing thought came while he was thinking about death and how quickly it came for some. He didn't believe the adage, "only the good die young." Oh my God, had they already killed Savannah?

Robert's thoughts turned sinister. He swore he would kill Lily if Savannah had been harmed in any way.

He didn't want to wait until Mark came to help, but he knew five ex-Navy SEALs wouldn't be enough to deal with dangerous criminals like the cartel.

He paced as he walked, trying to clear his head of the haze.

The truck driver jumped out of his semi and examined his truck. He saw Robert leaning down at the end of the tractor-trailer, studying the car under it.

The burly man with a bald head and a white beard that reached the middle of his chest spoke to Robert.

"Do you know these people?"

"No, I have no idea who they are, but they aren't from Virginia. Looks like Florida plates."

The driver bent over to look at the sedan. "I think you're right. I recognize the green and white plate. Could be Vermont, though."

Robert pointed at the license plate again. "Vermont doesn't have oranges on the plate. And see the FL in the twisted piece on the left? Those are definitely Florida plates."

"Yes, I agree. I see an orange now that you mention it. Why would anyone from Florida be here trying to kill you?"

"I'm not sure. It must be idiots killing people in drive-by shootings. A woman was killed in Virginia Beach a couple of days ago."

"I'd say it's a mob killing. I'm a retired policeman from New York. I've seen my share of this kind of shooting. Name is Peter."

Robert shook his extended hand.

"I'm Robert, an ex-detective from West Palm Beach. Thank you for not running over me. I'm sorry about your truck, though. Where are you headed?"

"Palm Beach Gardens, Florida. That's where I live now."

"I'll be damned."

Peter looked at Robert and sincerely said, "Look, I know you don't know me, but I was a cop for forty years. I smell a rat. You're in trouble. Want to tell a brother what is going on?"

"Only if you want a ride, and a room and board at my home in Norfolk while your truck is being repaired. I can pay you back for sparing my life."

"There's no fixing this piece of shit. She'll go to the junkyard for scraps. I'll take you up on your offer."

*****

The police and tow trucks finally arrived. After two hours, Robert's car was the first to be removed from the scene.

He finally called an Uber.

Robert and Peter told the police officers their stories about what had happened, suspecting a drive-by shooter.

Robert gave them Dr. Clark's name and his company business card. Peter gave his information with his name and number. He reached inside the cab of his truck and placed a blue hat on his head. The hat had a badge and the name of his police department, along with the time he had served on the force.

They all shared police stories as they waited. The police officers were friendly and just as bored while they waited to clear the area, waving motorists along as they stopped to gawk at the scenery.

The police were still waiting to remove Peter's truck when the Uber arrived. Peter jumped back into his truck and removed a duffel bag and several shotguns in brown casings made of thick canvas. He quickly placed them in the Uber's trunk before the policemen could question him about them.

Robert gave the Uber driver his address.

*****

The men sat in silence until they reached Robert's home. Robert was in turmoil and shaken from the kidnapping, accident, and murder of Dr. Clark. His muscles were sore from the accident. He had difficulty thinking, but he knew one thing for sure: Lily was behind the murder. He also realized that Lily had Dr. Clark's will, which was taken from Savannah, and she no longer needed Dr. Clark. So why was she still keeping Savannah hostage? He had a headache and took two Tylenol. He tried breathing techniques to calm his anxiety. His mind raced with the things he needed to do next. Then he remembered his dog. Ana always had a way of calming him down.

While Peter stashed his property in the upstairs guest room, Robert called his neighbor to ask if Ana could stay with her for a few more days, starting tomorrow. But he needed her home tonight. He explained that he had important business and would be gone for a week or two.

Peter came into the kitchen and gladly accepted Robert's cold beer. He sat at the counter while Robert made ham sandwiches. Ana came bouncing into the room, and Robert laughed at her while she raced in circles, so happy to see him.

Peter watched Ana's antics and laughed, but said, "Okay, Robert, it's time to tell me what's going on and how I can be of service."

Robert took his time and carefully chose his words. He didn't know this man, after all. Just because he said he had been a cop doesn't mean it was true, so he started by asking the man about his time on the force.

Peter began by telling multiple stories. Some were downright hilarious and made Robert laugh. Some were downright scary, and he knew that Peter was telling the truth. He had always been a good judge of character, and he decided he liked and trusted the man.

Slowly, Robert began telling him what he knew about Lily Mason-Clark. He told him his thoughts on why Lily wanted her husband dead, but he wasn't sure why Lily was trying to kill him or why she had Savannah kidnapped.

It felt good to get the story out.

"This sounds like a bad movie, and I would have difficulty believing it if I hadn't seen it for myself. What are your plans to get the girl back?" Peter asked.

"My buddy is flying in tomorrow with some of his pals who were in special forces. We also have five ex-Navy SEALs. We'll all meet and formulate a plan of action now that we know where the warehouse is. Dr. Clark told me the layout before he was killed. I'm sure Savannah is being held there."

"Is she your girlfriend?"

"She isn't. She lives in Florida, but I admit, I've always been in love with her. I'm worried and feel guilty that she was asked to come to Virginia to help Danielle get better."

Robert left out the part where Savannah was the child's mother. He felt Savannah would be upset that he told her secrets to a stranger.

"Well, you haven't asked, but now that my rig has been totaled, I have nothing on my plate. I'm a widower, and my two children are grown. I have experience with breaking into warehouses and can offer my services. Sounds like you can use all the help you can get. But answer me one question. Why aren't you getting the police involved?"

Robert opened up two more beers and stood across the counter.

"Because we're dealing with an evil woman who has hired the cartel. The police would go by the book and take too long with an investigation first. Savannah may not survive that long. I want warriors, not everyday street cops who may not have the experience these guys have."

"No FBI or SWAT teams?"

"Again, I want to go in quickly. I don't want a guy standing by a car with a bullhorn saying, 'Come out with your hands up', because they have to be politically correct and follow the rules.

I don't want helicopters flying overhead and making these guys nervous. I want stealth action; quietly overtake them before they realize what is happening."

Peter took a sip of his beer and held out his hand to Robert. "I'm in. I may not be able to climb walls anymore, but I am very good at strategic planning. I can help. Besides, I miss the action."

Robert shook Peter's hand.

"Let's have a beer and a cigar on the deck and talk."

"Cuban?"

Robert laughed. "No. I only smoke Davidoff. Much milder and smoother than a Cuban."

"My kind of cigar."

They walked out to the deck, and it was getting dark. Robert shared the bits and pieces Dr. Clark had given him about the warehouse's layout. "Tomorrow, we'll drive by the actual building and take some pictures of the outside before we meet with the other men. Michael Mason has a large blackboard in the conference room at DM Yachts. We can lay out the interior of the building on it. It's kind of like how the coaches of football teams provide diagrams of their plays."

"Sounds like a good place to start. You're a smart man, Robert. I hope you're just as wise and not going into this thing because you're in love with this girl."

142

"Savannah Hayes is no ordinary woman. She's a doctor. She's strong and hardheaded. I'm sure she's giving them a run for their money."

"Oh my God. Savannah Hayes? Doctor Hayes from Palm Beach? I know her. She treated me in the emergency room after my car accident in West Palm Beach. What a small world. I'm definitely in. She's a great doctor."

"And you, my new friend, are prone to vehicle accidents."

They chuckled.

"Then you understand that she is special."

"I understand. Now, I must get some sleep to get ready for the excitement."

Peter left Robert alone with his thoughts. He prayed that Savannah was still alive.

He decided to watch the 11 o'clock news and sat traumatized as he had to relive the horror while the newscaster showed videos of the wreckage. The anchor described how one of the most beloved doctors in the community was allegedly murdered and mentioned that Dr. Kyle Clark might have been a victim of a drive-by shooting. He also mentioned the woman who was killed in Virginia Beach a few days ago. He noted that the police are withholding the names of the Mercedes and truck driver pending an investigation.

Robert was thankful his name wasn't mentioned in the report, but he knew he would be questioned by the police soon. He would stick with the drive-by-shooting story. He switched off the television and calmed himself down. He was angry, confused, and mortified.

He needed to sleep, so he took an Ambien.

He helped Ana into his bed, thinking about Savannah and her mantra: Just when life seems to be going well, there's always a but.

He suddenly sat upright. When would he have time to purchase another car? He would have to rent one. He felt lost without his car. Will Lily have a funeral for Dr. Clark? His mind was still racing.

Everything that was happening didn't make sense to him. All he could do was pray that he could save Savannah and put Lily Mason-Clark in prison for the rest of her life.

He lay back on the pillow, and Ana snuggled beside him. He closed his eyes and prayed, waiting for the sweet balm of slumber.

Chapter 15

Robert's phone started ringing off the hook early the next morning. Michael Mason called first.

"I watched the story unfold on the news. Videos of your accident and interviews with witnesses are plastered on all the local television stations. The community is in shock and grieving over the loss of Dr. Clark. Are you okay, Robert?"

"I'm traumatized, I'm not gonna lie. And now I'm without wheels. How did you know it was me? Did they mention my name?"

"No. I recognized the Mercedes, and they reported about Dr. Clark's death, so I knew it was you. I guess you need a new ride now, Robert. I can loan you one of the company's trucks until you buy a new car."

"I don't think that's a good idea, Michael. Lily probably knows your vehicles and could follow me again."

"Anything else you need?" Michael asked.

"Yes, Mark Jenkins is flying in today with a few of his buddies. I would appreciate it if you could pick them up at the Norfolk airport and take them to a hotel. I'll take an Uber to the nearest rental car agency this morning. Then I'm checking out the warehouse where Lily must be hiding Savannah."

"I can do that, but they can stay aboard The Lady Jane. They will be freer to talk and hide any equipment they bring."

"Good idea, Michael. Gotta go; I'll connect later."

The second caller was David Atkins, AKA Atlas. He had also watched the news and had talked to Michael Mason earlier.

"How can I help? What's the plan today?"

Robert explained how he had met Peter and that they would surveil the warehouse.

"I have a drone. Give me your address and I'll pick you up. I can be there within the hour."

"That will be very helpful. I appreciate it, David."

"See you soon, Robert. Text me your address."

Robert called his neighbor to take Ana.

Meanwhile, Peter came downstairs carrying one of the canvas bags concealing his shotgun and entered the kitchen as Robert made pancakes. Robert caught him up on the news and phone calls.

"You can stay here while we scope out the warehouse."

"Are you kidding me? You'll need a wingman and a lookout if someone comes along unexpectedly. I'm going with you."

They high-fived each other and chatted about the next few hours while eating breakfast, especially about the importance of being careful.

Robert's phone rang again. The Suffolk, Virginia, police were calling. The policeman wanted him to make an appointment to help with their investigation immediately. Robert explained that his car was totaled and he would need a rental.

"Give me your name again and tell me how I can reach you. I need to find a rental car soon and will come to your precinct within the next few days. As a matter of fact, I invited the truck driver who sacrificed his truck to save my life to stay at my home, and I will bring him with me. That way, you can kill two birds with one stone."

Detective Jim Mathews hesitated and wasn't happy about the delay, but he understood the circumstances and agreed.

While Robert was on the phone with his insurance company, David knocked on the door. Peter answered, and the two big men made introductions. They chatted at the door, waiting for Robert to finish his call.

Robert hung up. "Are you guys ready for a little action today?"

The men nodded.

"Then let's roll."

David drove his green Ford Bronco to the warehouse district in Norfolk. They turned off the main road and entered an abandoned warehouse district. They moved slowly past old brick buildings that must have stood for centuries. Most of the warehouses still appeared to be abandoned because no cars or people were around.

They slowly drove down a one-lane dirt road at the end of the warehouses. High, dense cogon grass and weeds stood in a field on the right side of the road. Overgrown tall fescue grew on the left side. Robert thought a man could easily hide in the cogon grass and no one would see him. The dirt road was entirely hidden from the main road.

David stopped the SUV when they rounded a slight curve in the road. Ahead, at the dead end, they saw a two-story brick warehouse about 50 to 60 yards long. It had a flat roof and dirty windows. Some of the windows were broken, but most remained intact. Several white vans and a Jeep Cherokee were parked on the old, torn pavement. Blades of grass were growing up between the cracks.

Most importantly, they noticed two black SUVs parked in front of the loading dock in the middle of the building. The dock had a concrete three-step stoop with a closed, corrugated metal door that could be opened vertically upwards, similar to a garage door. Faded red letters on the side of the building said 'Browns Meats.'

David backed up the Bronco to the beginning of the curve to hide from view.

He turned the SUV around, making a dent in the weeds, turned off the engine, and placed his key in the cupholder. He jumped out and opened the tailgate to retrieve his drone.

Peter slid behind the wheel. Robert jumped out and placed a revolver in the waistband of his khaki cargo shorts.

"Peter, if you see anyone coming, honk the horn and drive away. David and I can hide in the grass. I'll text you where to meet when the coast is clear." Robert said.

David swiftly flew the drone toward the warehouse. Robert slightly bent his knees, hunched his back, and ran as quickly and quietly as possible to the right side of the loading dock, being careful not to be seen by the cameras. He noticed two cameras attached to the roof and angled toward the cars and loading dock. He realized he would be seen if he used Dr. Clark's key on the door next to the bay door.

He ran to the right of the dock and stood on his tiptoes to peer inside one of the dirty windows. He couldn't get a good view, so he moved to his right to look inside another cracked window. He gently tapped the window with the butt of his gun, and a large piece of glass fell by his feet, giving him a clear view of the inside. He removed his cell phone and began videotaping the interior of everything he could. Then, he took pictures of five metal doors lined in a row straight ahead of him. He assumed Savannah must be behind one of them. From a large, open, metal staircase that led upstairs to a glassed-in room, he noticed Lily opening the door, which he assumed was the office. He snapped a fast picture, returned to the Bronco, and jumped in the back seat. David was back in the driver's seat.

"Go, go, go! Drive to the parking lot of the first warehouse, and let's talk about what we just saw. I need to think."

As they sat in the Bronco talking, David finally asked, "Where do we go next?"

Robert thought for a minute, deciding what to do next. He knew he had to get a car and make an appointment with the detective, Jim Matthews.

"Drop me off at the nearest car rental agency and meet me back at my house. I left a key under the doormat so you can get in. I'll meet you there as soon as I can. My friend Mark Jenkins is flying in today with some of his retired special forces buddies, with whom Michael and I have contracted."

Peter said, "I'm staying with you, buddy. Let's get you a rental car, go to the police department in Suffolk, and give our statements to the detective. Let's get that out of the way."

"You're right, Peter. I'm still a little traumatized, and I'm not thinking clearly. That makes more sense."

Robert turned to David. "Okay, David, as soon as Peter and I finish our chores, I will call you. We'll see you later at the house, then we can meet up with the other guys at DM Yachts tonight, view the videos and photos, and devise a plan of action."

Before David turned on the car, they saw Lily fly by in her Jeep. They had no idea what had just transpired.

Chapter 16

Earlier, Lily Mason-Clark was in a foul mood at the warehouse. She didn't care enough or have the time to bury her dead husband, but she knew she had to pretend to mourn, at least in public.

After all, the community loved Dr. Kyle Clark, so donations graciously flowed into the organization, A Lil Help, believing the money was helping people receive new kidneys. They encouraged family members, even strangers, to donate their kidneys. The doctors ran television commercials and gave interviews to reporters, which brought them fame and fortune. Kyle had initially started the business because he genuinely wanted to help people. The organization was legal and above board all the way. His fellow doctors were supportive, donating their time and skills to people who couldn't afford to pay for surgery. However, they reaped the benefits of people with good insurance, and the doctors were rewarded monetarily. The community applauded them, which, in turn, brought them new patients. Eventually, the well ran dry of donors, and the doctors became so busy with their practices that the phones stopped ringing. All the volunteers who answered phone calls left the business to find something else to do. That's when Lily stepped in and took control. She purchased the old warehouse and moved the offices from the previously rented space in a Winn-Dixie shopping center. Her wit and ability to scheme kept the organization alive for a while. After a year of doing business legally, she began hiring men to kidnap people experiencing homelessness off the streets and bring them into the warehouse. They would be housed in a room with a bed, a sink, and a handmade toilet.

So many homeless people were brought into the warehouse that she had to design each room to accommodate six people. She psychologically controlled her "patients" by shaming them into believing they should be grateful to offer one of their kidneys. After all, they got a bed to sleep in and were fed twice daily. The people with drug addictions were given their drug of choice. Soon, she hoped at least four of the five rooms would be filled again with patients for their organs or young teens that could be sold to the highest bidder. She kept one room with just one bed. That room was designed for her special guests. It's where she stashed the man or woman who wasn't homeless but was unlucky enough to find themselves in a bad situation. It was the room where Savannah was now.

The police were getting suspicious because so many homeless people were missing, so Lily had to pivot and get more creative. That's when she found a willing partner in Jesús. He had brought several of his gang members to Florida from Mexico, and that's when she had been lucky enough to meet him while on her much-needed vacation in Miami. She convinced him she could provide protection and make him a multi-millionaire, without much effort. She felt that together, they could expand the business by adding human trafficking and illegal drugs. The doctors were getting hard to handle, even though Dr. Paul Wilson and Dr. Kent Stone continued performing surgery on the surgical tables she had placed in the open hall of the warehouse.

Jesús had agreed to work with her because he knew he was being watched by the FBI and needed to leave Florida.

However, today, she was upset with the new partner and employees. She was also upset that she had to wear black clothing to honor her dead husband, which washed out her pale, white complexion. She took her anger and frustration out on her new employees.

She was pacing the wooden floors, which creaked with each step she took in her black high heels. Back and forth, back and forth. She hurriedly walked as she was yelling and berating the men in the room with her, using language only gangsters could identify with, and she didn't hold back. She was threatening them with their lives, pointing her index finger in their faces while she called them stupid.

Six men quietly sat at computers in the office upstairs in her warehouse, listening to her rants and raves, giving her all the attention she demanded. Four more men were missing, out in their vans looking for victims.

Each man on the computers had one job: stay on social media, stalk young girls and boys, and pretend to be interested in them romantically. They all had a cheat sheet in front of them. All the sheets said the exact wording designed to woo young teenagers. The men were to take their time, gain the teens' confidence, and eventually set up a place to meet after dark.

But for now, Lily demanded their undivided attention. Thankfully, because all eyes were on Lily, no one noticed or heard the drone or saw Robert taking pictures of the warehouse's interior.

Lily was a master planner and was proud of herself for having written the lies the men were spewing. She schooled the predators in the language of emojis and love words to inspire the young, naive girls and boys to send nude photos of themselves. Each man had a library of fake photographs that they used, depending on the age and gender of their victims.

Today, she was not satisfied with their results. None of them had hit their quota for the day. She expected to reel in at least two young bodies per man daily, and so far, there were only six teens in one of the four rooms outfitted with old hospital beds. The fifth room was the supply room.

One extra man was used to watch the monitors and security cameras. While Lily was yelling at the men, they sat motionless in their chairs, their eyes away from the monitors as they watched her pacing back and forth. The men became angry but were more fearful of the man sitting at Lily's office desk with his feet propped up on top.

Jesús, the cartel leader, sat with a shit-eating grin, looking amused. He toyed with the Colt 45 in his hands, twirling it in his fingers like a cowboy did in the movies. He sometimes needed to send the men warning signs with his facial expressions. His eyes would narrow with a look of seriousness, raise his eyebrows, and purse his lips firmly. He would maintain eye contact, making sure his men were paying attention. He could easily put a bullet in Lily's head had she been stupid enough to show him any disrespect in front of his men. However, he felt he was in on a good deal with her and away from rivals who wanted to kill him in Mexico and Florida. He sat quietly, watching and listening to her little pep talk. Lily soon recognized that Jesús and his men were strong on grit but short on brains.

Once she ran out of curse words, she left the office and slammed the door, almost breaking the glass in the upper part of the old, wooden door. She kicked the bottom of the door for better measure with her high heel and soon regretted the decision. She screamed when she saw she had scuffed up the toe of her shiny, black shoe.

The men watched her through the glass window, sat motionless as she looked back, and raised her tiny fist, leaving them with one last warning.

As she descended the metal stairs, she could hear the men laughing, which made her even angrier. She cursed when one of her heels went through the grate on the metal stairs. She removed her high heels and continued down, cursing the entire way.

Before she left the building, she had one more person to berate. She put her shoes back on at the bottom of the stairs and walked to one of the five rooms on the first floor.

She removed a key card from her skirt pocket and swiped it at the reader located on the door lock. The metal door clicked open.

She entered Savannah's prison cell. Earlier, Lily had one of the men handcuff Savannah to the wall, knowing she would chat with her.

Savannah was sitting cross-legged on the dirty mattress with her head lowered and now dirty, brown hair straggling down her face. She did not look up when Lily entered the room, recognizing the sound of high heels on the concrete floor, knowing it could be no one else but the evil bitch, Lily.

Lily approached the bed.

"Where is it?"

Savannah didn't answer.

Lily grabbed a handful of Savannah's hair and jerked her face up to look at her. Defiantly, Savannah asked, "Where is what?"

"My husband's will? What did you do with it?"

"I took it to the attorney's office as he asked. Your guys kidnapped me and took it before I was able to get it to Mr. Edwards. Why don't you ask your men where it is?"

Lily pulled a manila envelope from her large purse. She opened it, pulled out the contents, and shook the blank papers in Savannah's face.

"You took the wrong envelope, you idiot. Where is the will?"

"Why don't you ask your husband? I don't know. I thought his will was in that envelope. It's the only one that looked anything legal."

Lily was still furious. "I can't ask my husband, you bitch."

"Why not? The nurses won't let you near him. Who can blame them?"

"You're more stupid than I thought you were. He's dead, that's why. He died in a car accident yesterday, along with your stupid boyfriend. Why do you think I'm dressed in all black?"

Savannah sat numbly, shooting darts out of her eyes at Lily. She shook the hair away from her face, looked Lily in the eyes, and calmly said, "Who is the stupid one? You killed him for blank pieces of paper. You killed him for nothing."

Lily slapped Savannah as hard as she could. Savannah didn't flinch; she stared at her with eyes full of hatred.

Savannah was smart enough to know she could be next in line to be murdered. She was also smart enough to know Lily was a liar. Maybe Robert and Dr. Clark weren't dead, and she was lying to get information.

Savannah adjusted her body, closed her eyes, and mentally straightened her invisible tiara.

"Well then, prove it to me that they are dead. Prove it to me before I answer any more questions."

Lily released her grip on Savannah's hair and stood back. "So you do know where the will is. Before this is over, you'll tell me where it is. I have to go to the funeral home now, and when I get back, I'll give you the proof."

Savannah was obstinate. "What makes you think I have anything you want?"

Lily answered, "I'm not an idiot. I knew you were at the clinic for something. My men waited in the parking lot for you to leave with your boyfriend. They sent me photos of you carrying a large manila envelope."

Savannah turned her head to look at Lily.

"Show me the reports about the accident. You must have a phone to show me photos. I don't believe anything you say."

"I don't have time. We will do it my way. Just sit here and suffer over the loss of your friends."

"Uncuff me, or I won't say one more word. Give me more privacy and turn the monitor away so I can relieve myself in private when I need to use the toilet. And for God's sake, give me a clean sheet and pillowcase. If you refuse me, you won't get another word out of me."

From the room, Lily looked up at the ceiling monitor. "Uncuff her, move the monitor, and give her something to eat. I want her kept alive. Do you understand me? Blink the monitor if you do."

The monitor blinked.

"Bring her a sheet and pillow from one of the tables downstairs. And again, I warn you. I want her kept alive."

The monitor blinked again.

Lily continued, "And I advise you not to take my generosity as a sign of weakness."

Savannah watched as the camera was directed away from the homemade toilet, turning her head away from Lily and the monitor. She was done with any conversation, trying to comprehend what was said about Dr. Clark and Robert. She dared not show any emotion.

After Lily had left the room, Savannah straightened her back, adjusted her arms over her head, wiggled her aching hands in the handcuffs, and became mad. She was determined that Lily wouldn't make her weak or break her.

As her mind cleared, she began forming a dangerous plan that could end in disaster, but she didn't care at this point, especially if Robert was really dead.

Lily stormed out of the warehouse, jumped in her Jeep Cherokee, and sped off so fast that she fishtailed, but she managed to straighten the SUV.

She sped down the one-lane road past the tall grass and passed a green Ford Bronco parked in front of one of the dilapidated buildings. If she hadn't been so angry and deep in thought about the will and the money she was losing because of Jesús and his stupid men, she would have seen the three men in the green SUV, recognizing one as Robert.

Chapter 17

Savannah waited an hour for one of Lily's men to enter the room and release her from her handcuffs. She sat on the side of the mattress with her head bowed, her feet firmly on the concrete floor, thinking and praying her scheme would work. She also noticed that the lace on her right tennis shoe was loose, and she silently cursed.

When the man finally entered the room, she recognized his voice. He was the guy who was afraid of her tattoo.

He spoke to her as he stood by the open doorway.

In broken English, he said, "I come to give you food and bedding and uncuff you, okay?"

Savannah sat quietly and nodded, but did not look at him.

"I will put the tray down on the end of the bed, then uncuff you. You gonna give me the evil eye if I do you this favor?"

Savannah shook her head slowly and meekly.

The man hesitated, unsure if he trusted her, but he had no choice but to do what the boss told him. So he slowly moved to the bed, looking up to ensure the monitor was blinking red, indicating it was working correctly.

He placed the sandwich, an apple, and a bottle of water at the end of the dirty mattress.

Savannah didn't move. The man began to think the woman had to be exhausted by now, even though they had noticed she still had enough strength because they had watched her exercising in her room periodically. So he moved towards her slowly, put his hand in his pocket, and retrieved the key to the handcuffs.

"I need to use the toilet. Will you bring the bucket closer so I can pee first?"

The man saw no harm in that. He lifted the lid to the handmade chair with his foot and scooted the bucket underneath it until it was by the bedside. He held his breath because it smelled like urine. He noticed the plastic bucket had not been emptied, and he gagged as he looked at the contents.

Savannah looked up at him for the first time. "Please hurry; I'm going to pee my pants if you don't. Please. Now uncuff me quickly so I can pull down my pants unless you want to do it."

Savannah looked at the man with pleading eyes. He didn't want trouble with the boss, so he hesitated but uncuffed her.

She stood, unbuttoned her jeans, and brought her hands down to pull her pants down. Instead, she bent down, picked up the bucket, and threw the contents in the man's face. He screamed as the acidic urine splashed in his eyes. She quickly kicked him in his groin as hard as she could, watching him go to his knees while still screaming. She kneed him under his chin, and he fell flat on his back. She ran to the open door, slammed it shut behind her, and was thankful when she heard it click. Noticing that the downstairs was empty of men, she raced to the two operating tables in the middle of the giant hall covered in plastic, wishing she could hide under one, but quickly realized that wasn't an option. Then she saw a door beside a corrugated metal garage door. She lifted the lid on one of the surgical metal trays on a table next to the operating tables. She grabbed the largest scalpel from the container. She grabbed a package of Coban wrap sitting next to the container. She placed the scalpel in the back pocket of her jeans and ran to the door, praying it was unlocked. Luckily, she flung it open easily, stepped outside, and found herself on a stoop next to the loading dock. She heard men shouting from inside the warehouse, placed the Coban in her front pocket, and raced down the three steps on the left side. However, her loose shoelace came untied, and she fell, landing at the bottom. She caught herself with her hands as her body slid

165

across the old tar and gravel surface. She looked back to the right and saw a dead end. She looked ahead and saw tall grass that appeared dense and over six feet tall.

Not wanting to waste time tying her shoe, she hurriedly removed it, tucked it beneath her armpit, and willed herself to stand up and run as fast as possible. Adrenaline ran through her body as her sympathetic nervous system kicked in. Her heart raced as she ran the 20 yards to reach the end of the building. She ignored the pain in her right bare foot, knees, and elbows. She heard gunfire and men shouting in Spanish.

She stepped to the left at the end of the building so she wasn't in the open. She leaned against the brick building and took notice of her surroundings. The tall cogon grass was ahead, between another 5 and 10 yards. Could she make it without being detected? To the left was a high fence she knew she couldn't climb. She knew the grass had sharp edges and could cause skin irritation or minor cuts, but the men's voices were getting louder. She knew she had no choice, so she ran, fell again, and stood back up. Her life depended on it.

She finally reached the grass and ran into a giant spider web. She dropped her shoe as she raised her arms to block her face. She knew flailing her arms would only make the web adhere more tightly. She silently screamed and swiftly but calmly disengaged the web by brushing it from her face and arms. She bent over, shook her head, and ran her hands through her hair to remove the sticky substance. She looked around and was grateful she didn't see a spider. Based on the size of the web, she could only imagine what size the owner was.

She picked up her shoe and limped further into the grass, keeping low. She could see a road to her right and headed toward it.

Suddenly, she heard a car and stopped. She saw a white van driving down the lane toward the warehouse. She stooped and watched it as it parked next to several SUVs and other vans. A man exited the van, walked around to the passenger side, pulled the side door open, and yanked out four teenage boys who were handcuffed behind their backs. The driver yelled at them as another man left the warehouse to help with the struggling teens. She then noticed a man walking toward the grass with a rifle.

She got on all fours and crawled away from the road into the abundant reeds. She came eye to eye with a giant rat. She stopped, the rat stopped, and they stared at each other out of curiosity.

"Shoo, shoo," she whispered.

The rat didn't budge initially, but it started moving closer to her, mouth open and bearing sharp teeth.

Savannah drew a breath, slowly reached into her back pocket, and withdrew the scalpel. She swiped at the rat, nicking its head. The rat squealed loudly and scurried away.

She put the scalpel back in her pocket, put on her tennis shoe, and tied the laces tight on both shoes.

She looked back to see if the man with the gun had heard the animal's cries. Evidently, he had.

He was now running toward her, and she stood and ran. She followed the rat's direction because she knew rats had strong instincts to avoid danger and seek safety.

She was now flailing her arms to cut through the dense grass. A warehouse loomed ahead of her, and she prayed that she could safely reach a hiding place.

As she approached the building, she began checking the entranceways. She noticed broken windows and one large double door. She ran to the door and tried the doorknob. The door was locked.

"Shit," she exclaimed.

She ran to the nearest broken window, removed the Coban wrap from her pocket, tore off a piece with her teeth, and wrapped it around her hand to break the rest of the glass. She placed the wrap back in her front pocket. She stood on a large rock and lifted herself up and through the window. She managed to shimmy through without cutting her body, and she dropped to the wooden floor. She looked up at the 20-foot ceiling; the dim light made her squint to see missing plaster and holes in the roof.

Rows of old shipping containers filled the first floor.

She ran behind one, stepping over rats scurrying around. She pressed her body hard against the cold metal container and slowly peeked her head around. She saw a set of wooden stairs leading to a second story in the back of the room.

She studied the container to see if she could climb up to hide. She soon realized that she didn't have the strength to pull herself up 8 feet.

She stood quietly and listened intently for any noise outside, still hearing the rats scurrying around.

She hoped the man would be afraid of rats and would give up.

She moved away from the container, stood on her tiptoes, and looked out the front windows of the building. Was that car noise she was hearing? Was that a road in the near distance?

She figured it must be getting close to five o'clock, and traffic would be heavy. Could she reach the road and flag down a good Samaritan who could save her? Would someone hear the gunshots and call the police?

She thought about Robert, wondering if he was really dead. Her gut told her he was alive. She had always had excellent intuition. She prayed he would rescue her soon, but in the meantime, she could only save herself.

She quietly made her way around each container, stopping and listening each time she reached another one closer to the door, which also happened to be closer to a set of stairs in the back of the room.

She looked back at the stairs. The first floor had about 20-foot-high ceilings. Could she make it up all those stairs without falling?

She looked for a back door while quietly running toward the back of the building. When she reached an exit door, it was locked and bolted with heavy chains.

Suddenly, she heard gunshots. It sounded like the front double doors were being shot at, and she heard a bullet whiz by and ricochet off one of the containers.

She was now frantic. She was trapped on the first level with no way out. She thought she could play hide-and-seek with the man by moving between containers and eventually running out the doors he had blasted through, but she heard more men shouting outside the broken windows.

She ran up the stairs, taking two at a time, until she reached the second floor's landing.

Catching her breath, she looked around for a place to hide. The old wooden plank flooring looked just as dangerous as the man who was now inside the warehouse. The floors creaked, and pieces of flooring were missing. She walked carefully, testing the floor with each step she took. She peered into a hole and saw the man moving around the containers, searching for her. He heard the floor creak and looked up with a quizzical expression.

There was nowhere to hide because the second floor was empty except for spiderwebs.

She looked at the ceiling and saw a hatch door with a retractable ladder. A tattered rope was hanging down from the underside of the ladder. She prayed the rope wouldn't break from dry rot.

She calculated that the second-story ceiling was approximately ten feet high.

She simply had no choice but to try jumping up to reach the pull cord to unfold the wooden ladder.

The man was yelling, "Where are you, bitch?"

She jumped, trying to catch the rope, and failed, winching from the pain in her right knee.

She caught the rope on her third attempt and pulled hard to lower the old ladder.

She then began to climb, carefully testing each rung, fearing the wood on the ladder was as rotten as the old flooring.

She reached the top and tried to push up to open the hatch door. She used her shoulder to push up on it, but the wooden door had swelled and settled after many years of no use.

Meanwhile, the man's voice was getting closer; she was getting desperate because she heard him coming up the stairs.

One more hard push, and the access door gave way. The ladder became unstable with her movements and began to wobble.

She heard a snapping noise and realized the old aluminum catches were corroded and breaking. Hurriedly, she pulled herself up through the hatch.

The man was yelling something in Spanish that she didn't understand. He placed his rifle strap over his shoulder, reached for the ladder, and began to climb. When he was halfway up, the force of his weight caused the middle aluminum catches to break. The ladder collapsed, and he fell backward to the floor, cursing when the ladder hit him in the head.

Savannah watched as the man held his hand to his bleeding forehead. He angrily pushed the ladder off his body and stumbled when he stood.

She closed the hatch door, ran on the flat roof, and hid behind one of the old air conditioner units. While waiting, gunshots were heard.

The man was shooting up through the roof, so she climbed on top of one of the units.

She sat there for at least half an hour, gathering her thoughts and calming her body and mind.

She finally became aware of the scrapes on her palms and knees. She blew on her hands, took the scalpel, and picked out small bits of gravel from her hands and knees. She was also upset that she now had a hole in her jeans at her right knee. Her knee was swollen, and she gently rubbed it with both hands to ease the pain. She was thankful she had the foresight to grab the Coban because she knew she had always tended to fall when she ran. Thankfully, she didn't need any stitches.

She wrapped her knee with the Coban and studied the many scratches from the grass on her arms. They weren't deep, but she knew they should be cleansed before any infection set in.

Then, the realization hit hard. How was she going to get down from the 30-foot-tall building?

No longer hearing gunshots, she limped to the back of the building, where numerous pine trees grew. The closest tree was at least a foot away. She wondered if she had the nerve to jump that far. If she missed, she would die from the fall. What other choice did she have?

She limped to the east side of the building, hoping there might be a fire escape, and looked down.

She meekly sat back down on one of the units, feeling it to be a powder keg, and adjusted her invisible crown. She removed the thin scalpel from her back pocket and slipped it into a side pocket on the right side of her jeans. She stood and jumped up and down on her good leg to see if it would fall out or could be seen.

Once satisfied that the scalpel was securely hidden, she sat back down and waited. Anger and disappointment crept into her weary soul.

She had just seen two men with guns climbing up a tall, metal ladder anchored to the side of the building.

Chapter 18

While Robert and Peter were getting a leased vehicle to drive, Michael Mason picked up Mark Jenkins and his three buddies at the Norfolk airport.

Mark brought Lee Hunt, Tom Brown, and Jim Bailey, all ex-Green Berets who had served together in the U.S. Army. Lee Hunt had been their captain in a unit called the A-Team. They had remained friends after retiring. They still served their community as private citizens whenever they were needed.

Mark made the introductions, and the men fist-bumped.

Once the men were settled in the company SUV, Mark asked about Robert and Savannah.

"Robert didn't tell you anything?"

"No, he called me in a frenzy and told me Savannah had been kidnapped. Then he asked me to gather some buddies and bring guns. That's all I know. So I hope you can tell us what is happening here."

As Michael drove toward the marina where the yacht, The Lady Jane, was docked, he told the men as much detail as possible.

Mark was visibly upset when he heard the story.

"Oh my God, this sounds like a bad movie script. It's unbelievable—and poor Savannah. That poor woman has been through horrible and challenging times. I know she is Robert's true love, and he must be beside himself with worry."

"Yes, he is, Mark, he's barely eating and obsessed with finding her. We are all worried. I feel guilty, thinking it's my fault for asking her to fly here from her peaceful life to help us with our daughter."

"How is your daughter, Danielle, doing, by the way?"

"Since Savannah told the oncologist taking care of Dani what she and the family expected of him, he discontinued the chemo treatments, and Dani is feeling much better. She's still in the hospital, wearing a little tiara and telling everyone she is a princess."

"Ahhh, Savannah's famous tiara trick." Mark chuckled.

The three ex-Berets looked confused, and Mark explained what he meant—another ah-ha moment.

Michael continued telling the men about how they met David Atkins and his retired Navy SEAL friends, and he could feel some tension coming from the men in the back seat.

"We are retired Green Berets, and we can kick Navy SEALs' asses," one of the men said with a laugh.

Michael frowned and became worried.

"Men, are we up for this challenge with the cartel, or will you be challenging David and his buddies? If you don't feel you can work side by side, I will turn this car around and take you back to the airport."

Lee Hunt, who still acted as the team leader, laughed heartily.

"No worries, Michael. We are both highly trained special forces and have a friendly rivalry. We may joke and poke fun at them, but they are respected. I worked with many frogmen on missions and admired their strength and patriotism for our country. You may hear some friendly banter between us, but I assure you, we will work as a team. Isn't that right, men?"

"Hooah," the three men said in unison.

Michael was satisfied and tried remembering the difference between the team's battle cries: Hooyah versus Hooah.

He thought he was starting to understand, but he was never in the military, and the shouts were a little confusing to him.

Once they reached The Lady Jane, the three ex-soldiers blew a low whistle, staring at the beautiful 125-foot yacht.

The men unloaded their luggage and gear, and Michael led them to the yacht and showed them to their staterooms.

"Mark," Michael said, "Robert is picking up a rental car and should be at the police department helping them with their investigation as we speak. I have left a car in the parking lot for you to use. It has GPS, and you can easily find your way around. There are restaurants and grocery stores nearby. I'm sorry, I don't have a crew on board to cook or clean, but it's quieter than a noisy hotel. Robert has asked everyone to meet at DM Yachts at six tonight."

Michael reached into his pocket and handed Mark the keys to the vehicle.

Mark took the keys and said, "Hooah, Hooyah."

The two men laughed.

At a quarter to six, David Atkins and his team gave the guard at DM Yachts his name and license again.

Behind them were Mark and his buddies. The guard recognized Mark and his car as one of the company's cars and flagged him in.

Robert met all the men in the lobby. Robert and Mark hugged.

Robert thanked them all for coming and led them to the conference room. Michael, Adam Jordan, and Peter were already sitting in their seats.

The SEALs took the same seats they had at the last meeting, and the Berets found their seats. Introductions were made, and the SEALs and Berets shook hands. They shook hands with Peter, who admired all these warriors, regardless of the military branch they had served.

Robert stood and pulled down a large, white screen attached to the ceiling at one end of the table.

David stood and projected the video he had taken with his drone onto the big screen. David wanted to display the video on the screen so that everyone could get a good look and understand what they would be dealing with shortly.

The video came to life and showed an old, one-story, dilapidated brick warehouse approximately fifty yards wide by 40 yards deep, roughly 18,000 square feet. They saw the loading dock and bay door in the middle of the building. Three concrete steps led to a stoop in front of the corrugated garage door. There was also a metal door to the right of the garage door. They saw the faded lettering over the bay door, indicating it used to be an old meat slaughterhouse. They saw a flat roof with large skylights. On top of the roof were two air conditioning units, which appeared to be running. They saw the white vans, a couple

179

of sedans, two black SUV's and a white Jeep Cherokee parked approximately twenty feet from the loading dock.

Robert gasped when he saw one of the SUVs missing its front fenders and the hood smashed in. He realized he was looking at the vehicle that destroyed his Mercedes. He was angry, but it proved he was on the right track. It also showed the road beside the tall, dense cogon grass field on the east end of the warehouse. They saw David's green Bronco sitting on the edge of the grass near the end of the road before it became an open parking lot.

On the west end, there was a dead end. A ten-foot-high stainless steel chain link fence ran from the dead end around the entire back of the building and ended on the east side near the grassy area. Overgrown weeds peeked through the fence, and a heavy forest of pine trees lay beyond and behind the warehouse for at least a quarter of a mile.

David turned off the video. "Any questions?"

Everyone shook their head; no.

Robert used the same screen and brought up his pictures of the interior. Beginning at the front of the building on the north side, the men could understand the direction of the layout.

First, the men noticed the ample, open space in the interior, with concrete floors and walls. Some concrete was missing on the walls, and brick peeked through. The ceiling was about 40 feet tall. On the east side, metal beams were placed in a grid, approximately ten feet square, and held a variety of dangling hooks. The various sizes and shapes of hooks hung close to the floor, but several hung about seven feet off the ground. They were on a pulley system to raise and lower them. Below the hooks were trenches and holes dug into the concrete to catch the blood from slaughtered animals.

On the west end, two operating tables covered with clear plastic were located. Beside each bed, a table held containers with lids. A tall metal cabinet with two doors sat beneath the office's flooring on the far northwest wall.

At the far southwest end, metal stairs led up to a landing and a large room that ran north and south with windows all around. Robert had taken a fast photo that showed Lily kicking the bottom of the door and several men standing in a dimly lit room.

On the south side were five metal doors lined in a row that appeared to be doors to rooms. Each door had a keyless pad that would unlock the door with a swipe of a magnetic card. Evidently, Lily had installed the keypads.

Robert had also taken pictures of the placement of the security cameras.

"Any questions?"

Lee Hunt asked, "Why the hooks and operating tables?"

"We're not sure. I guess we're about to find out."

Robert sat down in his seat. "Listen, the woman I love is in that warehouse. Some very evil men and one woman, who is the ringmaster, are hiding Savannah and possibly more innocent people behind those doors. We're dealing with psychotic cartels who don't care about human beings unless they can make money off them. Behind one of the doors could be a room full of fentanyl and different drugs. I don't know, but I know these people are dangerous."

Robert continued, "Dr. Kyle Clark had a key that he said was to the door to the warehouse. However, one of the doctors, Dr. Stone, said he went to the warehouse with Dr. Clark once, and Lily wouldn't allow them inside. That shows me Dr. Clark might have been lying about the key. I took a key ring from him the day of the accident. All his keys were labeled."

He reached into his pocket, pulled out a bag of keys, and dumped them on the table.

"Before the meeting, I had his key reproduced for each of us. Whoever can get near the door without being seen can see if it works. If not, we need to find another way in. We also need to find a way into those interior metal doors. That may mean we must take the key from one of the cartels or Lily Mason-Clark. Lily is in the photo upstairs, kicking the door. Don't hesitate to shoot her, but don't kill her in case she is keeping Savannah hidden somewhere else."

David Atkins said, "I think I know a better way inside without a key."

Robert walked out of the room. Moments later, he returned, rolling a large chalkboard in front of the screen.

"David, tell us what you're thinking. Let's put all our heads together and devise a solid plan. We may need to practice our strategy. Michael found another area nearby online with empty warehouses similar to Lily's."

Michael's cell phone rang. "Yes? Yes, let him in."

"I'll be right back."

He quickly left the room.

The men all talked at once, giving suggestions.

Michael soon came back carrying eight large pizzas.

"Help yourself, men. It's gonna be a long night."

While the men ate, Robert dismissed himself and walked into his office next door to the conference room.

He pulled Savannah's purse from a side drawer. He had heard it ringing several times, but never had time to answer. What would he say to the caller, anyway?

He guessed her code to be her birth year, and the phone opened and showed Savannah's wallpaper. He smiled when he recognized a picture of them in Nassau ten years prior.

He read the many texts from her work. A man named Jason May texted at least twenty times. The texts became frantic when Savannah didn't answer. He could tell from the writing that Jason was frustrated, worried, and angry.

He demanded to know why she wasn't back to work or answering his calls.

Robert looked through the list of numbers and found Dr. Jason May listed. He surmised this must be the same Jason.

The phone rang again. It was Jason.

Robert decided to answer it and speak for Savannah. A good-looking man wearing a white medical jacket appeared on the screen.

"Hello?" Robert asked.

There was a moment of silence.

"I'm sorry, I must have the wrong number."

"Are you trying to reach Dr. Hayes?"

"Yes. Who are you? Please put Savannah on the phone."

"I'm sorry. I can't help you. Savannah is tied up at the moment." Robert noticed the irony of his words.

"Listen, tell her no one here at the hospital has heard from her for at least a week. She could lose her job if she doesn't call in. We are all worried about her well-being."

Robert hesitated, unsure what to tell the doctor, but he didn't want Savannah to lose her job.

"Are you Savannah's boss or boyfriend?"

"Yes, I'm her boss. I work with her at the hospital, and we are friends."

Jason then asked, "So, who are you?"

"I'm also a friend. A very good friend. I guess someone there needs to know what is going on. Savannah has been kidnapped."

Jason laughed, "You're joking, right?"

Jason stopped laughing as Robert told him a short synopsis of Savannah's tragedy without mentioning names or the cartel.

"Listen, can you cover for her, Jason? An elite team is going to rescue her soon. She will probably be traumatized, but I'll have her call you when she can."

"Will you keep me updated, Robert?"

"I'm sorry. I am very busy with the men. Rescuing her is my priority. Please tell the hospital staff that Savannah fell ill and needs more time off."

"I can do that for Savannah. We need and miss her here in the ER."

"Thank you, and please stop texting and calling. Savannah's phone will be turned off and locked in a drawer in my office. No one will hear it."

"Yes, yes. Okay, but please tell Savannah we love and miss her when you see her."

"Will do. Goodbye."

Robert turned off the phone, put it back in her purse, and locked it in the desk drawer.

He returned to the conference room. "Okay, did I miss anything I need to know?"

Michael said, "Not much, but I need to leave you guys. I need to go home and get to bed early. Cathi and I are forcing Dr. Stone to release Dani from the hospital tomorrow. If he refuses, he will be fired, and I will have my attorney file a complaint against him with the hospital, the Department of Health, and even the AMA if necessary."

Robert said, "I'm happy Dani is well enough to go home. Go, be with your family. I will lock up when we leave here."

When Michael Mason left the office, Robert asked, "Has anyone come up with any good ideas?"

A couple of the SEALs made suggestions, which the Berets disagreed with.

Adam Jordan said, "I don't know what I'm doing here. I'm just a CPA; I can't help. I'm going home, too. Good luck."

Mark Jenkins laughed, "If you need a pilot, I'm your man. I'm not a strategist, but you have my support."

Robert sighed. It truly was going to be a long night.

Chapter 19

Michael Mason had been intrigued by what he saw and heard in the conference room. Before heading home, he wanted to know the location of the warehouse for himself before darkness set in. The warehouse district was on his way home.

He drove slowly up the one-lane road and stopped at the end of the field of grass. He turned off the engine of his Mercedes, removed binoculars from the glove box, stepped out of the car, and walked as close to the end of the grass as he could without being seen.

He crouched and looked through the binoculars, seeing the layout. He panicked when he saw movement by the dock and thought he had been caught. Then he realized the binoculars made everything look closer than it actually was.

He exhaled a sigh of relief.

He started backing away to get in the car to leave, but he saw a girl dressed in white. She stood out from the men, who were dressed all in black.

He removed his phone and snapped a picture for Robert.

He watched as the men struggled with Savannah. One man was on her right side and had her by her arm, forcing her to climb the steps. She had her hands handcuffed behind her back, and her hair was in disarray. It looked like she had a bandage around her knee. Two men walked behind them carrying rifles. They stopped at the bay door, and the man released her arm and grabbed something out of her front pocket. He eyed the Coban, put it back into her pocket, and roughly grabbed her by the arm again. One of the men behind her slapped her on the butt. Savannah yanked her arm away and turned around. She was now facing the grass. She thought she saw Michael. To distract the men, she spat on the man she thought had slapped her. The other two men laughed at her.

It was clear that she was angry and was trying to wrestle free from the man's grip.

Michael watched until the men forced her inside the metal door next to the corrugated bay door. He wondered if Savannah had seen him when she turned around because she had looked right at him.

Still crouching, he slowly backed up, stood when he knew he couldn't be seen, and ran to his car.

He put the car in reverse and drove backward until he reached the abandoned warehouse where Savannah had been fleeing. Of course, he had no way of knowing what had just transpired. He backed into the lot by the warehouse, put the car in drive, and drove as quickly as possible to the highway.

He tried calling Robert, but he didn't answer. He pulled off on a side street and parked. Then, he texted Robert the picture he had taken.

When he was back on the highway, his phone rang. Robert was gleeful and thanked him profusely for the picture.

Robert was grateful for the evidence that Savannah was alive.

Was that crying he heard coming from Robert? He didn't judge the man for his tears. If that had been Cathi, he would have cried, too.

Once the men had Savannah back inside, the angry and embarrassed man she had thrown the urine on and kicked came down from the office. He limped up to Savannah and put a gun to her head. The man's face was distorted and filled with hatred. He felt his peers disrespected him now, and he wanted revenge.

The men started yelling in Spanish and wrestled the gun away from the man.

The man holding her arm said in English, "Miss Lily and the boss say we are to keep her alive for some unknown reason.

When the time comes, you can be the one to kill her. But for now, put the gun away."

The angry man took back the gun and stashed it in his belt. He was satisfied that he would be the person who would finally kill her.

The men walked Savannah to her cell door, opened it with a swipe of a card, uncuffed her, and pushed her inside so hard that she slid across the cement floor. She rubbed her bad knee, stood up, and limped to bed. She was grateful that she at least had one clean sheet and a pillow.

She was exhausted, so she lay down, covered herself with the sheet, and turned on her right side, facing away from the camera.

As she lay there, pretending to sleep, she slowly reached under the sheet and retrieved the scalpel from her pocket. Carefully, she used it to cut a slit on the side of the mattress, just small enough that no one would notice the cut but large enough to insert and hide the blade.

She lay there wondering if the man she had embarrassed was going to kill her. She prayed. She thought about the two people she loved the most, Robert and Danielle. She wondered if Dani was going to live or if she would meet her in heaven. She regretted that she couldn't give Dani the bone marrow transplant she needed. Tears ran down her face.

Was Robert alive?

She heard the door open and lay still.

"What now?" she thought.

She heard high heels and knew Lily was back to torture her.

"Did you have a nice little outing?" Lily asked sarcastically.

Savannah didn't move.

"Look at me, bitch. Tell me where my husband's will is."

"Why should I tell you? You'll kill me afterward."

Lily contorted her face. "Then I will kill the little Mason girl that you came to save. You're not doing your job very well, are you? Do you want out of here? Then tell me where the will is and save Michael's precious brat."

Savannah lay still and said, "Show me the photos of the car accident. I don't believe Dr. Clark or my friend is dead."

Savannah rolled over and sat on the side of the bed, defiantly facing Lily.

"If I must."

Lily opened her phone and showed her the news video about Dr. Clark's death. Robert's name was not mentioned.

"Now, do you believe me? Tell me what you did with the will."

"I'm tired, hungry, and thirsty. I can't think. As you know, I've had a long and tiring day."

"You'll tell me before too long, but I need your doctor skills now."

Savannah was angry. "You want me to help you? Stop making me laugh."

"Let's just say you have company in the room next door. One of the guests needs a doctor."

A tall man whom she had never seen before walked into the room and handcuffed her in the front. She wondered how many men Lily had exactly.

Savannah eyed the bottle of water sitting on the floor.

"Do you mind? I need water. And I'm hungry. I need food."

"Oh, alright, hurry it up."

Lily grabbed the bottle of water. After removing the cap, she placed the bottle in Savannah's hands. Savannah held the water with both hands and gulped down the warm liquid.

"Thank you, Lily."

"Don't thank me, Dr. Hayes. I know what you're trying to do. Don't think you'll get better treatment by being nice to me."

Savannah stared at her, knowing that to be the truth.

The tall man took Savannah by her arm and led her and Lily to the room next door. Savannah stood quietly as he unlocked and opened the door.

Lily walked away while the man shoved Savannah inside, uncuffed her, and closed the door.

Her heart went into her throat at what she saw. Six scared, young teenage girls sat on beds similar to hers. They were all dressed in hospital gowns. They looked up and noticed Savannah, thinking she must also be a prisoner because of the handcuffs.

"I'm a doctor. I was told someone needed help. You can call me Dr. Savannah."

No one spoke because they were unsure if the woman was telling the truth. They had been lied to so often that they didn't know the truth.

Savannah sensed their hesitation.

"I have a room next door. I was also kidnapped because the person who had you brought here knows I have vital information that I'm keeping from her. You don't need to fear me. I'm here to help."

One of the girls asked, "What happened to your arms and knee?"

"Well, I tried to escape but got caught. I fell several times while running."

"Are you a real doctor?"

"Yes, I work in an emergency room. I was a nurse before I became a doctor."

The girls leaned closer, showing interest in the beautiful woman, who seemed caring.

"Now, please tell me how you got here and which of you needs medical attention?"

A pretty, fresh-faced blond said she had made a mistake by talking with a cute guy on the internet. She continued telling her story about how she snuck out of her house when her parents went to bed. The story ended when she was brought into the room about a week ago. She had overhead one of the men saying in Spanish that she would be sold. She took Spanish in school and understood. She was too scared to fight.

All the girls began telling their story. A couple had been snatched off the street while walking home from school.

A girl in the farthest bed from the door raised her hand, cowering in her bed. She looked about 13 or 14 years old.

"May I approach you?"

The girl nodded her head.

Savannah walked and stood by the girl's bed. She was a beautiful brunette with large eyes and full lips.

"What is your name, honey?"

"Tess."

"How did you get here?"

"My parents wouldn't let me go to a party, so I ran away from home. I stayed under a bridge with some other runaways. I was kidnapped and thrown into a van. I want to go home."

"Are you in pain?"

The girl nodded and started crying.

Savannah noticed bites on the girl's arms and legs. She showed no emotion but tenderness toward Tess. Immediately, she recognized the bites as bed bugs.

"You have bed bug bites and need a corticosteroid cream to help the itching and inflammation."

All the girls screamed and jumped out of their beds.

Savannah noticed unused gowns on a chair beside the small pedestal sink. She walked over and effortlessly ripped the cheap material into large strips. She wet the gowns at the sink and applied the cloth to the girl's skin, pressing down to use them as a cold compress.

She had the girls sit up to check their backs. That's when she noticed a large, bloody surgical pad over Tess's left kidney, or at least where her kidney had been. Savannah touched Tess's forehead to see if she had a fever.

Savannah whispered to Tess, "Did a doctor perform surgery on you recently?"

"Yes, about a week ago, I think."

"Did he do the surgery on one of the tables out in the warehouse?"

Bile came up in Savannah's throat. The realization hit hard: Lily was into organ transplants and child trafficking.

"Yes."

"Can you describe him?"

"No, I was blindfolded."

"Did the doctor say his name?"

"No."

Savannah looked at the monitor and spoke loudly.

"This poor girl needs medical attention, NOW."

The monitor blinked.

"Are there any antibiotics here?"

The monitor blinked.

"Show me where they are. The girl needs antibiotics and Tylenol. She needs a dressing change. She also needs cream for bed bug bites and a new mattress."

There was silence. The monitor's red light stayed steady.

"Damn it, do you hear me?"

Five minutes later, the door suddenly opened, and the tall man motioned for Savannah to follow him after he put her back into the cuffs.

She reassured the girls that she would return shortly.

Once outside the room, she says, "Uncuff me. I can't change the girl's dressing while my hands are in cuffs. I'm a doctor, and this girl needs me. I swear I won't try anything funny."

Another man with a gun joined them. He held the gun on Savannah while the other man uncuffed her. They led her to a large metal cabinet near the operating tables and opened it with a key.

Savannah searched for the proper antibiotics: Tylenol, antibiotic cream, Benedryl, and toothpaste tubes. She also chose antiseptic swabs, surgical dressings, paper tape, sterile gloves, and disposable masks.

She found a small bedpan and placed all the supplies in it.

She turned to the man with the gun.

"You must remove the mattresses and exchange them for new ones. The girls have bedbugs. The young girl who had surgery has a fever, and she's bleeding from her wound. She could die, or do you care?"

The tall man whispered to the gunman, "That is the pretty one. Miss Lily wants to sell her."

Savannah overheard the conversation but pretended she didn't hear it and kept picking up supplies.

The man with the gun spoke Spanish into a handheld radio in his pants pocket. He received a response in Spanish.

"Pick up your things and follow me."

The men led her to a third door, shoved her inside, and closed the door.

Savannah stood inside the room and looked around. There were ten beds, and she noticed the old mattresses looked relatively cleaner than the dirty ones in the other room. She sat in a wooden chair, placed the supplies on her lap, and waited.

Fifteen minutes later, the door opened, and the teenage girls were ushered into the room. They had been given washcloths, hand towels, soap, clean gowns, and bed sheets.

The girls helped Tess to a nearby bed.

199

Savannah instructed the girls to wash and change. She opened the box of Benedryl and rolled her eyes when she only saw six pills in the package.

She picked up the tubes of toothpaste. "See this, girls? If you have bites and run out of cream, put this on. And try not to scratch. It'll only make things worse. Understood?"

They all nodded.

Savannah turned her attention to Tess. She donned gloves and gave Tess one of the Benadryl and two Tylenol. She washed her body with soap and water, applied cream to her bites, and then helped her into a clean gown.

"Okay, honey, lie down and roll on your good side so I can change your surgical dressing."

Savannah almost gasped when she removed the old, bloody dressing. The wound was red and swollen, along with a cloudy green discharge. The wound was infected. She prayed it wasn't MRSA, which was highly contagious.

She put on her invisible doctor's hat and started doing what she did best: fixing things.

After cleaning the wound as best as possible with her few supplies, she changed the dressing and handed Tess four antibiotic pills. She watched as Tess took the pills with water.

She instructed the oldest girl, who appeared to be around 15, to watch for signs of bleeding or any color drainage on the pad and not to touch the girl's surgical bandage. If Tess's fever worsened, she should tell the man on the monitor that Tess needed the doctor.

Savannah stood under the camera. She swiped her hands back and forth, suggesting that she was finished. She picked up an unused gown and washcloth, discarded the old dressing and her gloves, and rolled them up. There was no trash can. She laid the item in the bedpan, now empty of her supplies.

She cautioned the girls about using the Internet. She was going to tell them always to be aware of their surroundings, but evidently, she had not.

Tess reached out her hand to Savannah. She sat beside the young girl and took her small hand in hers.

"Help us, please," Tess whispered.

Savannah leaned down and whispered in the girl's ear, "Help is coming soon. Right now, you need to heal and rest. I'm just a couple doors down. I'll come back when you need me, I promise."

Tess smiled weakly and closed her eyes.

The tall man entered the room, and the girls scooted farther back into their beds, their eyes wide open with fear.

"Get up."

Savannah stood, picked up the bedpan and a clean washcloth, looked at the girls, and gave them a thumbs-up.

"I'll see you brave girls soon. Stay strong."

The girls sat in their beds, looking at Savannah with pleading eyes.

When Savannah left the room, the girls gathered around Tess and asked her what Savannah had whispered to her.

Quietly, Tess told the girls that help was on the way, and it gave them hope. They believed the beautiful doctor.

The fifteen-year-old took charge and said, "Get back to your beds and get some sleep. We'll take turns watching over Tess."

The girls obeyed and crawled into their beds.

The tall man took Savannah back to her room. She handed him the bedpan with the rolled-up gown and told him to throw it away. She also said that Tess would need more antibiotics, Tylenol, and dressing changes because she had an infection, and she was hoping he understood.

Once inside her room, she gave the man on the monitor the exact instructions.

She noticed the handcuffs were dangling from the wall above her bed again.

She turned her attention to her own body. She washed her face and neck with the clean washcloth from the girl's room. She continued to wash her arms, armpits, and hands. She removed the wrap from her leg and washed her knee. The wrap had helped with the swelling. She saved the rest of the wrap for later. The red scratches on her arms from the grass were no longer a worry. They would heal on their own.

She felt good about being somewhat cleaner and helping the girls, but worried about them, especially Tess.

She ate the sandwich left on her bed during her absence. She lay on the bed, said goodnight to the monitor, and gave him the finger underneath the sheet.

She closed her eyes and prayed she wasn't imagining seeing Michael. She thanked God that she finally had some hope. But why had Michael come without Robert? She refused to think about Robert being dead. She felt sorry that poor Dr. Clark was dead.

Then she thought about the will and the prenup. Did Lily believe she was that stupid to drive all the way to Virginia Beach to deliver blank sheets of paper? Not to mention embarrassing herself when Mr. Edwards opened the envelope to find nothing.

Chapter 20

Michael and Cathi Mason hurriedly ate their breakfast. They were excited knowing they were bringing their little girl home today.

At 8 a.m., Michael called Dr. Kent Stone on his personal cellphone.

"Hello, Michael."

"Hello, doctor. I'm informing you that you will release Danielle from the hospital today. We no longer require your service."

Kent Stone hesitated. "But she's not ready to go home yet. One of her kidneys still isn't functioning correctly. I want to monitor her. I have ordered more blood tests to make sure she's in remission from her cancer."

"She seems well enough to come home. At least for a break from the hospital. Savannah, I mean, Dr. Hayes said Dani can live with one functioning kidney."

"But, Michael, I've found her a compatible kidney. I had planned to transplant the kidney today. Don't you feel your daughter deserves to have two good-functioning kidneys? We have gotten most of her immune system back to normal. In my opinion, she is ready for the next step."

"My wife and I have lost all confidence in you, doctor. We want you to discharge her today. If you refuse, you will be fired and off the case for inadequate and poor quality of care. My next phone call will be to my attorney."

Kent Stone frowned. "I see I have no choice in the matter. I'm sorry you feel that way. I am going to Dr. Clark's funeral this morning. I'll call the hospital and let them know Danielle can be discharged later today. I must sign the order, so give me a few hours."

"Understood. Just make sure you don't forget. If you do, we will discharge her against medical advice. You can't stop us."

"Michael, I don't advise any patient to leave a hospital AMA. It doesn't look good on the patient's record. Your insurance company could deny payment, and you'll be stuck with the bill."

Michael laughed, "So be it. But I assure you, I won't be stuck with the bill. YOU will. When my attorneys get through with you, they will know anything and everything you have ever done wrong in your entire life. You will lose everything you care about, so I highly advise you to discharge Dani today."

Dr. Stone was visibly sweating. He was glad Michael couldn't see that his hands were shaking. Michael's threat had more significance to him than facing Lily today.

"I won't forget. You can take your daughter home later this afternoon. But won't you be going to the funeral with Dr. Hayes? She worked for Dr. Clark, after all."

"No, I don't believe we will be attending today. Thank you, doctor. I have to go now. Goodbye."

Michael hung up the phone and hugged Cathi.

"I need to call Robert. Then we can get dressed and go to the hospital."

On the other end of the phone conversation, Dr. Stone hung up and wondered why Dr. Hayes would not attend the funeral. He thought it possible that she had gone back to Florida.

The Masons arrived at the Children's Hospital at 10 a.m.

They found Dani sitting up in a chair, reading a book while wearing her tiara, still attached to IVs, a heart monitor, and oxygen. Cathi stayed with Dani while Michael called the security company to inform them their service was no longer required. He left the room and spoke to the guard outside the door. He shook his hand and thanked him for the service, but was free to leave later that afternoon.

He went to the nurses' station and spoke to the head nurse.

Nancy was in a foul mood and didn't bother to look up when Michael talked to her.

"Nancy, I want you to check my daughter's chart and see if Dr. Stone ordered the discharge yet."

Nancy jerked her head up. "What? Wait, I mean, what did you just say? Danielle is scheduled for surgery today at 2 p.m. She's been NPO since midnight."

Michael was furious. "She is NOT having surgery today. Dr. Stone is discharging her today. I demand you remove her IVs and prepare her for discharge this afternoon. Order up a breakfast and lunch tray for her. And do it, NOW."

Michael glared at Nancy. She seemed befuddled.

"Okay, okay. Give me a minute."

She opened her computer and pulled up Danielle Mason's chart. She looked at Michael, surprised that no one had told her that Dr. Stone had called in discharge orders.

"Yes, the order is here. However, our hospital's standard practice is for the doctor to sign and legally authenticate the discharge orders before the patient leaves. He must sign it personally. We no longer allow electronically signed orders. It's hospital policy."

"So, I'll have the nurse remove the IVs asap. The poor child must be starving, and I'll order her food now. Anything else?" Nancy gave Michael a strained smile, and he thought she was a very strange individual.

When Michael left the nurse's station, Nancy berated the attending nurse for not telling her Dr. Stone had called in discharge orders. She ordered the nurse to remove all tubing from Danielle and call the kitchen for breakfast and lunch based on Danielle's strict diet.

She then went to her office and closed the door. She picked up the phone to call Lily Mason-Clark.

*****

The funeral service was held at Dr. Clark's favorite Baptist church. The room overflowed with mourners, and Lily didn't understand why so many people were crying. Lily sat in the first pew, wearing all black. She kept her head down as if in prayer, so no one would talk to her. Two men dressed in black suits stood by the front door, guns secretly tucked into their pants at the waist.

Lily almost screamed, "Enough of the damn preaching and music, get to the gravesite and get it over with," but she knew she had to suffer through pretending to be a grieving widow.

She glanced at the closed coffin once. She felt nothing but had a slight regret that the handsome doctor's face was halfway blown off and couldn't be repaired enough to have an open casket.

Sitting with her head down and hands folded, she stopped listening to what the minister was saying.

She was getting anxious about finding the will. Was her original prenup with the will? If Savannah didn't tell her where it was soon, then she would kill her, take her organs, and sell them. She would also take her gunmen to Brett Edwards's office and coerce him to tell her what Kyle had instructed him to do about the will.

But she also knew that she had to keep Savannah alive because she was the only one who knew where her treasure was.

She knew the spouse would inherit 100 percent of the deceased's assets in Virginia without children or a prenuptial agreement. She wanted to ensure that the will had not been modified to exclude her interest in the clinic. She needed the clinic, damn it. She also had to find the original prenup to destroy it. The prenup took precedence over the will.

She had been stupid enough to agree to Kyle's wishes and had signed a prenup before they were married the second time. She didn't care back then, but now, for her successful business to continue, she needed the clinic more than the real estate, the million dollars in the bank, or the cars. He left no life insurance policy. The prenup was all about the clinic.

One of the smartest things she had done was hiring a thief to break into the one-person attorney's office the day after his death and steal the only copy of the prenup and will. She burned them.

However, she vaguely remembered blurting out her secret one night when she was angry and drunk. Did she really tell Kyle what she had done, or did she dream of it? She couldn't remember, so now she couldn't take any chances.

Nevertheless, she knew Kyle had the original will and prenup she couldn't find. She assumed they were somewhere in the clinic because she had turned the house upside down looking for them.

She also assumed that Savannah had been in the clinic to retrieve the documents when JoAnn forced her out. Instinctively, she knew Kyle had asked Savannah to take them somewhere, so she had them followed. She put two and two together when the tail ended up in Virginia Beach.

Savannah and her boyfriend were going to Brett Edwards. He was the attorney who had drawn up Daniel Mason's will so tightly, without any loopholes, that she couldn't fight it after his murder. The man was brilliant.

She also had another big problem. Nancy had called her earlier to tell her Danielle Mason was going home in the afternoon. She was upset that the scheduled surgery had been canceled. Dr. Stone had assured her that the child would die on the operating table. The surgery would have been profitable in more than one way.

Things weren't going her way, and she was very frustrated. The longer she sat through this ruse, the angrier she became.

Thankfully, after a boring hour for Lily, the first part of the funeral service was over, and it was finally time to go to the gravesite.

Two police officers on motorcycles escorted Lily's limo and cars filled with mourners to the gravesite. She rode with two men in black suits who didn't speak.

Once inside the area, Lily demanded that the limo driver stop the car.

"I'll get out here."

The driver stopped, opened the passenger door, and offered Lily his hand. She refused it. Who did he think she was? A helpless woman grieving over her dead husband?

She exited the limo with the two men and told the driver to wait.

The officers instructed the driver to move forward. He assured the officers that he would. The officers nodded and left, now that their job was done.

"I have to pull the car up, Ma'am. More people are coming, and they need room to park."

"I don't care about them. As soon as the casket is in the ground, you need to take me to the Hilton downtown. We are having a Celebration of Life there afterward. I'm not walking further than I need to return to the limo. So do as I tell you. Do you understand?"

The man had a flashback of his cruel mother. He recognized evil when he saw it.

The two men opened their jackets slightly, showing their guns, so the driver didn't argue.

Cars lined up behind him, hanging out on the boulevard, waiting to drive in.

He stood behind his limo, shrugging his shoulders and lifting his arms with his palms up, indicating he was sorry and helpless to the other drivers.

Horns began blowing. He wished the officers hadn't left.

The road was a one-way lane that circled the graveyard like a horseshoe. He could have easily driven to the opposite side, where the limo now sat. The gravesite was halfway in the middle of the circle, and Lily could have walked the same distance to the limo, except on the other side.

A lot of cars were blocked. The driver became frustrated, so he pulled the limo to the left onto the grass and allowed the cars behind him to continue around the horseshoe.

Lily didn't care about the other mourners as long as she didn't have to walk further. Her heels were sinking in the soggy grass, and it started to drizzle. A man with an umbrella walked up beside her at the gravesite. He opened the umbrella and offered to hold it while they stood together.

She looked at him with disdain, took the umbrella from the man, and pushed him away.

When the man tried to retrieve his umbrella, Lily snapped her fingers, and the two bodyguards led the man away by his arms.

People could not believe their eyes. They had heard rumors about Lily, but now witnessed the evil woman in action.

People stayed away from her. She impassively stood with two dangerous-looking men dressed in black behind her. She looked neither left nor right.

She stared at the minister and caught his eye. She tapped her wristwatch to indicate, "Hurry up." She was growing impatient with the long-winded man.

When the casket began to lower into the ground, she walked away from it and past the crowd of mourners, cursing under her breath that her shoes were wet.

As she neared the limo, she saw Kent Stone. She pointed at him and motioned for him to meet her at her ride. People were still waiting at the gravesite for the casket's final destination.

Dr. Stone meekly followed her.

She instructed the men to get inside the car. Then, she stuck her index finger in Kent Stone's face and shamed him.

"One doctor down, Kent. Which doctor will be next? I warned you that harm would come your way if you didn't do as I say. I warned you, didn't I?"

"But, Lily."

"Don't but Lily me, Kent. I have a couple of bones to pick with you. Come to the Hilton and bring the other doctors."

"Okay, what bones?"

"Danielle Mason's discharge, for one. The other is the teen girl."

Kent flinched and looked worried. His entire body stiffened with fear.

"How do you know about the discharge? And what teen?"

"Do you recognize the name Tess?"

"Yes, what about her?"

"Do as you're told, Kent. See you later at the Hilton. You'll find me celebrating in the conference room."

She and the gunmen got into the limo, and the young driver shut the door, leaving Kent standing alone.

She was angry again because the limo driver had disobeyed her. Cars lined the entire length of the horseshoe-shaped road. How were they supposed to leave? They were now blocked. She was too stubborn to admit she had caused her own problem.

The gunmen sat, waiting for orders, while Lily yelled and screamed at the driver.

"Back up on the grass until you hit the boulevard. Do it NOW. Get me out of here."

"I can't do that, ma'am. I'm not that experienced with backing up a limo that far. We'll have to wait until the other mourners leave."

Lily looked at the men, and they removed their guns and pointed them at the driver.

"Can you do it now?"

"Yes, ma'am."

The driver removed his cap, adjusted the side and rearview mirrors, and turned around in his seat to look out the back window. He didn't have a backup camera, so he asked the men to lower their heads so he could see. He slowly backed the limo, trying to avoid hitting all the parked cars on the right. The driver's side was scraped by fallen, dead branches and overgrown weeds on the left. He wondered how he was going to explain the damage to his boss.

When they finally reached the main boulevard, he asked the men to check whether it was safe to continue backing up.

The men looked both ways and told the driver to hold until a traffic light turned red down the block so he could safely pull out without being hit.

Lily started relaxing as they drove to the Hilton. She couldn't wait until the service was over.

Chapter 21

Lily arrived at the Hilton 40 minutes before everyone else. She paid the driver with cash and released him.

She had parked her Jeep Cherokee in the hotel's lot earlier. She had the two men drive one of the black SUVs to the hotel and instructed them to park beside her.

She didn't want anyone to know where she lived. After all, the men belonged to Jesús, and she didn't trust any of them.

So she hired the limo driver to pick her up at the hotel along with the two men and drive them to the church, the gravesite, and back to the Hilton. She had planned to change out of her black mourning clothes at the hotel after the Celebration of Life and go back to the warehouse.

The limo driver exited the luxury car to open the doors and faced Lily when she exited the vehicle.

"Please give me your insurance information so I can repair the limo. My boss is going to be furious."

Lily innocently looked at him. "I have no idea what you are talking about."

The driver growled, "You know exactly what I'm talking about. My boss may fire me for this damage."

Lily laughed. "Then you need another profession or learn how to drive."

She shot a warning look at the two men. Once again, they opened their jackets to show their guns.

Because they stood alone in the lot, when one of them put his hand on the butt of his gun, the driver became afraid and jumped in the limo, squealing his tires as he left the hotel. The men laughed.

The men followed Lily into the hotel and stood by the front door, watching people as if they were Secret Service guarding the President. Lily walked up to the front desk to announce her arrival.

"I'm Mrs. Clark. I'm expecting many guests to celebrate my husband's passing—I mean, his life. Is the room ready?"

"Yes, Mrs. Clark. Food and drinks have been set up in the room. My condolences. May I say you look awfully familiar?"

"No, you may not. Where do I find the room?"

Lily recognized the hotel receptionist from the years she had worn a wig to disguise herself when she had her illicit affair with Kyle. She couldn't believe the woman still worked there after all these years.

As a bellman led the way to the rented room, Lily couldn't help but think about how ironic the situation was. Her love affair and life with Kyle Clark began in the hotel when they had their rendezvous while they were married to other people. Now, their lives together were ending here. Did they live happily ever after? Well, she certainly was happy now. She had riches and, hopefully, Kyle's established medical clinic.

*****

The mourners started straggling into the large event room.

Lily sat at the table nearest a podium that had a microphone. At the back of the podium was a long, rectangular table filled with different species of beautiful white flowers. Lily had placed many photos of Kyle and herself. However, feeling unselfish, she put one large picture of Kyle by himself. A black guest book with a pen from the funeral home lay on a small round table next to it. It was just for show. She had plans of tossing it afterward. Non-alcoholic drinks, a large tub of ice, and an assortment of finger foods were on a side table, along with paper plates and plastic silverware. A large trash can sat at the end of the table.

There were white tablecloths and vases of flowers on each round table. She stopped counting the chairs when she reached 100.

Lily sat at her table, never bothering to get up and greet anyone. She was unaware of how inappropriate her actions were. She assumed everyone should approach her and offer their condolences. After all, she was a grieving widow.

The tables were filling up fast. Everyone felt unwelcome and uncomfortable, but wanted to pay their respects to Dr. Clark and leave as soon as possible.

They whispered about Lily's strange behavior.

One man told his wife, "By the looks of it, Dr. Clark is better off dead. He was probably in torment with that witch of a wife." The wife shushed him but laughed.

The man continued, "Look at her, sitting alone at the table, looking at her phone, acting like she is a queen. No one dares to sit with her. And who are those two men standing on each side of the door?" They both looked at the men and then at Lily with smirks written all over their faces.

A man who sat with eleven guests at one table said Lily reminded him of someone, but he couldn't place who. Another man asked, "Joffrey, from *Game of Thrones?* " They all laughed.

The room was noisy with chatter.

Lily finally looked up from her phone and searched the table reserved for Dr. Stone and the other doctors in her organization.

When everyone was seated, she finally stood and walked to the podium. She spoke to the crowd in a monotone voice, showing no emotion.

"Hello, thank you for coming. Kyle would be pleased to see so many people who have come to say goodbye. I'm too distraught, as you can imagine, to say anything, but if any of you would like to say a few words, please feel free to come up to the podium. In the meantime, help yourself to food and drinks."

She looked toward the doctor's table. "Dr. Stone, if you and the other doctors with you would be so kind as to meet with me afterward, it would be appreciated. Once again, thank you, thank you all for coming."

JoAnn stood. "What about the clinic, Mrs. Clark?"

Lily kept her temper in check but was furious that Kyle's office manager had the nerve to question her in front of everyone. But it was evident from the change in her facial expressions and rigid posture that the question perturbed her.

"The clinic will remain open. It's one of the reasons why I will be talking to the doctors today."

JoAnn asked, "Do the nurses still have their jobs? Our patients need their chemo treatments."

Lily was losing her patience and tried to answer calmly, "Yes, now sit down unless you want to come up and say something about your boss. This is not the time or place to discuss these matters. You'll have all your answers soon enough."

JoAnn was not afraid of Lily. She was the first to approach the podium. Lily sat down and went back to her phone.

Soon, JoAnn had everyone laughing. She could weave a story and had many funny ones. Even Lily had a chuckle or two. JoAnn had worked with Kyle for over 30 years and knew her husband better than she did.

After ten minutes, Lily tapped her watch; JoAnn cut the stories short and asked others to talk.

While people ate the food and told their funny stories, Lily left the room, telling the two men to stay. She needed a drink and went to the hotel's bar. She was tired of listening to how much people loved Kyle.

She drank two glasses of chardonnay and returned to the room, thankful that people had finished talking and eating.

Soon, everyone but the doctors left without saying goodbye to her.

She stood before the round table where the doctors sat, glaring at each of them as she circled it.

"Greetings to our organization of doctors: Dr. Kent Stone, Dr. Paul Wilson, Dr. Roy Hart, and Dr. Kyle Clark."

She waited for a response and then laughed, "Oops, I'm sorry. We seem to be missing one, such as an unfortunate accident with a drive-by shooter. It's amazing how many people die from accidents."

She continued to walk around the table as all the doctors sat quietly. She clicked her tongue against the roof of her mouth, making a tsk-tsk sound.

"Sure hope that doesn't happen to any of you."

Dr. Stone got up his nerve and said, "We get it, Lily. You can cut out the theatrics. Just tell us what you want!"

"First of all, Kent, explain why you're discharging Michael Mason's child and not performing the surgery today. I went to extreme lengths to make sure a bad kidney would be delivered to the operating room. And you would accidentally remove the good one."

"Oh, my God, Lily," Paul Wilson said. "I'm the nephrologist and was scheduled to be in surgery with Kent. I had no idea you were trying to kill the child. Did you, Kent?"

Kent looked down at his folded hands on the table and didn't answer.

"I can't believe this. Your schemes are getting out of hand, and I want no part of it."

Paul stood to leave.

The men at the door once again showed their guns.

Lily sternly said, "Sit your ass back down. I'm talking to Kent, and I want answers."

Kent raised his head. "I had no choice, Lily. The Masons threatened to fire me and call an attorney. Michael said I would be investigated. That means an investigator would find something, and we would all lose our medical licenses. Worse yet, we could all go to prison."

Roy Hart said, "He did the right thing, Lily. You know he did. He doesn't have a choice. Can't you see that?"

Kent Stone said impatiently, "So, if you'll excuse me, I told the Masons they could take the child home around 2 p.m. I need to sign the discharge papers. It's already 1:00 p.m., and I must get to the hospital."

Lily continues creeping around the table, thinking.

Kent said, "Dr. Savannah Hayes will go through the chart with a fine-toothed comb. She was already questioning the staff. What if she asks the right questions to the right people? And now that Dr. Clark is dead, she may be suspicious. After all, you almost killed her boyfriend, too. We're not dealing with stupid people here. Michael Mason is a billionaire. He doesn't care if he signs the child out AMA. The hospital bill will be pennies to him. One way or the other, he is taking his child home today, and none of us can stop it. Believe me, I tried."

Lily absent-mindedly said, "Oh, you don't need to worry about the doctor; I have her locked in the warehouse."

"WHAT? Lily, what have you done? Are you crazy? Her boyfriend and Michael Mason have probably already gone to the police." Kent was visibly upset.

"They don't know that it was me who had her kidnapped, nor do they have any idea about the warehouse."

Kent Stone didn't say another word. He knew his words would fall on deaf ears. He also knew Lily would kill him for telling Savannah's friends where the warehouse was located. He thought Michael Mason only wanted to talk to her. He had no idea the doctor had been kidnapped. Lily was getting more dangerous. She had to be stopped somehow, and he was secretly glad he had told the men where the warehouse was.

Lily spoke and pointed her finger at Dr. Wilson. "You may have caused me to lose a lot of money. You know the teen you operated on at the warehouse?"

"Which one?"

"The girl named Tess. She's the pretty one I had planned to sell to an older gentleman. She has a bad infection and fever from your inept surgery."

"Oh, my God. I'll check on her today. But what kind of gentleman buys young girls?"

Lily chuckled, "You'd be surprised. Anyway, there's no need for you to check on the girl. Dr. Hayes is taking care of her. It's best you all lay low for now."

She continued, "Okay, Kent, go discharge your patient. And find me an oncologist who can oversee the clinic for a while. I want that done ASAP. We need the patients to continue the organ transplants. I'm going back to the warehouse now to check on things. I'll call you when I need you."

Lily picked up her purse from the table where she had been sitting. She left the room, and the two men followed. She didn't bother changing her clothes as planned. She left the hotel, jumped in her Jeep, and raced out of the parking lot. The two gunmen weren't far behind in their vehicle.

The doctors sat talking. They had met a couple of times, but none had formulated a plan to get out of the mess they were all in.

"Kent, do I know you? Were you going to let the girl die on our operating table?" Dr. Wilson asked.

"Of course not; we weren't going to remove her kidneys. I had planned for the equipment to fail or the electricity to go out before we put her to sleep. I'm thankful Dr. Hayes had the Masons stop the chemo treatments and is taking her home. I could never commit murder. I swear! Anyway, I need to leave. I still don't know how Lily found out the girl was being discharged. The hospital has a mole, and I think I know who it is!"

Dr. Wilson said, "Kent, find out who the mole is and end it. The more people who know what we have been doing, the worse our odds are that we won't be caught. In the meantime, we must figure out how to escape this mess. I'm sorry we ever met Lily Mason-Clark."

"Amen." Dr. Stone said.

"Now, excuse me. I have to run."

Chapter 22

Danielle Mason was excited to go home. All the IVs, the electrodes on her chest, arms, and legs that detected her heart's electrical system, and the oxygen cannula had been removed.

"Will Uncle Robert be at the house when we get there?"

"No, sweetie. Somebody has to attend the business, but I'm sure he'll visit you soon. He knows you're being discharged today and sends you his love."

Danielle smiled and asked where Dr. Hayes was. "I haven't seen her. I want to thank her for making me feel better. I like her very much."

"We like her, too, honey. We haven't seen her either. She's probably busy helping other children." Michael hated to lie, but the statement was half true.

Little did they know.

Cathi opened a small suitcase. "Let's get you showered and changed out of the hospital gown. I bought you a pretty dress to wear home."

"Thank you, Mommy."

Danielle was excited when she saw the pink ruffled dress. Pink was her favorite color.

After the shower, Cathi used the hair dryer she had brought from home to blow-dry her hair. She helped her with the dress, escorted the child to a chair, and then slipped on white ankle socks with ruffles at the top and black patent leather Mary Jane shoes.

Danielle twirled in her new outfit.

"Now, let's comb your hair. I'll even let you wear some pink lipstick, but it's only because it's such a special day."

Cathi applied the light-colored lipstick to Dani's lips. She then decided to dot the child's cheeks with the satin lipstick. She made a dime-sized circle and blended the product with her finger to give her pale face some color.

"There, all done. Go to the bathroom and take a look."

Danielle reached for the tiara on the bedside chair and placed it back on her head. "Now, I really look like a princess, don't I, Daddy?"

Michael smiled. "You look like a beautiful princess, honey. And we love you so much."

Danielle twirled again and ran to the bathroom to look in the mirror. Cathi and Michael hugged, all full of smiles and joy.

A quick rap was heard on the door, and Dr. Stone entered the room. Behind him was a nurse with a wheelchair.

"You're all set to leave, I see. It looks as if the cancer is in remission. I advise you to take Danielle to a nephrologist in the near future. She still has one kidney that isn't functioning 100%."

He handed Cathi Dr. Paul Wilson's card, assuming she was the parent who made all the doctor's appointments.

Danielle walked out of the bathroom and ran into Dr. Stone's arms.

"Thank you for helping me get better."

Tears swelled in his eyes as he bent to hug the child. The nurse smiled, still waiting to take the patient outside the hospital for her parents to take her home.

"You're welcome, Princess." Dr. Stone said gently.

Cathi's heart melted, and she felt bad that Michael had spoken so harshly to him earlier.

Michael stood stone-faced, not appreciating the doctor's actions.

"Okay, doctor, we are leaving now. Dani, do you need help getting into the wheelchair?"

Dr. Stone tried again to get back into good standing with Michael.

"Michael, can we talk before you leave?"

Michael looked at him. "We have nothing to discuss. We are anxious to get our daughter home if you don't mind."

Dani got into the chair by herself, looked up at the nurse, and smiled sweetly. "I'm ready."

"Okay, Princess. Let's go."

As they left the room, Michael was glad the guard had already left. He didn't want Dani to question why a man was sitting at her door.

As the nurse wheeled Dani down the hall, they passed several children walking with IV poles, dressed in hospital gowns with different animals. They waved to her as they passed.

Michael ran to the elevators to press the down button as Cathi strolled beside Dani and the nurse.

Dr. Stone walked behind the nurses' station and stood behind Nancy, who was on the computer. He watched the Masons and the nurse enter the elevator. He tapped Nancy on her shoulder and said gruffly, "I want to talk to you."

She stood and looked at his face, questioning him with her eyes.

"Yes, doctor, how can I help you?"

"Let's go someplace that's private."

He followed her to her office and shut the door.

"How long have you been giving Lily Mason-Clark information about my patients?"

Nancy looked down and reached for the door. "I have no idea what you are talking about. Who is that?"

He kicked the door shut with his foot, grabbed her by the arm, and asked, "What is she using against you?"

"Let go of me, or I will scream."

He released her arm. In a softer voice, he began questioning her again, "I'm sure you realize by now that Lily is a very dangerous woman. How did she threaten you? Tell me, and maybe I can help."

Nancy relaxed and sat in her chair. "Will you use any information against me?"

"No, I want to help. Lily has been trying to harm the Masons because her son was killed in a plane crash ten years ago. She blames her ex-stepson, Michael, for the crash. She wants revenge and has been trying to harm their daughter. Thankfully, Michael

Mason put the guard by her room. So tell me, what information does she have on you?"

"Okay, I'll tell you. I am afraid of that woman. She found out that I was in a drug rehabilitation center. She threatened to tell the hospital if I didn't help her. I lied on my application when I took this job. She has been blackmailing me. I am thankful that Danielle Mason is going home, but I became frightened when I was the last to know about the discharge. I feared Lily would follow through on her threats against me if I didn't tell her. She wanted to know everything, and believe me, she wasn't happy when I told her about the guard and now the discharge."

"Has she asked about any of my other patients?"

"No, I swear—just the Mason girl. But I can tell you that she wears a wig and disguises herself. She comes to the floor pretending to be a nurse. She demanded that I let her look at all the patients' charts on my computer. She enters the children's rooms, but I haven't stopped her."

"Have you noticed if she types or changes nurses' notes or deletes anything?"

"Yes, she sits for hours going through the charts. My staff thinks she is a nurse with the Quality Assurance team."

"What name does she use to access the computers?"

Nancy opened her computer and looked through the patient's charts. She found what she was looking for.

"Bridget Harris."

"Bridget Harris died six months ago, didn't she?"

"Yes, I believe so."

"Okay, Nancy, thank you. Your secret is safe with me. You have stayed clean, correct?"

"Yes, I swear."

"Let me know if she continues to sneak up here. Could you secretly take a picture of her with your phone? Just don't get caught. We can use the photos for proof."

Nancy wasn't happy about being used again, but was relieved to have found a way out of Lily's claws.

Kent Stone was ecstatic. He had found his way out.

"Proof of what?" Nancy asked.

"It's illegal to look at patients' charts without permission due to HIPAA and other privacy laws. She could go to jail. With your photos for proof, we can call the police for impersonating a dead person, illegally going into patients' charts, and altering the records. That's a very serious crime on both state and federal levels."

Kent opened the office door and walked to the nurse's station with Nancy.

Nancy agreed, adding, "I can also get her for identity theft."

"Good point, Nancy."

They both felt the weight fall off their shoulders.

Kent Stone was feeling relieved and couldn't believe he had found a way out of Lily's clutches. He smiled as he walked energetically with a renewed bounce in each step toward the elevator. He couldn't wait to tell the other doctors the good news. He would call a meeting and celebrate at the Hilton tonight.

*****

The nurse wheeled Danielle in front of the hospital entrance and stopped at the designated area where all the patients would be discharged home. She would wait with the patient until the patient was safely inside her parents' vehicle.

Cathi stood with the nurse while Michael ran to get the car parked in the four-story garage.

When he stepped off the elevator in the garage, two men dressed in black sandwiched him and grabbed his arms.

"Come with us."

Michael looked around for help, but the third-floor garage was empty of people.

The men forcefully led him into the back of a utility van and climbed in beside him. They gagged him with a cloth and handcuffed him behind his back. They sat without speaking.

Michael was not a coward by any means, but he kept quiet, feeling the press of steel on his side.

He instinctively knew what was happening. Lily was kidnapping him. But why? Money?

A van pulled up in front of the hospital. Cathi and the nurse casually conversed and didn't think anything about the van.

The passenger's door slid open horizontally to the side. Two men quickly jumped out and grabbed Danielle Mason out of her wheelchair and threw her in the empty van, void of back seats. The driver sped away, squealing his tires.

Cathi screamed and chased after the van, but it was too fast.

The nurse pulled out her cellphone from her pocket and began to dial the police.

Cathi ran back to the nurse.

Cathi was intelligent and fast on her feet. She lied, "Put the phone down, please. My husband and I know who did this, and we already have the cops and FBI involved. These people are dangerous, and we don't want more cops involved. It may screw up the ongoing investigation. My husband will be here any

236

minute. Just go back inside, please. Don't tell anyone what you've seen."

"But, how do you know who these men are? I mean, they took your daughter."

"Why do you think we had a guard at my daughter's room? It's all about money."

The nurse knew the Masons were wealthy, and the explanation made sense.

"We're on it. Please, don't call the police."

The nurse turned to leave, but said, "Then why didn't you have the guard stand here with us? You put all of us in danger. You're lucky no one was hurt."

Cathi was embarrassed. She stuttered, "We made a mistake. I'm sorry. It was foolish and naive to believe it wouldn't happen here."

As Cathi was spilling lies, one of the men in the van in the garage got a call on his radio.

"All clear."

One of the men uncuffed Michael but left the gag in his mouth, opened the back of the van, and pushed him out with his feet. Michael fell to the ground and quickly rolled because the van was backing up.

He removed the gag from his mouth and ran to his car. As he started the car, he was grateful he only had to push a button. He backed out of the parking space and drove as fast as he could without endangering anyone.

As he waited for a car that was pulling out, he called Cathi, but couldn't get any service in the garage.

He finally reached the hospital's entrance and was thankful to see Cathi sitting on a bench. She was crying and wringing her hands. She didn't understand why Lily would want to harm Danielle. Did she know the child was Savannah's and Noah's? How could she know if she did? Or was it for ransom money? Lily hated Michael for removing her from the mansion and stripping her of all her riches after Daniel Mason died. So, was it purely for revenge? And why did she want to kidnap Savannah? Robert had said it was about Dr. Clark's will. None of it made any sense.

She was relieved and jumped up when she saw Michael. She ran to the car, swiftly opened the car door, and sat in the passenger's seat, screaming, "The bitch took our baby, Michael. I swear I will kill her. I want her back, Michael. Where the hell have you been?"

"We'll get her back, baby. Don't worry."

Cathi continued to cry, "Please call the cops. Please, Michael. And tell me what took you so long."

He rapidly told her about the men in the utility van, using voice commands on his phone as he drove.

"Dial Robert."

Robert answered on the third ring.

Michael frantically said, "They took Dani, Robert. We need to get her back, NOW."

Robert put his hands to his head and bent over. He couldn't believe what he was hearing, but he didn't want to sound alarmed so that he could support his friend. He straightened and tried to remain calm, but he began pacing.

"Tell me what happened. Where are you? How did they take her?"

Michael breathlessly said, "Cathi and I will come to you. Tell me where you are, and I'll explain everything."

"We're all practicing maneuvers at the warehouse you told us about. You're not far from the Children's Hospital. See you shortly."

When the conversation ended, Robert howled loudly to release his anger and emotional turmoil. The frightening scream startled the men, who looked at him, questioning what had happened.

Michael beat his hands on the steering wheel, cursing and screaming out of anger and fear. Cathi tried to console him and asked him to be careful while driving.

"Michael. We need to keep a cool head. Don't do anything stupid, please."

Chapter 23

Savannah was napping on her side when the tall man entered her room and awakened her.

She had braided her long hair in one plait down her back earlier because she had been unable to wash and comb her hair. The man was now pulling on the braid.

She rolled over to face him, stretching her arms and yawning.

"Now what?"

She was tired because she had been caring medically and spiritually for all the girls in one of the rooms. She wasn't getting proper nourishment, and the emotional turmoil was stressing her out. She hadn't slept well. However, she was grateful she was busy and could help these poor girls. She would rather be tired from being too busy than sit and do nothing all day, worrying about Dani, Robert, and her job.

Earlier, she had met six teenage boys in another room. The room was smaller than the girls' and had five bunk beds. At least the mattresses and sheets looked clean.

The tall man led her to a door next to the girl's room and opened it. He rushed her into the room, and her mouth dropped.

She introduced herself as Doctor Savannah to the unruly boys, who were fighting and yelling at each other.

It was challenging to converse with them because they didn't trust her and didn't believe she was a doctor.

She realized she didn't look like one, with dirty hair, dirty white shoes, and torn jeans. She probably had body odor, too.

She didn't want to tell them she had escaped and had been caught, because they would have asked her about the failed attempt. She feared that, with testosterone coursing through their veins, they would try to escape for themselves, and more harm would come to them.

She tried to convince them that she wasn't there to harm them. She asked if they had any questions for her.

Their only questions were about the operating tables and hooks at the east end of the hall that they had seen. She could have answered the questions, but she knew answering them about the tables would frighten them. The girls already knew because of Tess. In her experience, males seemed to be more

242

frightened of surgery than females, so she told them she didn't know.

However, she explained the gambrel and meat hooks, knowing that the boys could imagine pigs and cattle carcasses hanging in the old meat building at one time. They thought that was cool.

One boy said, "I bet they can hang people from those, too."

Savannah's thoughts exactly, but she kept quiet.

A pillow was thrown across the room, hitting the boy in the head.

"Shut up, stupid. They aren't strong enough to hang a person."

"Are so."

"Are not."

The boys started fighting.

"Boys, why am I here? Does one of you need a doctor?"

The older boy said snarkily, "Yeah, I have a boner I need help with."

The boys laughed.

Savannah looked at the tall man with pleading eyes to get her out of the room. He laughed and took her back to her room.

She suspected that Lily wanted her to know there were more victims now.

The incident had happened earlier in the day, but Savannah surmised it was now late afternoon. The warehouse's overhead lights had come on even though she could see daylight out the dirty windows.

The tall man had motioned for her to follow him to the cabinet near the surgical tables. In broken English, he told her to get needles and thread.

She had difficulty understanding him and asked him to repeat himself three times.

The man began to pantomime. He held an imaginary needle in one hand. He brought up an imaginary thread to the needle with the other hand after licking it, and pretended to push the thread through the eye of the needle. He hummed the song, *Eye of the Tiger,* hoping she would understand the eye part.

She stared at him. He raised the hand that held the imaginary needle to his eye, pretending he had poked himself, and said, "Ouch."

That made her laugh. The tall man had a sense of humor. He had always been nice to her. She sensed the man was a gentle giant, but short on brain cells. She was patient with him and gently urged him on, saying, "It's okay, you can tell me."

He pointed to the thread on his pants, and Savannah finally understood. He smiled.

"Oh, someone needs stitches? You want me to get a needle and thread?"

"Sí"

"Is it for the girl, Tess?"

He shook his head, "No, boy."

She wondered if one of the boys had been operated on and his stitches were coming loose.

The tall man took the key and opened the cabinet so she could retrieve supplies.

Lily had allowed her to care for the kids because she kept them calm, especially the girls. Jesús's men had complained about all the screaming and nonstop chatter between the girls. The man at the monitor turned the volume down, and Lily was angry. She wanted to hear what they said about Savannah.

The boys were a different story. The men loved watching the boys fight, so they turned the volume up and even bet on the winner. Once, they bet against the smallest and youngest to lose, thinking it was a sure bet, but the kid surprised them. It was the men's entertainment. They enjoyed the fighting and gambling. Sometimes when Lily or Jesús wasn't around, they would bring out the tequila.

But for now, the man at the monitor watched as one of the boys looked seriously hurt, profusely bleeding from his head.

The tall man unlocked the door and ushered Savannah into the room. A boy about thirteen had been fighting, but he wouldn't say who he had been fighting with. He knew enough from being on the streets to keep his mouth shut.

The young boy was lying on a lower bunk with his head on a grungy pillowcase. Blood had invaded the cotton threads and had spread.

Savannah tried not to look concerned, but she looked at the tall man and asked him to move the boys who surrounded the bunk away so she could examine his head.

She identified that the blood was coming from his scalp. Due to tiny arteries and veins, the scalp is very rich in blood supply. She was thankful the cut was superficial and only needed Steri-Strips instead of stitches.

She asked the tall man to take her back to the cabinet to get what she needed. In the meantime, she told the boy to hold a gauze bandage against his head to help stop the bleeding until she returned.

At the supply cabinet, she returned the needle and thread and scooped up more gauze and a bottle of sterile saline solution to cleanse the wound since she didn't trust the soap and water from the old faucet in the boy's room. Who knew how rusty the pipes were that could potentially cause an infection?

She was thankful the cabinet was well stocked with medical supplies. The doctor who had performed the surgeries in the warehouse knew what they were doing regarding supplies. However, she doubted the person's surgical skills and wondered if they were even a real doctor. Looking at Tess's wound, she doubted the person knew what they were doing.

She handed the tall man some supplies to carry in his large hands. With both of them carrying an armful of supplies, she felt she didn't need to keep going back and forth to the cabinet looking for more.

She stood, tired, hoping she had chosen the right supplies and remembered to grab some Tylenol.

As she reached back to place the medicine in the man's hands, the last of the sunlight streamed through the window, and something shiny caught her attention.

Was that a tiny tiara lying on the floor by the tall man's foot?

He kicked it across the room, and she watched as it tumbled across the concrete floor.

She dropped the supplies and ran toward the object. She picked it up and studied it.

"Oh my God, this is the tiara I gave Dani."

She dropped to her knees and looked up at the office on the second floor.

She yelled as loud as she could, "LILY!"

The tall man dropped his supplies and grabbed her arm, forcing her to stand.

He said, "No, no, no good."

She ignored him and screamed,

"LILY, YOU COWARD, YOU EVIL BITCH, WHAT HAVE YOU DONE?"

Savannah started crying, a waterfall of grief, placing her hands over her face, her shoulders shuddering with agony. The tall man gently wrapped his big arm around her, lifted her to her feet, and led her back to the boy's room. He knew precisely what Lily had done.

The tall man locked the door behind him and returned to gather all the supplies scattered around the floor. He looked up at the office and noticed no one was looking at him. He picked up the tiny tiara and hid it under one of the operating tables, realizing the toy was meaningful to the nice doctor.

The boys stared at Savannah when she entered their room, realizing she had been crying because her eyes were red and puffy. She was wiping her face with her naked arms of the tears from her eyes and the snot from her nose. She was visibly shaking. Her head was down, her body slumped, holding herself up against the wall.

The boys watched in awe at the obvious transition in front of them. She went from a crying, broken person into a Phoenix rising from the ashes. She took a deep breath and gathered her composure. She straightened her shoulders and looked at everyone with intent and courage. She adjusted her invisible tiara. She walked proudly over to the injured boy and sat beside him. She stroked his tears from his face and hugged him, telling him to stay strong. They both needed the human touch of kindness.

She spoke to all of them, and just like a mother would, she scolded them and demanded they stop fighting and hurting each other. Like a football coach, she demanded they work as a team.

The tall man entered the room with all the supplies in his arms and dropped them on the boy's bed. He noticed the fighting had stopped and saw all the boys were listening to Savannah. She wasn't asking for violence, but for peace.

Savannah looked at the tall man and thanked him.

She became professional, cleansed the boy's wound, and applied Steri-Strips. She was relieved to see the boy's platelets were working and clotting the blood. She assured him he would be okay, but he might have a headache. She gave him the Tylenol.

She willed herself to smile at him and became the doctor she was meant to be.

The boys sat quietly, wonderstruck, at what had made the doctor cry, respecting that she had become strong.

They stared at her and didn't move as she helped the bleeding boy. Knowing she was one of them, they felt her pain and admired her strength.

They sensed she had also been kidnapped and wanted to make her proud. They nodded in agreement as Savannah spoke and asked if they would behave.

The tall man led her back to her room as she said goodbye to the boys.

She lay on her bed, under the sheet, and searched for the scalpel she had hidden. She couldn't find it.

She closed her eyes in disbelief and tried searching for it again, reaching further into the mattress.

Her hand felt the hard metal of the surgical blade and sighed with relief.

She wondered which room Danielle was in. The poor child must be so frightened. She hoped she was with the girls and not in the room with the beds that had bedbugs. She would demand to see her.

She looked at the monitor and shouted sternly, "LILY, I demand that you let me see Danielle Mason, NOW."

The monitor didn't move or blink. She only hears her shallow, upper-chest breathing, a result of the stress.

Savannah was angry and frustrated. She willed herself not to cry again. She turned her back on the monitor and pulled the sheet over her. She slipped the scalpel into the side pocket of her jeans.

She prayed to God to forgive her, and fell asleep thinking about Danielle and how she was going to kill Lily.

Chapter 24

At dusk, Robert and his men parked their vehicles in the abandoned warehouse's parking lot, where Savannah had fled and been caught. The team exited their trucks and moved quickly with their equipment down the dirt road toward Lily's warehouse. They planned to secure the perimeter, taking positions to cover any escape routes and entry points. They would take out and neutralize Lily's men outside the building first. They would slash the van's and black SUV's tires with a knife so the men couldn't escape.

They moved forward as a trained unit. They covered each other, using hand signals as they walked around the men's vehicles and Lily's Jeep after David used a silencer to shoot out the two cameras on top of the roof. Finding the coast was clear outside, the three Berets, led by the team leader, Lee Hunt, wearing gloves and appropriate footwear, began using tactical harnesses and rope ascenders to climb up the east side of the building to position themselves on the roof.

Robert and the other six men ran back to David's monster truck and slowly drove to the end of the dirt road, waiting for signals from Lee Hunt, who was now safely on the roof with his men. He looked down one of the skylights and saw Savannah kneeling on the floor with her hands cuffed.

He gave the signal.

*****

Earlier, inside the warehouse, Savannah was awakened by noise. While lying in her bed, she heard the familiar sound of her metal door opening and high heels resounding on the concrete floor.

Lily entered the room with the tall man. He looked anxious, and Lily looked angry. The tall man kept his head down and would not look at Savannah.

Lily's eyebrows and mouth were downturned. She was in one of her bad moods again.

Savannah thought it was typical of Lily's demeanor and refused to be intimidated.

She had to pee.

"Damn it, Lily, can't a girl have any privacy? Go away and give me five minutes to use the bucket and brush my teeth."

Lily was in no mood to be generous.

253

"Pee or shit your pants. I don't give a damn. Tell me where my husband's will is, NOW, or else."

Savannah rolled her eyes. "I told you, I don't know where it is. How many times do I have to tell you?"

Savannah sat on the side of the bed and stretched, ignoring Lily's threats.

"Now, excuse me while I go to the bathroom. Come back later. We need to talk. I know you have Danielle Mason. If you let us go, maybe we can make a trade, and I promise to help you find the will and prenuptial agreement."

Lily laughed and snapped her fingers with an evil glare, and one of the gunmen escorted Dani into the room. He held the girl tightly by her arm and had a gun to her head.

Danielle was frightened. Her green eyes were red and swollen from crying. Her long hair straddled her face, her skin was pale, and her lips quivered from fear. All the blood seemed to have left her body, as did her hopes of going home. She was clearly in shock. She stood motionless and looked at Savannah without recognition.

"Talk, or I'll kill the girl."

Savannah became outraged. She suddenly stood and lunged at Lily. Lily stepped backward and almost lost her balance. The tall man grabbed Savannah's arms and forced her to sit back down.

"Put the bitch in handcuffs and bring them both to me," Lily demanded angrily.

Lily turned and left the room.

Savannah spoke, "Dani, Dani, it's me, Dr. Savannah. Do you remember me, honey?"

Dani stood staring into space as if in a trance.

The tall man placed Savannah's hands in front of her body and handcuffed her. She was thankful that he hadn't cuffed her behind her back.

He led her out of the room along with the gunman, who still held onto Dani's arm. The child allowed him to direct her without any fight.

Savannah looked at the tall man with pleading eyes to help her as he followed the gunman, but he ignored her.

Savannah couldn't take her eyes off Dani until she saw where Lily was standing.

She struggled, trying to fight off the tall man as yellow urine soaked her white pants, not out of fear, but out of necessity. She was not ashamed. She was only human, after all.

"No, no, you can't do this, Lily."

Lily had them walk to the east end of the warehouse, where the hooks were dangling from the ceiling.

Savannah fought, kicking and fumbling as the man raised her arms and applied the meat hook to the middle part of the metal chain between each cuff.

Lily handed the gunman a piece of rope. He put his gun in his waistband, tied Dani's arms together, and applied a hook to the rope. He pulled on the wire attached to a pulley system and lifted her a foot off the floor. Dani passed out. She dangled off the floor, her head fell, and her chin was now resting on her chest. Her hair swung down over her face.

He then pulled Savannah's wire, but she kicked him again and struggled.

Lily berated the gunman, "Are you stupid. Pull her up."

Savannah pleaded, "Please, Lily, why are you doing this?"

Lily stood in front of Savannah far enough away that Savannah could not kick her.

"As you already know, this brat is Michael Mason's kid. I want to destroy him as he destroyed my son, Noah."

Savannah looked Lily dead in the face and said, "Damn it, Lily. Then you'll be killing Noah's daughter. She's my child. Noah is the father. I allowed the Masons to adopt her when I went to medical school."

Savannah was yelling now, not caring who knew the truth, "SHE'S YOUR GRANDDAUGHTER, LILY. I SWEAR IT! Please don't hurt her. Do what you will to me, but I beg you to let her go."

Lily took a step back, not believing what she had just heard.

Savannah spoke rapidly, "I can prove it. I gave blood to test my DNA, as did the Masons. Dr. Stone can give you the results, Lily. Please, cut her loose. She's in shock and needs medical attention. You are killing Noah's child. Look at her green eyes. They are my eyes. Look at her curly blond hair. It's Noah's hair. Lily, please."

Savannah was crying now, pleading for her child's life.

Lily nodded her head to the men to bring them down. Dani slumped to the floor. Savannah kneeled in front of her daughter to feel for signs of life and was grateful when she felt a heartbeat with blood rushing through her carotid artery on the right side of her neck.

Lily looked at the child on the floor. Was she her beautiful boy's child? She instantly thought it could be true since Noah and Savannah were both on The Lady Jane in the Bahamas together over ten years ago.

Shouting interrupted her thoughts. Two of her men, guns drawn, were yelling in Spanish as they ran down the metal stairs from the office.

Up on the roof, Lee Wilson had already signaled to David.

The powerful truck moved quickly, grinding through gears as it climbed the three steps, until it crashed through the corrugated garage door.

The deep rumble and roar of the massive engine and crushing metal were deafening. Fragments of metal clanged and bent, and the debris flew upward and landed with a loud bang. The door collapsed to the ground in utter destruction, and David rolled over the torn metal inside the warehouse and finally stopped the vehicle.

Meanwhile, Lily ducked from debris and hurriedly told both men, "Grab them, and follow me to my car. Shoot anyone who comes close."

The tall man grabbed Savannah, and the gunman picked Dani up and swung her over his left shoulder, holding his gun in his right hand.

The warehouse was in total chaos, with men yelling and bullets hitting their targets and ricocheting. Anger and fear swept through the room, contributing to the pandemonium.

Lee Hunt and one of his men dressed in military fatigues crashed through the skylights in the roof above them, descending on ropes while firing their M16 assault rifles into the office windows on the second floor.

As the berets began their descent, the seven men in the truck jumped out with their automatic AK-47 rifles, positioned themselves behind the vehicle, and started shooting, taking out the two men who had descended downstairs.

Bullets were flying from both sides.

Robert looked to his right and saw Savannah being dragged backward by a tall man and Dani over another man's shoulder, leading them toward an exit door.

"Hold your fire," Robert yelled over the noise. "Lily has them. Don't shoot them."

Savannah and Robert locked eyes. He silently cursed because they didn't disable Lily's Jeep.

He nodded and gave her a small, encouraging smile. She nodded back, but the men positioned themselves behind the two females to use them as shields. Lily was behind the tall man, and they backed out the front metal door, down the steps, and to Lily's Jeep.

Robert and David kept their guns aimed at Lily and the men, watching every step they took.

When they reached the Jeep, David, who had been a sniper in the military, stood behind his truck, aimed, pulled the trigger, and killed the gunman with a bullet to his head. Savannah reached out and caught Dani before she hit the ground. The tall man knelt behind the two victims and picked up the dead man's gun. Lily hid behind him, instructing him to put her hostages in the back of her Jeep.

David did not have a good shot now because the tall man made Savannah stand before him, holding the gun to her back. He was taller than she, so he bent his knees to make himself shorter.

The tall man yelled, "I have a gun. I will kill. Stop shooting."

Savannah held the limp Dani upright under one of her armpits.

Adrenaline rushed through her, giving her enough strength to maintain her balance and support Dani's weight. The man pulled and tugged on Savannah, who struggled to hold Dani up, dragged them behind the Jeep, and opened the tailgate. He placed them both in the cargo area, closed it, and jumped into the backseat. Lily had already jumped in the driver's seat and ducked down, using the remote in her pocket to start the car. Then, Lily sped off.

Meanwhile, gunfire continued in the warehouse.

Jesùs was hit in the head by a bullet that had crashed through the office windows. He died instantly.

With their leader dead, the men ducked from flying glass and bullets and hid behind the desks, knowing they didn't have a chance of survival because they were overpowered. They yelled in Spanish that they surrendered, yet continued to shoot through the windows and the office's wooden door in case the men came up the stairs.

Another Beret was still on the roof. He shot out the glass of the skylight above the office and began shooting down. Lee Hunt advanced up the metal stairs and emptied his magazine full of ammo into the office. He reloaded with more ammo.

Suddenly, all the firing stopped. The warriors believed all the men in the office were dead or at least injured.

Robert yelled, "Anybody hurt?"

Peter sat on the floor, leaning against a back wall, and yelled back, "I've been hit."

The other soldiers downstairs yelled that they were ok.

Robert ran to Peter, thankful that a bullet only wounded him and did not kill him. Peter was bleeding from his left arm. Robert removed his belt and used it as a tourniquet.

While Robert attended to Peter, David motioned for one of his men to follow him up the stairs. Each SEAL, like the Berets, wore bulletproof vests, military gear, and gloves. They expertly carried their rifles, ready to start shooting, but knew Lee was in the office and had them covered, unless he was dead.

The men carefully and quietly walked up to the office and kicked the door in. With rifles raised, they slowly walked over broken glass and found ten men lying dead on the floor.

Lee sat on a desk, rifle secured, and said, "Took you long enough." David did not laugh.

"Clear," David shouted out the broken windows.

David and the men looked at the monitors and saw the children in the rooms. They left the monitors running so the police could see what they saw and use it as evidence against Lily. One of the men retrieved the keys to the doors from the dead men's pockets to unlock the rooms downstairs.

They returned downstairs.

The other Beret on the roof descended through the skylight and joined his men, who were now busy checking the perimeter of the building.

David offered one of the keys to Robert, who sat beside Peter on the cold concrete floor.

Robert thanked him and took the keys.

He stood and walked to the nearest door on the southeast side of the warehouse, opening it with a swipe of the key. It was empty; he guessed it must have been Savannah's prison cell.

He moaned, and tears swelled as he realized Savannah's situation.

He spoke out loud, "I'll find you, baby. I'm coming to get you."

He left the door open and walked next door to the second room, which was also empty. He almost cried when he saw the empty beds with the dirty mattresses. He asked himself, "What evil could do this to another human?"

He walked out and left the door open.

He walked next door to the third room, opened it, and found the teenage boys sitting on their beds, talking at once. They had heard the gunshots and shouting, wondering if the good or bad guys had won. Or were they all bad?

The room became silent as they stared at Robert, wondering who he was and if he was there to kill them.

"Boys, I am a friend of Dr. Savannah's. We came to rescue her and you. Don't worry, the men who brought you here will not be hurting you anymore. I'm locking the door when I leave for your safety until the police arrive. You haven't seen me, okay?"

They stayed silent after thanking the man and nodding their understanding.

Robert shut the door behind him and walked to the fourth door, next to the boy's room. He opened it and suddenly heard screaming from the young, frightened girls. They were all huddled together in a corner of the room.

"Shhh, shhh, I'm one of the good guys. I'm here to rescue Dr. Savannah. The police will he here soon. They will take care of you. Be brave."

Tess spoke, "Dr. Savannah said the same thing. We will. And, thank you, sir. Is she ok? Can we see her? I want to thank her for taking care of me and making me better."

Robert wasn't expecting questions or gratitude.

"I'm sorry, girls, I have to leave. The police will be here shortly. I'm shutting the door for your protection. You haven't seen me, okay?"

The girls nodded in agreement.

He shut the door quietly and left the room, hoping the children wouldn't identify him to the police.

He unlocked the fifth door, next to the girl's room, and found boxes stacked to the ceiling. He removed his Swiss Army knife from his pocket and carefully opened several boxes.

On one side of the room, the boxes held medical supplies. On the other side of the room, Robert found a copious amount of drugs. He didn't touch them, fearful they contained cocaine and fentanyl. He let out a low whistle and couldn't believe the amount of money invested. He estimated the street value would be in the millions. He left, closing the door behind him.

He asked one of the men to look for tape in the medical supplies.

When one of the men returned with the surgical tape, he used the scissors on his knife to cut pieces about two inches long. Then, he began taping a key to the closed doors for the police to find.

In the meantime, Peter's arm had been bandaged by one of the men who had found the medical supplies. Thankfully, a bullet had only grazed his arm.

All the men stood milling around in the warehouse, waiting for Robert's orders.

"I'm going up to the office and will call the police from one of the dead men's cellphones. Then we need to get out of here. Let's meet back at DM Yachts to discuss our next move. Clean up any evidence."

"Hooyah"

"Hooah"

Each team started gathering their gear and supplies and began covering up any evidence by collecting all the expended bullets from their guns, while Robert called the police.

When Robert returned downstairs, the ex-military men, including Peter, the ex-cop, stood in a disciplined line at attention, waiting for him.

"All done?" Robert asked.

"Yes, sir. All done," David answered.

"Then let's get the hell out of here."

*****

When the police swarmed in and found the dead men, the drugs, and the unharmed children, one of the uniformed policemen asked each of them to describe any man they had seen.

None of them had an answer. They all denied seeing any man.

Chapter 25

Lily drove her Jeep toward her home in Norfolk, five miles over the speed limit so that she wouldn't be stopped by the police for speeding. She was stoic, never uttering a word, focused on her driving, while thinking about her next steps.

The tall man, now the only survivor of Jesùs' men, sat in the back seat, holding a gun on Savannah and the girl who were in the cargo area.

He was wondering what the evil Lily had planned for him now. He thought of the men they had left behind. Were they all dead now? He had no idea, but he was smart enough to know the men who crashed into the warehouse were trained gunmen and would probably be looking for them.

Savannah had positioned her body close to her child, who was still out cold.

Savannah had no inkling that Dani was feigning to be asleep, but was aware. Dani felt she was good at pretending, like when she pretended to be sick to avoid a school day. But she knew Savannah was lying close to her, so she couldn't roll around in the moving car. She instinctively understood Savannah was trying to protect her, so she kept her eyes closed and her body limp.

Savannah was still handcuffed and couldn't examine Dani, but could only pray they would both survive their discouraging circumstances. She wondered where Lily was taking them, hoping against hope that Lily would uncuff her to attend to Dani. She was thankful no one had checked her pockets and found the scalpel. She began formulating a plan to talk her way out of the cuffs, even if she had to grovel, which was so unlike her stubborn self. But in this case, she had no choice. She would do whatever it took to survive. She had to protect Dani.

Once Lily reached her home, she opened the garage door, pulled her Jeep in, and closed the heavy door with a remote.

"OUT," she shouted.

"Carry the child upstairs to the bedroom on the right. The doctor can stay with her, but keep the cuffs on her," she said to the tall man.

The man carried Dani upstairs to the bedroom on the right and gently laid her on the bed. Savannah begrudgingly followed him up the stairs and into the bedroom.

Savannah whispered, "Please tell me your name."

"Mateo, doctor."

"Please call me Savannah. Mateo, you know Lily is an evil woman who doesn't care about any of us. You can't trust her. You know this in your heart, don't you?"

Mateo stared at Savannah, but nodded.

"Si," he said.

At this point, he knew he was also a captive. He thought about fleeing, but didn't know where he was or where he would go.

"Please, release me from my handcuffs so I can attend to the child. Please, Mateo. We are in this dangerous game of Lily's and must stick together."

Savannah hoped that using the tall man's name was a psychological means of survival. She was trying to gain his trust and make him distrust Lily.

Mateo stood quietly, trying to comprehend the circumstances. He realized that Lily was evil, and he was afraid of her. He decided to self-preserve and walked away, shutting the door behind him when he left the room. After all, he did have a gun to protect himself.

Savannah sat on the side of the bed and gently shook Dani, who was lying on her back. She was relieved that Dani had some color back in her face and was breathing normally. She felt for a resting heart rate and found it beating around 70 beats, as far as she could tell. The child moaned and turned over away from Savannah.

"We are safe, Dani. It's Dr. Savannah. You know I won't hurt you, sweetheart."

Dani rolled onto her back and cried. "What is happening? Where are we, doctor?"

Savannah didn't lie. "I'm not sure, but I think we are in our captor's home. Your Uncle Robert tried to save us with some men, but Lily managed to drag us out of the warehouse and put us in her Jeep. He won't give up. He'll find us again. You passed out in the warehouse. How are you feeling?"

"I don't remember anything. I must have fainted again. I do that sometimes, but I feel okay now. I'm still scared and tired, though. I'm glad you're with me."

Savannah smiled and ran her fingers through Dani's hair. "Would you like me to lie with you as you rest? Then we can shower when you feel up to it.

"Yes, please. My mother sings songs to me when she lies beside me. Can you sing me a song?"

Savannah smiled and said, "My mother used to sing songs to me, too. I'll sing you my favorite. Now, close your eyes."

Savannah started singing her childhood song.

Hey, hey, oh playmate,

Come out and play with me.

And bring your dollies three.

Climb up my apple tree.

Slide down my rain barrel.

Into the cellar door

And we'll be jolly friends

Forever more, more, more.

So sorry, playmate

I cannot play with you

My dolly's got the flu

Boo hoo hoo hoo hoo hoo

Ain't got no rain barrel

Ain't got no cellar door

But we'll be jolly friends

Forever more, more, more.

Dani drifted off to sleep, and Savannah sat up and looked helplessly around the spacious bedroom. She noticed remnants of old bloodstains on the white wool carpet that looked like someone had tried to scrub them to no avail. She got out of bed and walked to a closed double door. She opened the closet doors and saw men's clothing hanging neatly. She saw folded sheets and blankets on a top shelf. She checked the pockets in all the clothing, looking for something to help free herself of her handcuffs. She only found receipts and a prescription pad. Evidently, this had been Kyle Clark's bedroom before Lily had him murdered.

She opened the dresser drawers and searched, moving her hands under the neatly stacked rolls of socks and underwear, but found nothing.

She walked into the ensuite bathroom and opened the medicine cabinet. She found nothing of value there either.

Exasperated, she decided to see if she could reach the scalpel hidden in her pants pocket. She walked to the bedroom door and locked it from inside. She held her ear to the door and listened for any sounds of movement or talking. When she was satisfied she might be safe, she walked back into the bathroom, slid the shower curtain over, and sat on the edge of the tub. She carefully unzipped the pocket on her right upper leg and pulled out the scalpel. She hoped she could use it to unlock the cuffs.

She tried to insert the blade's end into the keyhole but found the tip was too large. She placed the scalpel back in her pocket and zipped it. Then, she opened the bathroom cabinet drawers, searching for tweezers, a bobby pin, or anything that could fit into the keyhole.

She suddenly heard the bedroom doorknob shake and a loud knocking. After closing the drawers, she froze in place momentarily and tiptoed to the door.

"Food. Unlock, por favor."

Savannah opened the door. Mateo stood with a tray of sandwiches, cubes of different cheeses, and two bottles of water. He thrust the tray toward Savannah, urging her to take it.

She thanked him, took the tray with both hands, and balanced it while walking toward the bed. She managed to set the tray down and noticed a wooden toothpick inserted into a cube of cheddar cheese. It was just like Lily trying to be perfect in every way.

After Mateo closed the door, she removed the pick and tried inserting it into the cuff's keyhole, but she became frustrated when that didn't work either. She was not experienced with unlocking handcuffs, so her only solution was to coerce Mateo to set her free.

She lay back on the bed, covering Dani with a blanket she had found in the closet. She ate sitting up in bed while listening to her sleeping child's soft, light breathing.

While she chewed the cheese, she looked at the bedside stand. She had not searched it yet. She opened the drawer and found an old cellphone and a small flashlight. The flashlight worked. Excitedly, she turned on the phone, but the battery was dead. She stood, scooped her hands under pieces of paper and old photographs, and felt a rubber cord. BINGO. It was a charger for the phone. She quickly plugged one end of the charger into the phone. She looked around the room for an electrical outlet. She wanted to use an inconspicuous outlet that her captors wouldn't find the phone.

She decided to pull out the heavy, oversized bedside stand, which was situated between the bed and a side wall. She struggled, but took her time to inch it away from the back wall, and scooting it on the thick carpet wasn't easy. She leaned over and saw where the lamp was plugged into an outlet behind the furniture. She moved the lamp to the side, lay her body over the nightstand, and stretched her arms to plug the other end of the charger into the wall socket under the lamp's plug.

She fiddled with inserting the plug. After several attempts, she unplugged the lamp to improve her vision and plugged in the power adapter into the lower outlet. Then, she plugged the lamp back into the top receptacle.

She was ecstatic when the phone dimly sprang to life.

She looked at the time on the phone. It was 4 p.m.

She dropped the phone on the floor behind the nightstand. She would wait an hour to see if it was half-charged. Then, she sat on the floor and scooted the furniture back into its place with her feet.

She rested back on the bed, thinking Lily wasn't as brilliant as she thought she was. She had made a colossal mistake.

*****

Downstairs, in the back of the house, Lily had forced herself to eat to sustain her energy. Mateo sat at the kitchen counter, growing weary, watching her pace the kitchen floor. She suddenly swiveled on her heels and walked up the hallway to the foyer at the front entrance. She stood on the black and white checked marble floors as she peered up the stairs to the right of the front door. Holding onto the open railing, she wondered if the child upstairs was truly her granddaughter. She thought about going up to speak to her, surprising herself that she actually had feelings. She had loved her son, Noah, so much and had hardened her heart after his death. She vowed no one would ever make her grieve so hard again, so she became cold and bitter.

She hated everyone and everything. She promised Noah and herself that she would make Michael suffer because he allowed Noah to fly on the company jet that had mechanical problems. She was angry that she never got to say goodbye to her boy. She was furious that his body was never recovered from the wreckage, and the Atlantic Ocean was his graveyard.

But now, with the possibility that part of her boy's DNA was this close, she couldn't help but soften her heart a little. But she needed proof.

She also needed a drink. Looking down the hallway from the foyer, she saw the closed, back sliding glass door straight ahead that would lead to a patio. She could see Mateo's left side, sitting on a counter-height stool. Although she couldn't see the kitchen because it was to the left of the hallway, she knew he was still sitting at the kitchen counter. She returned to the kitchen and ignored Mateo.

She opened a cold bottle of Chardonnay she had retrieved from the refrigerator and poured herself a glass. She continued pacing the floors around the downstairs, back up the hallway toward the foyer, turned right through a wide open doorway into the spacious dining room. She could see the living room in front of the house that would lead to the foyer. Fluted columns separated the two rooms. She carried her wine back and forth between the two rooms, drinking as she walked and thought. She circled the elegant, traditional heirloom cherry dining table. She admired the eight high-end, upholstered Hepplewhite chairs in an off white damask silk fabric.. She turned on the crystal chandelier to provide light. She ran her hand over the beautiful hutch that encased her fine China from England and France. She entered the living room through the columns and admired the custom silk sofas, elegant furnishings, and window treatments. Then she walked back to the kitchen only to pour more wine.

After her third glass, she picked up her cellphone on the kitchen counter and dialed Dr. Stone's private cellphone.

"What do you want, Lily?" Kent Stone asked.

Lily slurred, "Did you take blood from Dr. Hayes and the Masons for DNA testing?"

"Yes, why?"

"Bring me the results."

"I didn't follow through on it because it didn't matter then."

"Well, run the tests."

"It's too late, Lily. The blood has been thrown away."

Lily poured another glass of wine and emptied the bottle. "Do you know where I live?"

"No, why?"

277

"I want you to come tomorrow and bring three DNA testing kits. I will text you my address. I expect you to be here in the morning after you make your rounds at the hospital."

"Who are they for, Lily?"

"Never you mind, Kent Stone. Just do as I say or I'll make you regret it."

She hung up, texted her address, became angry, and threw the empty bottle of wine across the kitchen.

Mateo wasn't paying attention. He was too busy eating his sandwiches. The bottle hit him square in the nose, landed on the quartz countertop, bounced, and hit him in the chin before breaking in front of him.

Blood poured from his face.

Mateo stood abruptly, knocking over his stool. He felt pain. He reached up to feel his face and looked at the blood on his hand. He felt nauseous.

"La perra." He screamed in Spanish.

"You bitch, I need a doctor," he angrily said.

Lily laughed, thinking it was funny.

"Calm down, it was an accident, for God's sake."

Lily opened a door, walked into Kyle's office, an addition added off the end of the kitchen, into a cabinet, and pulled out the doctor's medical bag containing supplies.

She handed the bag to him. "Here, take the first aid kit up to the doctor. She'll take care of you. Now go. I need to think."

Mateo headed upstairs for help, leaving a trail of blood on the tile floors and the carpet on the stairs.

Lily had a flashback of Kyle dripping blood everywhere after she shot him.

Instead of dwelling on it, she opened another bottle of wine. She picked up her wine glass and the bottle and headed to her downstairs bedroom.

She closed and locked the door and stumbled to the bathroom ensuite. She laughed as she laid the glass and bottle on the small table beside the large clawfoot tub in the middle of the room. The tub was six feet away from the open double doors that led back to the bedroom. She always sat headfirst to face the doorway to see anyone who dared to disturb her.

She turned on the water to fill the large clawfoot tub, returned to her bedroom, and walked to her bedside stand. She opened the drawer and pulled out her Colt 45.

She returned to the bathtub and laid the gun next to the wine. She turned down the lights to a soft glow and turned on music with a remote. She checked the water temperature, undressed, and stepped into the tub.

She laughed and said, "Oops" when she slipped and fell into the tub.

As she settled in with her head propped up on a waterproof pillow, she said out loud to her dead son, "Noah, I've had one heck of a day. I'm sorry I almost killed your child. Here's to us, my dear boy, and to me kidnapping her. We can finally have our revenge."

She poured herself another drink, celebrating because she was now a grandmother.

Then she had a stream of consciousness.

The heck with the will. She no longer cared about the clinic. She had no love lost for the dead men back at the warehouse. She had enough money to live comfortably from her illegal businesses. She had at least 10 million in cash stashed in a safe that no one knew about. She had enough stocks and bonds to sell down the road, if needed. She would change her name to Diana and Danielle's name to Noella and take them by private plane to someplace where no one could find them. They would be happy. She needed to find her stored photo albums in the attic to show Noella pictures of her handsome father and tell her stories about how wonderful and generous he was.

Yes, they would be happy together. But first, she had to have proof that the girl matched her DNA.

She drained the water while sitting in the tub and fell asleep dreaming of a better life.

Chapter 26

Mateo heavily rapped on Savannah's bedroom door, tightly holding the large, black leather medical bag in his right hand.

"Doctor, need a doctor."

Savannah moved to the door. "Why? Who is hurt?"

"Me."

Dani sat up in bed, her green eyes wild with fright. Savannah assured her they would be okay.

Savannah opened the door to see fresh blood dripping from Mateo's face and ushered him into the bathroom. After closing the lid, she motioned for him to sit on the comfort height toilet.

She removed the medical bag from his hand and opened it. Inside were sterile gauze and a small bottle of saline. She also found gloves and arduously slipped them onto her hands while watching blood drip from Mateo's chin onto the tile floor.

She also saw Dani standing at the bathroom doorway, holding onto the doorjamb, curious about what she saw.

"Tilt up your head so I can see your chin," Savannah told the man.

Mateo didn't know the word tilt, so Savannah lifted her head so he could mimic her. He understood and lifted his head to look at the ceiling.

Savannah gently cleansed his nose and chin, but the bleeding continued.

She looked back into the bag and found a small bottle of Novacaine and syringes. She also saw a curved needle and non-absorbable suture threads.

"Mateo, you need stitches on your chin and nose. You need to remove my handcuffs. I can't help you with these on my wrists."

Mateo reached inside his right pant pocket and removed a key.

Savannah was relieved, but said, "Mateo, look at me. I will only help if you promise to leave the cuffs off me."

Mateo was feeling faint at the sight of his blood dripping on the floor.

"Si."

Savannah asked, "What did you say yes to?"

"Leave esposos off."

283

"Say in English, Mateo."

"Leave off coughs."

"Do you mean cuffs, not coughs?"

"Si, doctor. Coughs. Please, hurry."

Savannah extended her arms to allow Mateo to uncuff her. The cuffs hit the tile with a loud bang. She prayed Lily had not heard the noise and come upstairs to investigate.

She stretched her arms, rubbed and rotated her wrists to get the blood circulating.

Savannah turned to Dani. "Go to the nightstand on my side of the bed. There's a small flashlight in the drawer. Bring it to me."

Dani dashed to the nightstand and returned with the flashlight.

Savannah said, "Good girl. Now hold it under his chin so I can stitch it up. Can you do that?"

Dani nodded, turned on the flashlight, and held it under his chin as directed.

"Mateo, I'm going to numb your face because you need stitches."

She pointed to the stitches on his jeans, as he had in the warehouse when he tried to make her understand when Tess needed stitches.

"Ouch?"

Savannah held her thumb and forefinger together on her right hand and said, "A little sting."

"Okay, sting? Like a bee?"

"A little bee."

As Savannah prepared the syringe with the Novacaine, she turned to Dani.

"You can turn your head for this."

Dani stood firm. "No, I want to watch. I'm going to be a Veterinarian one day."

"Alright."

Then she proceeded to inject Mateo's face with the numbing solution, hoping he wouldn't feel the stitching in his nose and chin.

Mateo fainted at the sight of the needle in the syringe.

Savannah pushed his body to rest against the sink cabinet.

She chuckled, remembering when a 6'7" man fainted in the emergency room. He saw a vial of blood being taken from his

285

daughter's arm, and down he went. He became a patient after hitting his head on the floor.

Dani leaned down, put the flashlight on the counter, picked the cuffs off the floor, and helped Savannah put them on the man's wrists. Then Savannah slowly lifted the gun tucked inside the waist of his pants and the key inside his pants pocket. She quietly stood and walked with the gun and key to the bedroom. She placed the gun under her pillow on the bed, and the key in the nightstand's drawer.

When Savannah returned to stitch him up, Dani stood and watched at the bathroom door.

Savannah was so proud of Dani's bravery. She was her child, after all.

Savannah told Dani to hide under the bed. She had no idea how Mateo would react to being handcuffed when he woke up. Would he charge at them like a bull? What was he capable of doing when he was angry? She had to be ready for anything. She also unzipped her pocket in her pants, took out the scalpel, and hid it under the pillow along with the syringe filled with Novacaine. If he lunged at her and took the gun, she would stab him with the Novacaine in the carotid, then slice his throat with the scalpel. She would do whatever it took to protect herself and Dani.

She sat at the head of the bed, steadying her nerves, and brought the gun out from under the pillow. She sat, facing the bathroom door, while removing the safety. Luckily, her father had taught her about guns at a young age when he was in the military. However, she had not actually shot a gun before, but there's always a first time for everything.

She practiced removing the syringe and scalpel from under the pillow several times. She practiced several scenarios in her head while she patiently waited.

Finally, Mateo woke up, shook his head, and laughed when he realized his compromising position. He stood at the bathroom doorway, laughing. He was so tall that his head barely fit beneath the 80-inch-tall doorframe.

Savannah held the gun on him. She was smart enough to know that she had to let him go. Otherwise, Lily would come looking for him, probably loaded with guns.

"Mateo, I will throw you the key to the handcuffs once you're in the hallway. You can leave, but I'm keeping the gun. Do you understand?"

"Si. You smart woman, doctor."

"Yes, Mateo. Now you can help us or die. It's only a matter of time before my friends find us—your choice."

Mateo chuckled. "No choice. I live, you live. I go."

Mateo opened the bedroom door, walked to the hallway, turned around, and raised his handcuffed hands.

Savannah lifted the key from the nightstand drawer and threw it at him. She raced to the door, shut and locked it again.

Mateo had been in handcuffs before. He was adaptable to unlocking cuffs with different items, so having a key was easy. He unlocked the cuffs, put them and the key in his pocket, and stood thinking. He wasn't an evil man; he got caught up in a gang because of his brother, one of the men at the warehouse. He hated guns, but now he wished he had one. He had never killed anyone before. He liked the nice doctor. She had been kind to him, but he couldn't risk his life to help her or the girl.

On the other hand, the little blond bitch was evil. He had no protection against her except for his size, which might overpower her. However, she had guns. She wouldn't hesitate to kill him. He made a decision. He would call his mother to send him money to get home to Mexico. He was through with gangs. He would work in his uncle's garage. He had always been good with his hands.

He descended the stairs and walked out the front door, carefully closing it behind him.

Savannah had shut and locked the bedroom door. "Dani, come help me move some furniture in front of the door."

Dani wiggled her way out beneath the bed. She stood and helped Savannah move a heavy accent chair in front of the door.

Savannah went to one of the bedroom windows. Looking out, she realized the room must be over the garage. She saw a large portico to the right that extended from the front of the building. It was too far from the window. There was no way they could tie bedsheets together and climb down, as she had seen in the movies.

But she had one glimmer of hope while still looking at the front yard. She motioned for Dani to join her at the window.

Mateo was in the driveway.

Dani asked, "What's he doing?"

"I'm not sure, but I hope he's leaving."

He sensed her looking at him, looked up, and waved goodbye. Savannah and Dani waved back, and then he continued toward the sidewalk. They watched him walk the tree-lined street until he disappeared, hoping he had no plans of returning.

Savannah turned her attention to pulling out the nightstand again. Dani tried to help her. Once again, Savannah leaned over the piece of furniture and grabbed the cellphone.

She showed Dani what she had found. Dani softly clapped her hands.

Savannah sat on the bed, trying to remember Robert's number.

"Dani, do you know Robert's number?"

"No, but I know Daddy's."

"Give it to me. Let me talk to him."

Dani repeated the number several times, but they only heard, "The number you have dialed is no longer in service."

"Do you know your mom's number?"

"I don't. I only remember the old numbers. But now I remember they changed their numbers because a man Daddy fired had been calling and harassing him."

Savannah looked at the time. It was now 6 p.m. The battery seemed to be draining fast, showing about 20% energy left. She knew DM Yachts would be closed by now and didn't want to waste time.

She dialed 411 for directory assistance.

She asked for Robert Malone's number.

"Dani, remember the first three numbers after the area code, and I'll remember the rest."

The operator gave her the number.

Savannah excitedly dialed the number, but it went straight to voicemail. Robert never answered numbers he didn't recognize.

She left a message: "Robert, it's me. I'm with Dani. We are both okay. We are hiding in an upstairs bedroom over the garage at...."

The phone died, so Savannah put it back on the charger. She hoped Robert would get the message and call the number again.

She picked up the phone, turned the ringer off, and put it on vibrate, so Lily wouldn't hear it ring.

Savannah suddenly realized that they were alone in the house with Lily.

"Dani, help me move the chair. I'm going downstairs to check things out. I'll take the gun. If you hear the phone vibrate, it's Robert, so answer it and tell him we're at Lily's house, okay?"

"Okay."

Savannah hugged her.

"When I return, I'll knock twice like this."

She quickly tapped twice.

Dani nodded and did as she was told after Savannah left the room.

Savannah descended the stairs, stopping and listening with each step. As she inched closer to the entry hall, she saw that the front door was unlocked.

She stopped when she heard music playing.

She could go back upstairs to get Dani and sneak out the front, but curiosity got the best of her. She had to know where Lily was and whether they were alone in the house. She didn't want any more surprises.

She crept into the hallway and saw the drops of blood on the black and white marbled floor. She followed the drops down a hallway past the grand living room and dining room on her left, careful not to step in the droplets of blood. She saw a light on in the back of the house. She tiptoed, keeping the gun raised with both hands toward the back of the house. She peeked around at the end of the hallway and saw the kitchen to the left. She saw a broken wine bottle lying in blood on the kitchen counter. She realized that Lily must have thrown the bottle at Mateo. To the right, she saw double doors off a vestibule. The doors were shut, and she could hear music coming from behind the doors.

She checked the back sliding doors on the right of the kitchen counter, which were locked. She lowered the lever to unlock them in case Robert and his men needed fast entry.

She backed up slowly until she reached the stairs. She raced up the steps and quickly rapped on the bedroom door twice, which Dani opened.

"Come quickly." Savannah ran to get the phone. "We must hurry."

Savannah put the phone in her pocket, leaving the charger behind, and then put her scalpel back into her pocket.

She placed the gun in the waist of her jeans and took Dani's hand to guide her down the stairs.

She opened the bedroom door, but stopped in her tracks when she heard the doorbell ring.

"Ding dong, ding dong, ding dong."

She then went to the window and looked out. She couldn't see who was beneath the portico at the door.

She went back to the bedroom door and kept it partially open.

She then heard a man's voice shouting. The voice was muffled, but she knew it was a man. Fear ran through her, and the hair stood on the back of her neck.

How lucky her timing was. She almost got caught.

She heard pounding on the front door, then "Ding dong, ding dong" in rapid succession.

Lily yelled, "Alright, alright, I'm coming."

Savannah snuck to the top of the stairs to listen.

Lily noticed the unlocked door. She hesitated and looked around, wondering where the man who was supposed to guard her was.

She stood on her tiptoes and looked through the peephole. She flung the door open.

"What the hell, Kent? You weren't supposed to be here until tomorrow."

"I decided to get this over with, Lily. I have a busy day in surgery tomorrow."

Savannah recognized Dr. Kent Stone's voice.

"Well, don't just stand there, come in before somebody sees you. Did you bring the test kits?"

"No, Lily, I was just in the neighborhood and thought I'd stop by," Kent said sarcastically.

Savannah wondered what Lily was talking about. Test kits? Could she possibly mean DNA test kits?

Savannah quietly shut the bedroom door, removed the gun and phone from her pants, and slid them into the nightstand drawer under the old photographs. She told Dani to get in bed and pretend to sleep. She moved the club chair back into its place, unlocked the door, sat on the bed, and waited.

The bedroom door opened, and there stood Lily and Dr. Stone.

Dr. Stone visibly looked surprised. He arched his eyebrows, his eyes widened, and his mouth formed an "O" shape. He looked at Lily, raised his voice, and said, "For God's sake, Lily, what have you done?"

Dr. Stone ran to Savannah.

"Are you okay?"

He looked at the child under the bedding and recognized the curly blond hair belonging to Danielle Mason.

He turned to face Lily, who was standing in the hallway.

"What is going on here?"

Savannah said, "I'll tell you. Lily kidnapped me because she thought I had Kyle Clark's will, which I don't. She kidnapped Dani and threatened to harm her to make me talk."

Lily walked into the room.

"Shut up. I'll do the talking here. Yes, I took the doctor to make her tell me where she hid the will and my prenuptial agreement, Kent. Don't you see, we need the clinic to keep our business going. I had this bitch where I wanted her, but then she told me the girl is my granddaughter. She had an affair with my son, Noah. I want proof."

Savannah wasn't going to tell them that Noah raped her in front of Danielle, who was now sitting up in bed trying to comprehend what she was hearing.

Dani looked at Savannah with tears in her eyes. "Is that true?" she asked.

Savannah put her arms around her. "Yes, Dani. It's true. I can explain it to you later."

"But, who is Noah?"

Lily said, "If Savannah is telling the truth, Noah is your real father. He was my beautiful son, and Michael, your alleged adopted father, killed him. That means I am your grandmother. Don't worry, I won't harm you if the DNA test results are as I hope."

"That's a lie," Savannah shouted, "Noah died in a plane crash."

Lily answered, "True, but it was Michael's fault." She would never stop blaming him.

Kent Stone yelled, "Enough. Everyone just shut up."

"Savannah and Danielle, would you both be willing to take a DNA test?"

Savannah spoke, "But I've already given blood. You should have the results."

Dr. Stone lied, "Unfortunately, the blood was tainted. But I believe I have the results for the Masons and your friend, Robert Malone. They gave blood early in Danielle's hospitalization before you came to town to see if they could help with the bone marrow transplant or to give blood, if she needed it. As you know, our patient here was anemic."

"Shut up, Kent. You've said enough," Lily screamed.

Savannah and Danielle were both confused.

Lily added, "I have let him swab my mouth for a DNA test. Now it's your turn. We'll know the truth in a couple of days."

Kent opened the kits and had Savannah and Danielle swab the inside of their cheeks. He allowed them to dry, then placed the swabs into the collection tubes, sealed them, and wrote their names on the correct tubes.

Suddenly, they heard a vibration.

Lily looked around, wondering where the sound was coming from.

She hunted around as Savannah prayed silently for the phone to stop, cursing herself for not turning it off.

297

Lily yanked open the nightstand drawer and found the phone and the loaded gun.

"You bitch," Lily screamed and slapped Savannah across her face. Savannah stood defiantly.

Kent caught Lily's arm to keep her from slapping Savannah again.

Lily wiggled away from his clutch and reached inside the drawer. "I'll take these. Who were you calling? Did you call the police? Did you steal this gun from my man? Where is he, anyway?"

Savannah and Danielle were speechless. Savannah finally said, "The phone was dead when I found it. I didn't speak to anyone. I don't want the police involved. Robert will eventually find us. Don't call the police, Dr. Stone. You won't be helping. Furthermore, how would I know where your man is?"

Lily looked concerned, not knowing if she believed Savannah.

"Wait in the hallway, Kent. I have tools in the hall closet. I want you to flip the doorknob so I can lock it from the outside. Then, we have business to discuss."

Kent did as he was told because he saw the gun she was holding in her hand. He knew she wouldn't hesitate to kill him.

After Kent installed the doorknob, Lily slammed the bedroom door, locking it from the outside. Lily forced Kent down the stairs at gunpoint.

Danielle fell into bed, crying. Savannah felt helpless and let the girl cry herself to sleep.

She had planned to wash her jeans and underwear in the bathroom sink, but was too exhausted.

She wondered about Dr. Stone's involvement in Lily's business and continued thinking of past events. She was horrified when she remembered him saying that Dani needed a kidney transplant. Her eyes drooped, and she thought, "I'll rest my eyes for a few minutes, then get up."

The few minutes turned into seven hours.

Chapter 27

The following day, Kent Stone took the DNA samples to the lab he knew would expedite the results quickly. He paid an extra fee and told the head technician, Sally, that it was an emergency. Sally never questioned why but promised to get right on it.

In the meantime, he went to his buddy at the hospital lab and requested the Masons' DNA results. His buddy promised to get right on it.

Before his surgery began, he thought about calling Michael Mason.

However, he called the other doctors instead and warned them not to take Lily's calls. He told them he had no time to explain but would contact them after hours. He added that they were no longer obligated to Lily before hanging up.

He also thought about calling the Police, but he was afraid they would discover his involvement with Lily.

After looking at his watch, he decided to call Michael Mason after his surgery. He was running late.

*****

Downstairs at the house, Lily prepared a tray of scrambled eggs and toast for Savannah and Dani and took it upstairs. She unlocked the upstairs bedroom door, hurriedly placed the tray on the carpet, and quickly shut and locked the door again.

She returned downstairs and turned on the local news while she sat at the counter, drinking coffee and toast.

She had finally cleaned up the mess made when she hit Mateo in the face with an empty wine bottle. She had double-bagged the bloody towel and said, "Good riddance," and threw it in the trash can under the sink.

She was still angry that he had skipped out on her.

She slowly ate her toast while watching the news. She became worried when the news anchor described the deadly scene in the warehouse in Norfolk. She anxiously, but morbidly, watched the dead men being brought out on stretchers and placed in an ambulance. She watched the children walking in a line out the warehouse door and down the steps to more waiting ambulances. Dozens of police swarmed the warehouse.

She switched the channels from Fox News to CNN and MSNBC. She was horrified that the story was streaming nationally. Pictures of the operating tables and the captives' rooms flashed across the screen. Luckily, no names were given due to an ongoing investigation.

She stood and paced the floor, thinking of her next move, knowing it was just a matter of time before the police came knocking on her door.

She ran to Kyle's office and began searching for the address of his cabin, which was about an hour away in the woods in Suffolk.

Kyle thought she didn't know about the cabin, but Lily had known everything about his whereabouts. She instinctively knew Kyle had been heading there to hide on the day she had him followed and killed.

She opened the cellphone she had taken from Savannah and searched Maps for recent places he may have been with it. However, she soon realized this was not the phone he had used daily. That phone was found in the wreckage, and she had already called the cellphone company and discontinued the service after the funeral.

She opened the *settings* on the phone she had taken from the nightstand to find the service provider's name.

Kyle had been a brilliant doctor who was meticulous about everything in his life, including record-keeping. She hoped to find the receipt and the address he used when he set up the phone—she hoped it would be the cabin's address so she could put it in the GPS in her Jeep.

She searched for the key to unlock his desk drawer and began pulling out his medical books from the bookcase, discarding each book onto the floor after rifling through the pages.

Medical papers and files flew across the room, landing on the wooden flooring with a thud. Because of her height, she could only reach certain levels of the bookcase.

She ran from the office to the utility room and found a small three-step folded step ladder. She carried it back to the office and disengaged the lock.

Finally, she could reach the top three shelves of books, discarding them one by one onto the floor after looking through them for anything that might help her.

Suddenly, she came upon a green, leather-bound book with no title on the spine. She opened it and found that a compartment within the pages had been hollowed out to transform it into a safe. She quickly removed a key and rushed to the desk. The top drawer opened easily, and she rifled through the files until she found what she sought.

The file was labeled *AT&T.*

She opened the file and found receipts for the cellphone mailed to the Suffolk address. She wrote down the address on a piece of notebook paper with a pen she found. She had to press hard because the pen was almost empty and the writing was light. She ripped the paper out and folded it neatly.

Excitedly, she ran to her primary bathroom to shower and dress without cleaning up her mess in the office.

She would take her victims to the cabin to hide out and wait for the DNA results.

Upstairs, Savannah had found cleaning supplies under the sink in the bathroom. She cleaned up Mateo's dried blood with a towel engraved with Kyle's initials. She draped the towel over a towel bar so it would be easily found.

While Dani slept, she unbraided her hair and stripped off her clothes. She turned on the shower and waited for the water to come to a comfortable temperature.

Minutes later, she stepped into the tub, stood under the showerhead, and felt the soothing water wash over her dirty hair and body. She used Kyle's men's shampoo and soap. Unfortunately, there wasn't a conditioner to help untangle her wet hair. She wished she could have leisurely soaked in a hot bath, but Dani would be awake soon, and she had to shower next.

She stood, enjoying the water washing away the filth. She hurried because she didn't want to use all the hot water. Begrudgingly, she turned off the water, stepped out, and wrapped herself in a clean towel.

She opened the top cabinet drawer, found a new toothbrush and unused toothpaste, and scrubbed her teeth and tongue so hard that they almost bled.

She walked into the bedroom and opened the closet doors. She examined Kyle's leisure clothing, wondering if they would fit her. He had been slim with an athletic body. She pulled a white T-shirt off a hanger and slipped it over her head. She realized that she had lost weight, and the shirt hung loosely on her. She rolled up the sleeves, ready for action. She didn't care how the shirt looked as long as it was clean.

She tried on khaki pants, which were too large, and dropped to the floor.

She walked to the underwear drawer and slipped into a pair of men's boxer briefs. They were loose-fitting but acted as shorts.

She returned to the bathroom, found a hairbrush, and brushed her wet hair as best she could. It felt good to be clean again. She found another clean towel and washcloth and laid them on the toilet lid for Dani to see. She placed another clean toothbrush by the sink.

Suddenly, she realized the underwear didn't have a pocket to hide her scalpel. She had no choice but to put her dirty jeans back on, so she removed the boxers and stepped back into her jeans. She checked to make sure the blade was still in the pocket. Satisfied, she put on her tennis shoes and walked to the bed to wake Dani.

She shook Dani awake.

"Dani, wake up, honey. You need to get in the shower."

Dani yawned, stretched, and sat up in bed.

"What do I call you now? Mother?"

Tears rolled down Dani's cheeks. Everything she had known had all been a lie.

Savannah hugged her. "You can call me Savannah. Cathi and Michael are still your mom and dad. They legally adopted you when you were a baby. I was just the lucky one to bring you into the world for them. You have been such a blessing to them, and they love you very much. Now, let's get you showered and your teeth brushed."

"You sound like a mom," Dani said, and smiled. Savannah smiled back as she hugged her again.

Dani seemed satisfied with Savannah's explanation, so she walked into the bathroom to shower.

As Dani showered, Savannah ate a piece of dried toast that Lily had left inside the door earlier, planning her next move.

She walked over to the dresser where she had previously seen an array of Kyle's items. She opened the drawer and found several old credit cards.

She rushed to the bedroom door and slid the card between the door and the frame near the latch. She wiggled the card and was surprised by how easily the latch retracted. She turned the knob and opened the door.

She shut the door back carefully and waited in the club chair for Dani to shower and change.

After Dani showered and changed back into her outfit, she felt better. She was regaining her strength every day.

Savannah sat on the bed with Dani standing in front of her. Savannah held Dani's hands and said, "Listen carefully, Dani. We're going to the hallway, and I want you to stand at the top of the stairs. I will sneak down, see where Lily is, and unlock the front door. When the coast is clear, I'll motion for you to come down the stairs. You'll need to run down as fast as you can without tripping. Let's remove the patent leather shoes and socks because they are slippery. I'll carry them down and put them on the first step. Do you know I wear an invisible tiara when I need to feel strong? Just because you can't see it, doesn't mean it's not there. You have one too, so put yours on."

They both placed their hands on their heads and adjusted the invisible tiaras.

Danielle smiled and removed her shoes. She stuffed her socks into her shoes and handed them to Savannah.

Savannah snuck down the stairs and peeked down the hallway toward the kitchen. She stood and listened for any sound. Hearing nothing, she quietly unbolted the front door, then motioned for Dani to run down.

Savannah picked up Dani's shoes, holding her hand out to grab her if she stumbled.

Dani made it down safely and walked to the door beside Savannah.

Savannah had her hand on the door when they heard Lily say, "Going somewhere?"

Startled, they both turned to see Lily standing in the hallway, gun in hand.

Lily continued, "Good. You saved me from climbing the stairs. I was just coming to get you. As a matter of fact, we are taking a little road trip."

Lily motioned with her gun to walk toward her until they reached the door leading to the garage behind the stairwell.

"Savannah, you are driving. Danielle, you get in the backseat and put your seatbelt on. I will sit in the passenger's seat. I loaded the back with food and drinks, so let's go."

Lily forced them into the Jeep, pushed the garage door opener, turned on the GPS, and inserted the destination in Suffolk. She pointed the gun at Savannah and said, "Drive. Follow the instructions."

Savannah put the Jeep in reverse. Lily closed the garage door with the remote and said, "No funny stuff, or the girl dies."

"You'd kill your own grandchild to save yourself?" Savannah questioned incredulously.

Lily sat motionless and didn't defend her actions.

Savannah said, "You're a piece of shit."

Lily laughed an evil laugh, and Dani trembled and clutched the seatbelt. Her green eyes widened, but she kept them downcast, afraid to look at Lily.

Savannah recognized that Dani was cowering in the backseat, making herself look small.

"Dani, Lily is only trying to scare us. Don't worry. Put your tiara back on. I noticed it fell off. Nothing bad will happen."

Lily looked at Savannah like she was crazy, but softened. "Look in the back. I brought your Daddy's old teddy bear for you. He would want you to have it. Go on, take it. It's next to the food and drinks."

With encouragement from Savannah, Dani reached back and found the stuffed animal.

Dani said meekly, "Thank you."

Lily asked, "Thank you, who?"

"Thank you, Grandma."

"You're welcome, Noella. That is your name from now on. And my name is Grandma Diana. Let's have some fun."

Savannah asked, "Where are we headed, Lily?"

"We are heading to Kyle's cabin in Suffolk. I looked at it on Google Earth, and it has a lake and a park-like setting. We can fish off a dock and roast marshmallows by a fire at night. It will be like camping out, but with a nice cabin to sleep in."

Savannah drove toward Suffolk, wondering how Robert and his men would find them in the woods. Hopefully, when Lily gets the DNA results, she will soften toward her granddaughter and let her live. She knew Lily would kill her, though, and take Dani somewhere. It sickened her that Lily had the gall to change Dani's name to Noella. She plans to replace her dead son with Dani.

She prayed Lily had brought along bottles of wine. She would wait until Lily passed out and slit her carotid arteries.

Savannah was formulating a plan as she drove west to God knows where.

Chapter 28

Dr. Kent Stone's surgery on his ten-year-old female patient was a success. The child reminded him of Danielle Mason. He wanted some fresh air as soon as he changed out of his surgical garb. He walked to the rooftop garden and was thankful he was alone.

He sat at one of the aluminum tables and pulled out his cellphone. He took a deep breath, then he dialed Michael Mason's number.

Michael was sitting at his desk at work. He looked at his phone to see who was calling. He smirked but was curious and answered, "Hello, Dr. Stone. What do you want?"

Kent rolled his eyes and wondered why he was bothering to help this rude man, yet he knew it was right.

"Michael, listen to me. Lily has kidnapped Savannah and Danielle and has them locked in an upstairs bedroom at her house here in Norfolk. Do you have a pen and paper handy? I'll give you the address."

Relief flooded Michael's body.

"Thank you, doctor. But how do you know this?"

"Because I was there last night. Lily demanded that Savannah and Danielle take a DNA test. Savannah says she is Danielle's birth mother, and Lily's son, Noah, is the father. Lily wants proof. Is that true, Michael?"

"Yes, it's true. So, does Dani know the truth?"

"Yes, Lily told her."

Michael scratched his head, a habit he had when he was anxious. He was worried about Dani and how she had taken the news. This was not how he and Cathi had planned to tell her about the adoption. Dani had once asked why she had green eyes and blond hair when her parents had blue eyes and dark hair. Now, she knew why.

"How is Dani? Is she okay? How did she take the news?"

Kent lowered his voice and sympathetically said, "She cried, but she seems to have bonded with Savannah. She was disheveled, but she didn't appear sickly anymore. We know she's in complete remission now. But listen carefully, Michael. Lily is a dangerous woman. She has a mental illness. She hasn't been the same since her son died. She has a gun or maybe guns and won't be afraid to use them. She is waiting for the DNA test results. I hope to know the results today or tomorrow."

Kent was relieved when Michael said, "Thank you again, but please leave the police out of this. I'll handle it."

Kent was grateful he wasn't the one who suggested the police should not be involved because he would have looked suspicious.

"Give me the address."

"What do you plan to do, Michael?"

"I plan on calling my wife and telling her Dani is safe. Then I'm going to save my daughter. I advise you to stay away from Lily and the house."

"Good luck, Michael."

"And Dr. Stone, I'm not sure you have seen the news today, but it appears Lily had doctors operate on children in a warehouse to sell their organs. I hope you weren't one of those doctors involved. Just saying. Nevertheless, I appreciate your help and won't forget it. I suggest you keep this conversation to yourself."

"No argument, Michael. Goodbye."

Kent hung up and became nauseous. Maybe this was a good time to take an extended vacation until this mess with Lily blew over. He also wondered what to tell the other doctors. He began wishing Lily would die, and all his troubles would end.

He had to find the nearest TV and watch the news. He felt his world was crashing down around him.

Michael called Cathi to tell her Dani has been found. He was going with Robert and the men to save her and Savannah. He didn't elaborate or tell her that Dani knew the truth about the adoption. He knew Cathi would want to talk about it, and there wasn't time.

They could talk later when Dani was safe in her bed at home.

He ran next door to Robert's office, where he was sitting with the men, trying to figure out how to get the location of the phone that Savannah had called from. When he tried calling back the number last night, no one answered. It said the mailbox was full and couldn't leave a message. They had been up all night. Robert had paced the floor and had exasperated the other men with his theories.

Lee Hunt and his two buddies had been placed on a plane back to Florida earlier that morning. Only three of the SEAL team remained because they were local: David, Knuckles, and Crusher. Peter also stayed. Robert liked having another cop around. Mark Jenkins and Adam Jordan stayed, waiting for anything positive to help their friends.

They all had looked up when Michael had barged into the room, waving a piece of paper.

"I've got Lily's address. Dr. Stone just called. He saw them last night when he was at the house. Get ready, let's go."

David asked, "Did he say how many men or guns she has?"

"He said Lily has a gun, possibly more, but didn't mention if there was anyone else there."

"It could be a setup," Robert said. "We need to be diligent and take the house by surprise. We know she's with a tall man with a gun. There could be more."

Michael said, "Right, give me a gun. I'm going."

"You're more dangerous with a gun, Michael, because you don't know how to use one. Have you ever heard about friendly fire?" David said.

Robert knew his friend well, and nothing would stop him from going. So he said, "Michael, you can go, but you need to stay behind us and do what you're told, okay?"

Michael nodded and handed Robert the paper. "Here's the address. Okay, let's go."

The men stood, grabbed some gear and guns.

Robert told Mark to hold down the fort while they were gone.

Robert turned to Peter and asked, "Peter, don't you think you should sit this one out? Your arm is still in a sling and healing."

Peter laughed, "And miss all the fun? No way. I've been shot worse than this before."

The six men took the Suburban SUV and followed the GPS to Lily's house. They slowly drove past it and parked down the street. Robert had looked up at the room over the garage, hoping to see Savannah at the window.

Peter spoke, "Look, guys. We're in an upscale neighborhood, and I'm sure not everyone is at work. We passed at least two landscape companies, and multiple cars were parked along the street. When I was a cop, we worked two men at a time. We need to be inconspicuous so we don't spook the neighbors.

The others agreed.

Peter said, "I didn't see any security cameras. Robert, park closer to the house. David, jump out, take one of your guys, and go to the back. Robert and I will take the front when you're out of sight. Michael, take the wheel and wait. The other remaining SEAL will be the lookout and protect Michael, if needed.

Robert nodded. "Sounds like a good plan. I have Kyle Clark's keyring. Thankfully, he labeled all his keys. I have it in my pocket. Let's go."

David and Crusher put on gloves, checked their guns, and put them in their waistbands. They jumped out and ran toward the back of the house by the garage, jumping a wooden fence.

Then Robert and Peter put on gloves, checked their guns, and placed them in their waistbands, hiding them under their shirts. They jumped out of the car and casually walked to the front door. Robert looked around and didn't see anyone, so he peeked into a window to his left as Peter stood under the portico. The living room was empty. Peter twisted the front doorknob and was surprised when he realized it was unlocked. He pushed open the door, and he and Robert drew their guns. They entered the house, guns raised, and quietly shut the door. They saw David standing at the end of the hallway inside the kitchen after finding the slider unlocked. They thought it was odd that Lily had left the doors unlocked. Was she waiting to ambush them?

The men started searching the house.

Crusher checked the main bedroom, gun raised, opening the closet doors and checking for people. David checked the dining room, living room, a half bath, and the coat closet.

Robert snuck upstairs and turned right into the bedroom, disappointed to find it empty. He saw Savannah's white top and a pair of men's briefs on the bathroom floor, and the blood-stained towel hanging over the towel bar. He was confused about the clothing, wondering if the man with Savannah had harmed her. He checked the tub and noticed the tile walls were still wet. Water dripped from the shower head. He became concerned, keeping his anger in check, and continued searching. He checked the other bedrooms upstairs, then opened a door leading to an attic. He slowly made his way up the stairs. He stood on a landing and looked around. He walked and began lifting sheets, uncovering pieces of antique furniture. Satisfied that the attic was only filled with boxes and furniture, he returned downstairs.

David checked the garage and looked inside the Bentley. He noticed standing water on the floor next to the car, suggesting another car had once been there, dripping condensation from the air conditioning or exhaust systems. He returned to the kitchen.

Crusher and Peter were opening drawers, looking for clues.

Robert found Kyle's office off the kitchen. He called Peter into the room and showed him all the books strewn around the floor.

"What do you suppose she was looking for, Peter?"

"I don't know. Let's look around."

They began picking up books until they found the book that had contained the desk key.

Robert went to the desk and looked through the files, but he had no idea what Lily had been trying to find. Nothing of significance jumped out at him.

While Peter kept picking up books off the floor, Robert sat in Kyle's leather chair and rolled it closer to the desk. He studied the contents on top of the desk. He saw a notebook and noticed

319

a piece of paper had been torn out of the binder, leaving jagged edges. He took a pencil and gently began rubbing the side of the lead pencil across the surface of the indentations left on the paper. He continued until words appeared.

"Peter, come look at this. This looks like an address. Kyle Clark and I were heading to his cabin in Suffolk the day he was killed. The day you and I met. I recognize the address. It's to the cabin. Now we know where Lily has taken them. I don't think we are too far behind because the tub and tiles were still wet in the upstairs bathroom."

Robert jumped up. Peter followed him to the kitchen and told the men they had to leave. He told them he knew where Lily was taking Savannah and Dani, but they would need more supplies and wait until dark to make their next move.

They all left the house through the front door.

As Michael drove back to DM Yachts, Robert told them the story about Kyle Clark and what he remembered the doctor had told him about the land layout and the secluded log cabin.

Chapter 29

Savannah turned off the main highway and drove down a narrow, dirt road. She came upon a heavy metal chain that stretched across the road, anchored on sturdy posts on each side. A visible "KEEP OUT" sign was attached to the chain.

Lily made Savannah leave the Jeep and remove the chain from one of the posts. She jumped back into the car, drove past the posts, stopped, and returned to reattach the chain.

She continued driving through a forest of trees, following the road for about a half-mile. At the end of the street, she turned left, parking in front of a cozy cabin.

The quaint, rustic log cabin was nestled among a dense forest of tall trees. It had a steeply pitched A-framed roof. The roof covering appeared to be corrugated metal panels. Moss and algae seemed to thrive on the aged roof, giving off a greenish cast. A stone chimney was in the middle of the roof, located at the top of the ridge. Two Adirondack chairs made from sticks and branches sat on a welcoming covered porch with a wooden railing. Two windows overlook the porch to the right of the front door. A small rectangular, multi-paned window was in the upper gable above the porch's roof. The wooden grids were dirty white. Savannah wasn't sure if it was a functioning window to a second-story room or was just for aesthetics. A stack of firewood sat next to the chairs. A dirt path laced with fallen leaves led to three wooden steps leading up to the porch, about 20 feet from where they were parked. The wide path continued in front of the porch and around to the right side of the cabin.

Lily forced them out of the car and retrieved the keys from Savannah.

She exclaimed sarcastically, "Well, isn't this nice? Why the hell Kyle built this dump is beyond me."

Savannah asked, "Have you never been here before?"

"Heavens, no. Do I look like a girl who could love a God forsaken place like this?"

Savannah said, "I think it's charming."

Lily looked her up and down, rudely saying, "Yeah, you would."

They were all standing at the back of the Jeep, looking at the cabin.

Lily urged Savannah to move. "Go check the door. See if it's open. If not, look under the mat to see if there's a key. Noella will stay with me."

Savannah wanted to correct her, saying her name is Danielle, but she kept quiet. It wasn't worth arguing about.

She walked to the door, which was peeling with green paint. She tried the door handle, but the door was locked. She thought, "What are all these damn locked doors I keep finding?"

She looked under the black rubber welcome mat but found no key. She looked under a heavy terracotta pot on the left side of the door with weeds growing out of the dirt. She screamed and jumped when a black snake crawled out of the weeds. Dani screamed too, fearing for Savannah's life. Lily told her to shut up.

"Try again. Find the damn key," Lily barked.

Savannah lifted the pot and found the key. She inserted it into the door and opened it. A musty smell poured out of the cabin, which had been closed up for so long.

Lily opened the Jeep's hatch with a remote and told her hostages to unload the supplies and take them into the cabin.

"Let me check for animals inside the cabin first, Lily. We don't want any surprises."

Lily was impatient, but agreed. "Alright, but hurry up."

Savannah entered, stopped at the front door after stepping onto wide pine-planked floors, and saw a large open room with tall ceilings. There was a large two-story stone fireplace about 20 feet in front of her. A scary bear head trophy was anchored above the mantle, open-mouthed, showing its sharp teeth. Savannah shuddered, looking at the bear. She looked inside the open firebox and saw a cast-iron kettle hanging from an iron arm attached to the sidewall that could swing out. Ashes lay beneath the pot from a previous fire.

She looked directly to her right. A kitchenette with four pine upper cabinets and four lower cabinets with brown and white speckled laminate countertops was on the side wall. Only a small metal container that said *breadbox* was on the counter.

In the center of the lower cabinets was a small sink, which had a single window above it. At the end of the cabinets, to the left, was a small, standing refrigerator with a single door. A small wooden oak table with two metal chairs sat in front of the sink. Next to the front door were two windows that overlooked the porch.

Still looking right, beyond the refrigerator, she saw wooden stairs leading to a closed door on the right of the landing. The stairs' railings appeared to have been created from honed pieces of thick tree branches.

Looking left, she saw a couch covered with brown and ochre plaid fabric. She saw the back of a brown leather chair facing the fireplace. An end table nearest the fireplace had a lamp. A wooden, rustic coffee table had stacks of medical books and fishing magazines in front of the couch. She entered the room and walked behind the two-way fireplace. In the short hallway, she leaned over, peered through the firebox, and could see the front door still standing open. She opened a door behind the massive fireplace and slowly opened it. She found a bedroom with a double bed covered in a blue quilt, a nightstand, and a lamp.

She thought about how brilliant Dr. Clark had been in designing his cabin. He could leave his bedroom door open at night and get the heat from the fireplace on a cold winter night.

She walked into the main living area.

She opened the window over the kitchen sink and the two front windows overlooking the porch to air out the cabin.

She opened the refrigerator door quickly and jumped back, expecting something to crawl out. To her surprise, the refrigerator was clean and still had electricity. It was fully stocked with sodas, bottled water, and jars of condiments. The freezer compartment on top of the refrigerator section had three trays of yellowed ice.

She turned on the faucet at the sink and ran the brown well water until it cleared. Then, she emptied the old ice trays and refilled them with clean water, placing them back in the freezer.

She had to use the bathroom and wondered where it was.

"Oh God, no, please, no."

She left the cabin and said, "Lily, the coast is clear, but I can't find a bathroom. I will check the side of the house to see if there's an outhouse."

"You've got to be kidding me. Well, then, go check." Lily shuddered, missing the comfort of her home.

Savannah walked to the right side of the cabin and saw a shower head coming out of the side of the wall from the kitchen. At least it had a concrete pad to stand on to shower. In front of the shower stood an outhouse of the same logs as the cabin. She quickly opened the door and jumped back in case an animal was there. She knew her imagination was getting the best of her, so she entered, sat on a wooden toilet seat embedded on top of a wooden bench, and peed into a hole. Stacks of damp toilet paper sat on a shelf to the right. She cringed, unrolled the paper several times, then used what she hoped was cleaner.

When she returned to the Jeep, she and Dani began unloading the supplies.

They carried the groceries and a small cooler and put them on the wooden table in front of the sink. Dani left the teddy bear in the back seat. She wanted no part of it.

Savannah opened up one of the top cabinets and found cans of food filling the space. She began opening the other three cabinets. They were all stocked. She noted mostly canned Spam, canned baked beans, packaged vegetable soups, and jars of crunchy peanut butter and jelly. She hoped Lily had brought something more appetizing.

She unpacked Lily's groceries from one bag. She unloaded three packages of hot dogs, buns, a variety of cheeses and Ritz crackers, packages of oatmeal and boxed raisins, a package of brown sugar, and, thankfully, three bottles of wine and a half gallon of milk in the cooler filled with ice. Dani found a box of graham crackers, chocolate bars, marshmallows, and long wooden skewers in another grocery bag. She smirked, supposed Lily had planned to act like a grandmother and make s'mores for Dani.

Lily entered, placed a sheet over the sofa, and cringed as she sat down.

Dani went to investigate the upstairs bedroom.

Savannah looked out the front windows and saw a clearing with a beautiful lake and a dock in the distance. Two more Adirondack chairs sat around a fire pit.

327

Suddenly, Savannah rushed to the front door, slammed it shut, and locked it. Then quickly ran to close the four windows she had opened.

She looked at Lily wide-eyed and placed her finger over her lips to warn her to be quiet.

A giant black bear had come out of the woods and investigated Lily's Jeep.

Savannah grew up in Virginia and knew they had to be near the Great Dismal Swamp, where bears were known to be.

Lily sat stoically on the sofa, raised her gun, aimed it at the door, and waited.

Dani headed down the stairs, and Savannah shooed her, whispering loud enough that Dani could hear, "Go back upstairs."

"Why? I'm thirsty and need to use the bathroom."

"Not now, Dani."

Dani sat on the steps halfway down, holding her privates with her hands. Then she let out a blood-curdling scream. The bear was on the porch looking in the windows.

Savannah raised her arms, waving them erratically and aggressively, yelling, "Get out of here, Git."

Lily joined her side and pointed the gun at the bear.

Savannah begged, "Don't shoot, Lily. You'll break the windows and make it mad."

Dani was screaming in a high-pitched tone, scared to death.

Savannah thought, "If this doesn't cause Dani to seek counseling for the rest of her life, then nothing will."

The bear had heard enough noise, walked off the porch, and ran into the woods behind the outhouse.

Savannah looked in the lower cabinets and found an iron pot. She found paper towels and ran up to Dani with the items. She wished the pots and pans had been aluminum so she could bang them together to make noise.

"Here, use these."

Dani nodded, climbed back up the steps, and turned, smiling. "Did I help? My screams scared a bear at our park one day. Mom said I was brave."

"Yes, Dani. Thank you for being so helpful."

Dani entered the bedroom and returned, saying, "By the way, there's a really cool bed up here made from trees." Then she disappeared back into the room.

Savannah was relieved and smiled. She knew then that Dani was a brave, strong girl, and she would be okay. She noticed she hadn't called Cathi Mommy, but had said Mom. Her tiara sat fastidiously on top of her head.

Lily sat on the sofa and said, "Find me a glass. I need wine. That was close."

"Be a dear and open the wine for me. I'm tired."

Savannah was weary of Lily's demands but opened the cooler. The wine had a twist-off cap, so she poured it into a tall plastic glass and handed it to Lily.

Savannah knew Dani must be hungry. She looked out the window to see if the bear had returned. It was getting dark out, so she had to hurry. She opened the door and ran for firewood, stacking as much as she could in her arms. She returned and threw them on the floor in front of the fireplace. She quickly closed and locked the door.

She swung the iron arm out from the fireplace. She stacked several logs on top of the ashes, then looked around for a lighter or matches. She found matches in a drawer. She ripped out pages of the magazines, crumbled them into a ball, and placed them around the stack of wood. After ten minutes of trying, she had a fire going.

The room began filling with smoke.

Lily yelled, "You idiot, you didn't open the flue."

It was too late to open the flue now. She would burn herself trying to find out how to open the damper inside the flue.

She ran to the sink, filled glass after glass with the well water, running back and forth to the fireplace and the sink, and poured the water over the smouldering fire, until it was finally out.

At this point, she had no choice but to open the windows to let the smoke out.

In the meantime, Lily berated her for being so stupid.

Exasperated, Savannah said, "Shut the fuck up, Lily. I'm a doctor, not a fireplace expert."

She gave up the idea of cooking the hot dogs. Instead, they would have to eat cold, raw hot dogs on a bun, cold soup, peanut butter, crackers, cheese, and chocolate bars for dessert.

Savannah chose the crackers and cheese and made Dani two peanut butter and jelly sandwiches on the hot dog buns while Lily drank her wine for dinner. Savannah hoped the bear couldn't smell the food. It was probably good that she hadn't been able to cook the hot dogs. She believed things happen for a reason, even if you didn't understand the reason.

She called Dani down for dinner, waving a dish towel to help remove the leftover smoke. At least the smoke covered up the musty smell in the cabin.

The smoke finally began to dissipate, and the musty smell returned.

The sun had set, and Savannah turned on the lamp on the end table. There was a soft glow in the room. She found a flashlight and candles in one of the drawers.

While they ate by candlelight, Lily continued to ask for wine refills, and Savannah and Dani watched the windows for bears.

After eating, Dani grabbed a fishing magazine and went back upstairs to read in bed.

Lily asked Savannah, "Did you love my son?"

Savannah looked at her sitting on the couch. The once meticulously groomed woman was a disheveled mess, physically and mentally. She almost felt sorry for her captor.

"No, Lily, I have only loved one man in my life. I love Robert Malone."

She surprised herself when she said it out loud, realizing it was the truth. She had always loved Robert.

Lily had tears in her eyes. "So you used my boy. What are you, some slut that sleeps with handsome men?"

"If you must know, your son raped me. He was a monster."

Lily stared at Savannah with daggers in her eyes but stayed quiet. She was trying to comprehend what Savannah had just said. She was slightly drunk on wine by now and couldn't think clearly.

Savannah continued, "Yes, Lily, he was a monster, just like his mother."

Lily pointed the gun at Savannah and slurred, "I should kill you for that. My boy was kind and generous. Michael is the monster. He killed my son."

Savannah said, "Lily, you've had too much to drink and haven't eaten. Why don't you eat and go to bed? We can discuss this in the morning. You should hear from Dr. Stone soon, and we can leave."

Lily stood and staggered. "I need to pee. Go with me to that outhouse."

"No way, Lily. It's too dark outside."

Savannah opened a bottom cabinet and pulled out an iron cooking pot with handles.

"Here, use this as a chamber pot. Take it to your bedroom, and go to sleep."

Lily staggered to the tiny kitchenette with the gun and opened the drawers with one hand. She removed all the knives and placed them in an empty grocery bag.

"Okay, but I'm taking these, in case you want to slit my throat in the middle of the night. Put the pot next to my bed."

Savannah did as she was told, and Lily staggered off to bed.

Savannah was relieved to be alone. She closed and locked the windows, then sat at the table, wondering if she could actually kill another human being. Maybe she would wait until Lily was asleep, then sneak into her bedroom and take the car keys. Then she and Dani could escape. But, then again, Lily would hire someone to find her and Dani. Lily would never stop hunting her down. She would possibly hurt Michael and Cathi. Hopefully, Dani might be safe once the DNA results prove she is her granddaughter. Thinking it all through, she knew she had to kill or be killed. She could see the headlines: Doctor kills woman in self-defense. Or, a Doctor loses her medical license over murdering a grandmother.

She rested her head on the table and soon fell asleep, exhausted.

Fifteen minutes later, Lily shakes Savannah awake, holding the gun to her head.

Infuriated, Savannah lifts her head. "Now what, Lily?"

Lily is now wide awake. "I can't use that pot, and there's no toilet paper. Take me to the outhouse, and hurry it up."

Lily pressed the gun against Savannah's temple.

"Alright, alright. Let me get the flashlight."

Savannah grabbed the flashlight, turned on the porch light, opened the front door, and flashed the light around to see if the bear was back.

Luckily, a full moon gave the women light.

Satisfied that they were safe, Savannah said, "Come on, hurry."

Lily followed behind Savannah as they made their way around the side of the house.

Lily grabbed the flashlight and entered the outhouse, shutting the door, leaving Savannah unprotected.

Savannah stood fearful outside the door, her senses heightened. Her eyes scanned the forest and the eerie silhouettes of the tall trees, searching for any signs of movement and listening for snapped branches.

She reached inside her pocket and retrieved the scalpel. She wondered if it would penetrate a bear's thick skin, but hoped she wouldn't need to find out.

Then she remembered a safety guideline: She shouldn't run, but stand her ground and slowly back away. She placed the scalpel back into her pocket so Lily wouldn't see it. She also didn't want to drop it in case she fell when she could run for safety.

When she saw movement, she felt overwhelming fear. She panicked and tried not to scream when she saw the large bear. She froze, her green eyes wide open, her mouth trembling. She positioned herself up against the door of the outhouse, hoping she blended in with the dirty white door.

The bear had smelled food and entered the house through the open front door.

Chapter 30

Robert, Michael, and two ex-military men followed the GPS in the Suburban to the cabin. Although the Suburban could seat between seven and nine passengers, Mark, Peter, and Knuckles were asked to stay behind, in case Dani needed to lie down in the backseat after being rescued.

Michael gave Knuckles the keys to the company truck and the address.

Robert said, "If you don't hear from us by eleven o'clock, come looking for us."

David brought Crusher. Robert brought Michael, knowing Dani would need him.

At 9 p.m., they turned onto the dirt road leading to the cabin and drove to the "KEEP OUT" sign. Robert turned off the SUV.

"Okay, men, put on your gloves and night goggles. We'll walk to the cabin from here."

Robert led the way as they walked stealthily down the dirt path, holding their rifles tightly. They knew that bears lived in the woods, so they scanned the woods as they continued moving forward. Wearing night goggles transformed the dark surroundings. The trees became bathed in a monochromatic glow of green. The smell of pine needles and the sounds of crickets created a calming background.

Suddenly, they heard women's voices. Then they heard gunshots and screams. They listened to a roaring bear. They started to run. As they neared the distant cabin, the moonlight created a halo effect, impacting their depth perception. They knew they were near their destination and removed the googles as they ran. The moonlight filtered through the trees enough to see.

Moments earlier, Savannah had quietly sneaked Lily to the passenger side of the Jeep to hide from the black bear and to get a better view inside the cabin.

"Give me the car keys, Lily. I will blow the horn to distract it."

"I don't have them. They're on the nightstand in the bedroom."

"Damn it," Savannah exclaimed.

"Stay here. I'll get closer to the cabin to see where the bear is. Dani is upstairs and didn't shut the bedroom door. Bears climb. I will draw attention to myself, and you shoot the bear when it comes out, okay? We have to work as a team if we're going to survive."

Lily was sober now and was worried and frightened.

She was mad at herself for feeling fearful. She wasn't afraid of any man, but the bear was a different matter. She couldn't care less if the bear killed Savannah, but realized she needed her help with the bear. Plus, she didn't know what to do with a kid. She always had a nanny when Michael and Noah were kids. She then thought they would drive across the state line tonight, head to the Outer Banks in North Carolina, and rent a beautiful place on the beach.

She answered, "Okay, save my granddaughter."

Savannah couldn't believe that Lily might have one decent bone in her body. That gave her hope that they would work together and Lily would shoot the bear.

Savannah fearfully snuck up the porch steps. She squatted, raised her head enough to peek in the front windows quietly, and saw the bear finishing her dinner of crackers and cheese. She clutched the windowsill for support. She was trembling with fear and pressed her hand against her mouth to stifle a sound. Her breath was shallow and rapid. Her heart raced, and chills went down her spine.

The black bear with shaggy fur looked powerful as it roamed around the kitchen looking for food. It had rounded ears and a short tail. Its exceptional sense of smell took it to the kitchen cabinets. It stood on its hind legs, measuring approximately 6 feet tall and 400 pounds. It swatted the cabinet doors with its claws and paws. It easily demolished the cabinets, spilling the canned goods to the floor. Now on all fours, its powerful jaws punctured a can of Spam. Unsuccessful, it rolled the can, then, using its sheer weight, aggressively jumped on it, then bit down on the can with its sharp teeth to allow access to the food inside. The bear furiously roared, bearing sharp canines. Then, it moved to the jars of peanut butter.

Savannah was in awe as she watched the bear open the screw-top jar with its paws and bite into the durable plastic container to reach the food. It was successful and stood on all four legs, quickly licking and consuming the peanut butter.

Savannah hoped the bear would leave on its own once it wasn't hungry.

Dani had awakened and began to descend the stairs. She screamed at the top of her lungs.

The bear turned its attention to Dani and started heading up the stairs, making low growls and huffing.

Dani ran into the bedroom, slammed the door, and hid under the bed. She stopped screaming and put her hand over her mouth to keep herself quiet. She willed herself not to whimper or cry.

A sudden rush of adrenaline rushed through Savannah as she ran to the front door, waving her arms and desperately shouting. "Here, here, come get me. You leave my child alone."

The bear backed down the steps and began running toward her.

Savannah ran down the porch steps, looking back over her shoulder.

When the bear was at the doorway, Savannah ran to her left toward the Jeep to get out of the way of the bullets, frantically screaming, "Shoot it, Lily. Shoot it."

Lily stood by the driver's door and fired the gun at the bear, but she was so shaky that she missed. She fired again, and this time, she hit her target. She emptied the gun of bullets, hitting the charging bear.

The small caliber bullets only provoked the bear, and it ran toward Lily.

Lily dropped the gun and dashed to the other side of the Jeep, where Savannah was hiding.

The bear jumped on the car's hood, roared, and clacked its teeth. Then, bouncing off the vehicle and pounding its paws on the ground, head down and ears pointed back, it aggressively charged the women.

Lily and Savannah started running to the cabin, screaming.

Lily had shorter legs and couldn't run as fast as Savannah.

The bear stood on its hind legs and growled. Lily stumbled and fell, stopping 10 feet from the cabin. She turned over and slowly stood, waving her arms. She turned and began running. The bear quickly charged and ambushed her from behind, knocking her back down to the ground. She started belly crawling, digging her nails into the dirt as she inched along; then she tried to get back on her feet. The bear pinned her down with one of its legs. It stood over her and sniffed her hair and body. It patted her with its paws, as if it were toying with her. Lily could smell the musky odor of its fur. She smelled the peanut butter on its breath. She lay motionless, trying to pretend she was dead. The bear could smell Lily's fear and bit her arm. Blood oozed.

Lily couldn't take it anymore. The pain was excruciating. She screamed, "Help me, help."

The bear growled as it attacked her, its claws tearing through her clothes and ripping her flesh. Lily continually screamed as the bear mauled her body.

Savannah stood helplessly on the porch, watching the gruesomeness. Her mind told her to run into the cabin and save herself and Dani, but her body was petrified with fear, and she couldn't move. She felt helpless, knowing she had no hiding place or a weapon to protect herself.

Robert and his men aimed and began firing at the bear. It opened its mouth and roared violently from the pain. It tried to stand to run away, but one last shot to the head killed it. It fell with a dull thud, with half of its body slumped on top of the dying woman, still pinning her down.

Savannah quickly looked to her right to see who had been shooting.

Robert saw Savannah on the porch and began running toward her.

Relief flooded her body as she ran and flung herself into his arms, enveloping him in a tight embrace. He pulled her closer, their bodies pressing together as their mouths met in desperate union. She clung to him, kissing him over and over.

Michael ran toward the house, interrupting the couple, shouting, "Where's Dani?"

Savannah finally said, "She's okay, she's upstairs."

Michael ran into the cabin, yelling Dani's name. Dani scrambled out from beneath the bed and flung the bedroom door open when she heard her father calling her name. She raced down the stairs, shouting, "Daddy," and jumped into Michael's waiting arms.

Michael checked her over. "Are you hurt?" Dani shook her head no.

David and Crusher examined the bear, ensuring it was dead. They rolled the bear off Lily, heard her groan, and rolled her over onto her back.

Savannah released herself from Robert's arms, walked over to Lily, and knelt, feeling for a pulse.

Lily's pulse was weak, and she looked at Savannah with glassy, unfocused eyes and asked, "Is it dead?"

"Yes, it's dead."

Lily looked at the twinkling stars in the sky, raised her right arm, pointed upward, and whispered, "Noah," before she died.

Michael walked out of the cabin with Dani. She saw Savannah kneeling on the ground next to Lily. She ran to her and hugged her tightly, glad they were both alive and hoping they were finally safe.

Looking down at Lily and the bear, she asked, "Are they dead?"

Savannah looked at her frightened daughter, stroked her hand, and said, "Yes, Dani. The monsters are dead. They can't hurt us anymore."

David and Crusher were picking up the spent cartridges.

"Now what, boss?"

Robert didn't hesitate. "Leave three cartridges near the bear. Leave Lily's gun where it lies. One of you gets the Suburban and drives it here. Leave it running with the lights on so we can see better in the darkness. In the meantime, I have Dr. Clark's keys to a locked closet in the upstairs bedroom. He told me he had semi-automatic AR-15 rifles. It has the same bullets as we use. I'll leave a gun downstairs with some ammo, to make it appear like Savannah shot the bear. Then, we will wrap Lily's body and place her in the back of the Suburban and take her to the nearest hospital. We'll give her name and explain that Lily was mauled to death by a bear. We won't provide any more specifics except for the address to the cabin."

While they waited for David to bring the car, Michael sat on the porch steps with Dani, holding her tightly, reassuring her that she was safe. Robert ran up the stairs and found the guns. He brought one downstairs and loaded the gun. He walked outside and pulled the trigger three times, emptying it into the woods. Then he carried it back into the cabin and laid it on the small dining table, leaving the mess of food on the floor. This way, the police would see the residue left behind on the gun and would know it had been fired. The demolished cabinets and food on the floor would prove that the bear had entered the cabin.

Savannah had picked up Lily's phone from her purse, removed the blue quilt from the bed, and brought them outside.

Robert told Savannah to enter his number into Lily's phone and call him. He would answer, place the phone in his pocket, wait five minutes, and then hang up the phone. The police would see that Savannah had called him to pick her up and help with Lily's body.

Savannah asked, "Why would I have called you. Why wouldn't I have just driven Lily's Jeep out?"

"Because you were in shock and too distraught to drive. Furthermore, you had enough empathy not to leave your captor's body lying where other predators would smell her blood, and you needed help with the body."

"And what happens when they find Dani's DNA?" Savannah asked. She suddenly remembered the teddy bear Dani was holding, which was still in the backseat of the Jeep.

"Lily is her grandmother. She would visit her periodically. They don't need to know about Dani. But you can explain that you had been kidnapped for Dr. Clark's original will, but luckily, the bear mauled her before she could kill you."

Savannah nodded. "Robert, the weird thing is, the envelope we took to Mr. Edwards's office contained blank sheets of paper. It doesn't matter about the will now, I suppose."

Robert looked surprised at this new information. His mouth dropped slightly open, and he said, "Yes, it does matter. Dr. Clark left you the clinic in his will, that is, if you want it. But I suppose we need to find it first."

As David and Crusher found broken branches with fallen leaves, they began sweeping the dirt from all the men's footprints.

Savannah laid Lily's phone on one of the Adirondack chairs on the porch. The police would find texts and phone numbers for her colleagues involved in her illegal activities.

David and Crusher wrapped Lily's lifeless body in the quilt and placed her in the cargo of their SUV.

Michael helped Dani into the backseat, placed her on his lap, and waited for the others. Dani soon fell asleep in her father's strong arms.

Savannah walked to the cabin, turned off the lights, and shut the door. She joined Michael and Dani in the backseat. Crusher was too large to fit comfortably with three people in the backseat, so he jumped in the front passenger's seat next to Robert. David squeezed in next to Savannah, who was sitting in the middle.

347

Robert turned the SUV around and headed to the highway.

No one turned around to look back at the cabin. The horror was over. It was time to look forward.

At the end of the dirt road, Robert stopped and asked his phone for directions to the nearest hospital. Maps appeared. He turned left onto the main highway, drove ten miles, and then turned into the emergency room entrance to the small hospital.

"Everyone, stay here. I'll take Lily's body inside and give them her name and the address to the cabin."

*****

Ten minutes later, Robert returned to the SUV and headed to The Lady Jane.

He asked the men to stay one more night there before going home. The next day, Adam Jordan, the company's CPA, would bring them checks for a job well done.

After arriving at the marina, the ex-soldiers hugged Robert and said their goodbyes.

Robert said, "This isn't goodbye. This is only the beginning of a beautiful friendship. Keep in touch, and I'll take you fishing."

Crusher and David said, "Hooyah" in unison.

Savannah joined Robert in the front seat. Michael called Cathi, telling her he was bringing their baby home.

When Robert pulled up to Michael's house, Dani jumped out of the car and met Cathi, who excitedly awaited their arrival on the front porch. She hugged Dani firmly, saying, "You're home now. You must be starving. I'll run you a hot bath, get you out of your dress and into something more comfortable, then fix you something good to eat."

Dani hugged Cathi, pulled away, then ran back to hug Savannah and say goodbye.

Savannah exited the car, knelt, hugged her warmly, and asked, "Are you wearing your tiara?"

Dani put her hands to her head, adjusted her invisible tiara, smiled, and exclaimed, "Yes."

"Good, me too. You're a brave girl, my darling."

With that, she and Robert watched the trio walk into the house with their arms wrapped around each other, then turn to wave goodbye. Robert backed up the car and headed home.

Robert asked, "Are you okay, Vanna?"

"Yes. Dani is a remarkable girl."

"Just like her mother," Robert added.

*****

349

Once safely at Robert's comfortable home, Savannah showered and put on clean clothes upstairs.

She entered the kitchen with wet hair and sat at the counter. She denied being hungry when he offered to fix some food.

Robert handed her a glass of Chardonnay.

She took it from him. "Funny, I will think of Lily every time I see a glass of wine now."

Not letting that stop her, she drank the wine and yawned.

Robert pulled her up to her feet and hugged her. "Will you sleep with me in my bed tonight?"

She smiled, and her eyes sparkled with a knowing warmth as she took his hand. They walked as one toward his bedroom.

Chapter 31

Early the next morning, Robert woke to his cellphone ringing.

He rolled over quietly, not wanting to disturb Savannah, who was still sleeping. He answered the phone, told Mark to hang on, and walked naked into the kitchen.

Robert said, "It's over, Mark. Savannah is with me, and Dani is back with her parents."

Mark answered, "I know. Peter and I stayed aboard The Lady Jane with the SEALs last night. Should I take an Uber to your house, or will you come get me?"

"I had plans to come get you and Peter, so get your luggage together. You guys will stay at my house tonight, and then I'll take you to the airport whenever you're ready to leave tomorrow. I'm sure Peter would appreciate it if you dropped him off at the West Palm Beach airport so he can return home."

Robert called Michael, who was at his desk at DM Yachts, and told him that he was heading to The Lady Jane. Michael said, "I had planned to send Adam, but I've decided to join you at the yacht. I will send David and his men off with a nice big check. They did one hell of a job. And, I also did as you asked. I have Savannah's purse and I'll bring it with me."

"How's Dani?"

"She's fine. We will get her some counseling. She keeps talking about her tiara, how it kept her brave when she saw the bear, and how her real mom protected her from Lily and her men. She stated she liked having two moms. She seems so grown up now."

"How is Savannah?"

"She's still sleeping. She's going to be fine, now that she is safe."

"Okay, see you at the yacht in 30 minutes. I'll leave now."

Robert dressed quietly and left a note on the kitchen counter.

Before Michael left the office, his cellphone rang. It was Dr. Kent Stone calling. He hesitated to answer, knowing he was to meet the men at the yacht, and he didn't want to be late. He prided himself on always being prompt, but curiosity got the best of him, so he answered.

"Yes, Dr. Stone, what now?" He asked firmly.

Kent Stone said he had heard about Lily's death on the morning news but didn't offer condolences. Since he had nothing to offer, he asked Michael how to reach Savannah. He assumed Dr. Savannah and Danielle were safe, now that Lily was dead.

"Why? Don't you think the poor woman has been through enough? If this is about the DNA, we already know that Savannah is Dani's birth mother."

"Well, something interesting has arisen. I need to speak with her about two important matters. One is about Kyle Clark's clinic. I believe she'll be interested in hearing what I say."

Michael scratched his head and said, "Okay, I will give Robert the message when I see him today. He'll have Savannah call you."

"Thank you, Michael. For what it's worth, I'm happy Danielle and Savannah are safe."

Michael hung up the phone without saying goodbye.

*****

Savannah woke up after another hour of sleep, showered, and slipped on one of Robert's shirts. She read the note as she made coffee and a big bowl of cereal and took them to the deck. She sat in the chair with her naked legs resting on an ottoman to get some sun on them. She felt relaxed as she watched the glistening waves dance onto the beach. She breathed in the salty

353

air, appreciating the surrounding beauty of nature and thankful for her freedom. She thanked God for keeping Dani alive and well.

Now that she was alone, safe, and without distraction, she calmed her mind. She gathered her thoughts about the future and made a few critical decisions as she sat, soaking in the sun's warmth and listening to the ocean.

Then, she adjusted her invisible tiara and smiled, letting the morning breeze soothe her body and the sound of the sea soothe her soul.

*****

A few hours later, Robert returned home with Mark and Peter in tow. He called his neighbor to send Ana home.

The golden retriever joyfully jumped on Robert, her tail wagging a mile a minute. She bounced from one person to the next, sharing her excitement.

Robert said, "You know, Peter, I've never known your last name."

Peter laughed. "That's because I never offered, and you never asked."

"So, what is it, then?" Mark asked.

"My name is Pietro Peters. Now you know why I only go by Peter."

Everyone laughed.

Mark teased, "Or we can call you Double Pete, or Peter Peters, pumpkin eater?"

Peter teasingly held up a fist and said, "Why, you, I'll get you for that."

Everyone laughed. Ana danced around the room, joining the camaraderie.

As the laughter died, Robert said, "I almost forgot." He reached inside a plastic bag, showed Savannah her handbag, and handed it to her.

He explained how it had been kept in his office drawer at DM Yachts for safekeeping.

Savannah thanked him, pulled out her phone, and plugged it in to charge.

Robert petted Ana and nonchalantly said, "By the way, Savannah, Dr. Stone called Michael earlier. He said he had some urgent news about the clinic. If you want to call him from here, I've placed his number in my phone."

He handed her his phone.

Peter and Mark knew the matter must be serious, so they walked to the deck to give her privacy.

She was curious. What could Kent Stone possibly want to tell her?

She hit send on the phone. It rang twice, and she heard the doctor's familiar voice say hello.

"This is Savannah, doctor. I understand that you want to speak with me. Now, what is this all about?"

Kent took a deep breath and began, "Two things, actually. First, I received a call from Kyle Clark's office manager, JoAnn, this morning. She had heard about Lily's gruesome death on the local news. She asked me to tell you that she is sorry that she allowed you to go on a wild goose chase to the attorney's office the day Lily had you kidnapped."

Savannah interrupted him, "But how did JoAnn know I had been kidnapped?"

Kent answered, "I swear, I didn't know Lily had kidnapped you and Danielle until that night at Lily's house. JoAnn continued calling me, so I had to tell her, Savannah. The woman wouldn't leave me alone. It actually felt good to tell someone. I instructed her not to call the police as you asked. I explained that your boyfriend was handling the situation."

Savannah knew JoAnn was tenacious and would never give up until she found out where Savannah was.

"Okay, that sounds like her. Continue."

"She wants you to know that she had to protect Dr. Clark. She knew Lily had shot him, so she knew the combination to his safe, took the will and the prenuptial agreement, and switched them with blank sheets of paper. She also knew Lily would come looking for the documents, so she took them home for safekeeping. She wasn't sure if Lily would be watching you or follow you to the attorney's office. She kept it a secret and didn't tell a soul in case Lily threatened you or anyone, forcing them to tell her where the files were. Anyway, she took the documents to Brett Edwards the following day. They are safely in the attorney's hands. She asks for your forgiveness. She also asks you to call Mr. Edwards. The clinic is yours if you want it. I have followed JoAnn's orders, writing the necessary medical orders for Kyle's patients to keep the clinic going. As you know, JoAnn is a force of nature; she is intelligent and knows the patients. However, I can't continue to help any longer. Evidently, Kyle left you his clinic. If you want the clinic, transfer your medical license to Virginia immediately."

Savannah sat stunned. Robert looked at her with a questioning look and mouthed, "What's going on?"

She sat next to him at the kitchen counter and turned the speaker on the phone. She had nothing to hide from him. She whispered, "The attorney has the will," to Robert.

She turned her attention back to the phone conversation.

"I have been wondering what happened to the will. That clears up that mystery. Thank you. Now, what's the second thing?"

"Are you sitting down?"

"Yes, why?"

"Because I believe you will be alarmed by my next information."

Savannah was curious and said, "Nothing you can say will alarm me unless you're going to tell me that Lily came back to life."

Kent chuckled nervously, but continued. "As you know, you took the DNA test with Danielle and Lily. The results confirm that you are Danielle's birth mother."

"Yes, I know that. What else?"

"Lily Mason-Clark was not her grandmother based on her results. Furthermore, Robert Malone's DNA test showed he is the father."

Savannah's eyes widened in surprise, her mouth dropped open, and she released the phone, which fell to the floor.

Robert picked it up and said into the speaker, "This is Robert Malone, and you have given me the best news of the day. I always knew in my heart that Dani was my child. That's wonderful. Thank you, doctor. But listen to me. You can never give that information to anyone else, do you understand? It could make Danielle's life more complicated than it already is. Along with the Masons, we will tell her when she's an adult. Savannah and I will always be a part of her life."

"Understood, Robert. Congratulations."

Kent Stone smiled as he turned off the phone and opened his office door to return to work. His smile suddenly disappeared. Two uniformed policemen stood to take him in for questioning about his involvement with Lily Mason-Clark.

*****

Robert picked up Savannah and twirled her around twice before putting her down.

"I'm so sorry, Robert. I didn't know. You're not angry? How can I make it up to you? I'm so, so sorry."

Robert put her down and got on one knee. "Then prove it to me. Will you marry me, Savannah Hayes?"

Savannah's eyes twinkled, and she squealed with excitement. She jumped into his arms, saying, "Yes! Yes, I'll marry you. I'll also take the clinic."

He kissed her tenderly, thankful that she finally said yes. He looked her in her eyes and said, "I have loved you for a million years. You have made me so happy. Do you know that?"

Savannah smiled, "I love you too, Robert Malone, and will love you for a million more. Thank you for saving me."

Robert jumped up and down joyfully, did a little jig, and yelled, "Did you guys hear that? We're finally getting married!"

The men clapped and yelled, "Woohoo," as they entered the kitchen and congratulated the couple. Today was a day for celebration in more ways than one.

The world seemed bright again.

The End.